Go ahead and scream.

No one can hear you.

You're no longer in the safe world you know.

You've taken a terrifying step . . .
into the darkest corners of your imagination.

You've opened the door to . . .

THE NIGHTMARE ROOM

R.L. STINE

THE NIGHTMARE ROOM

THE NIGHTMARE BEGINS!
BOOKS 1-2-3

◆ AVON BOOKS

An Imprint of HarperCollinsPublishers

A Parachute Press Book

Originally published in separate volumes as
Don't Forget Me!, *Locker 13*, and *My Name Is Evil*

Library of Congress Catalog Card Number: 2004097074

First Avon edition, 2005

AVON TRADEMARK REG. US. PAT. OFF. AND IN OTHER COUNTRIES,
MARCA REGISTRADA, HECHO EN USA

❖

Visit us on the World Wide Web!
www.harperchildrens.com

THE NIGHTMARE ROOM
DON'T FORGET ME!

CHAPTER 1

I wrapped my hands around my brother's throat and started to tighten them. "Die, monster, die!" I screamed.

Peter spun out of my grasp. "Danielle, give me a break," he groaned, rubbing his throat. "You're about as funny as head lice."

My friend Addie laughed. She thinks everything Peter says is funny.

"I know what we can do for the talent show at school," I told her. "A magic act. We can make Peter disappear."

Peter stuck his tongue out at me. It was purple from the grape soda he was drinking.

Mom appeared in the kitchen carrying a tall stack of dinner plates. She set them down on the counter next to the piles of bowls and cups she had unpacked. She blew a strand of hair off her forehead and frowned at me. "Danielle, stop saying things like that about your little brother. You'd feel terrible if anything happened to Peter."

1

"Yeah. Terrible," I said, rolling my eyes. "But I'd get over it in a minute or two."

"Mom, do you know what Danielle said?" Peter asked in a tiny, hurt voice. "She said her birthday wish is to be an only child!"

Mom scowled at me. "You didn't really say that to Peter, did you?"

"Of course not," I replied, glaring at Peter, who was still pretending to be hurt. "I mean, maybe I said it. But it was just a joke."

"Your face is a joke!" Peter said.

Addie laughed again.

Why does she think Peter is such a riot? Why do all my friends think he's so adorable and funny?

Mom narrowed her eyes at me. "Danielle, you're fifteen and Peter is nine. You're supposed to be the grown-up. You have to take care of him."

"No problem," I said. I raised my hands to strangle him again. "I'll be glad to take care of him!" I dove at him.

Peter laughed and squirmed away.

It was the kind of kidding around brothers and sisters do all the time. Nothing to it, really. It was all so innocent and good-natured.

I had no idea what was to come in the next few days.

I had no idea I really was about to lose my brother.

CHAPTER 2

It all started that day, the day Addie came to see our new house.

Mom had picked up a stack of china saucers and was carrying it to a cabinet above the stove. "Danielle, are you going to help me unpack this stuff?" she asked. "We've only got about a hundred more cartons to open."

"I'll open some!" Peter volunteered eagerly. He chugged the rest of his grape soda and tossed the can to the counter. "I'll open all of them!"

Mom shook her head. "I don't want to open all of them now. Just the ones for the kitchen."

"Let me help!" Peter cried.

I motioned to Addie to follow me. "I'll help right after I give Addie the house tour," I told Mom.

Addie tossed her blond ponytail behind her shoulders and hopped down from the kitchen stool. "I can't wait to see your new house, Mrs. Warner," she said cheerfully.

Addie is a very cheerful girl. That's her thing. She

even wears cheerful colors. Today she had a silky pink vest over a blue T-shirt and bright orange capri pants she bought at some thrift store for two dollars.

Outrageous colors! But Addie always looked really together.

The red-and-blue glass beads she wore every day clattered as she started across the kitchen. Addie has a lot of style. I like things kind of plain and simple. My favorite color is gray. She always makes me feel brighter just walking beside me.

"Whoa." Mom stepped in front of Addie, blocking her way. "Did you get your ears pierced again?"

Addie nodded.

Mom carefully examined the white and gold hoops in Addie's ears. "Three in each ear?"

Addie nodded again. "Yeah. Only three."

Peter pushed in between Mom and Addie. "Hey, Mom, can I get my nose pierced?"

Mom's mouth dropped open but no sound came out.

I picked up the hammer Dad had been using. "Here, Peter," I said. "I'll do it for you."

Peter stuck out his purple tongue again.

"Stop picking on Peter," Mom said.

"Boohoo." Peter rubbed his eyes and pretended to cry. "She hurt my feelings."

I dropped the hammer, grabbed Addie's arm, and tugged her to the kitchen door. "Come on. The grand house tour. I'm showing off this magnificent mansion." I stepped over a pile of carpentry tools.

"Be careful," Mom called after us. "The molding in the back hall was just painted. And there are still a few floorboards missing back there."

"We'll be careful," I said.

"I want to give the tour!" Peter shouted, running after Addie and me. "We can start in my room. I have the coolest window seat. When we unpack my binoculars, I can sit there and spy on the neighbors. And my closet's bigger than my old bedroom. And I think there's a secret compartment in the wall!"

"Very cool," Addie agreed, her long ponytail swaying behind her as she walked toward the front stairs.

"Peter, why don't you help Mom," I suggested. "I'm going to show Addie around myself. Maybe we'll look at your room later."

"No way!" he cried. "Addie wants to see my room first, right?" He clamped himself around her arm and started to pull.

Addie laughed. "Well—"

"Peter?" Mom called from the kitchen. "Peter? Can you come back here? I really need your help."

Peter groaned and let go of Addie. "I'll be back," he muttered. "Don't do my room without me." He stomped away, the cuffs of his baggy jeans scraping the floor.

Addie shook her head. "Your brother is so sweet."

I rolled my eyes. "Easy for you to say. I think he's totally annoying."

She snickered. "You're both such opposites in every way. You're so quiet and serious, and Peter never stops talking. Look at him. Red hair. Bright red glasses. All those freckles and pale, white skin. He looks like an elf. And then look at you. You're so dark and adult looking. Dark brown eyes, wavy brown hair. It's like you're not from the same family."

"That's because Peter comes from Mars," I said.

Addie stopped at the stairway and gazed around at the peeling wallpaper, the cracked plaster, the long, uncarpeted halls. "How old is this house anyway?"

"At least a hundred years old," I said. "It's a mess, isn't it?"

Addie nodded. "Kind of."

"My parents call it a fixer-upper," I said. The old floorboards squeaked under my feet. "You'd never know my parents worked on it for weeks before we moved in."

"I guess it'll be really nice someday," Addie said, brushing a clump of dust from her orange pants. "Right now it really does look like a creepy old house from a horror movie."

"Tell me about it," I sighed. "Actually, the best

thing about this house is that it's enormous. There are so many rooms, I'll be able to get away from Peter and my parents. I'll have my own space." Our old house on the other side of town was really tiny.

"Let me see your room," Addie said. She started up the stairs.

"Don't lean too hard on the banister," I warned. "It's kind of creaky."

I started after her, but stopped. "Oh, wait. Someone left the basement door open. I don't want the cat to go down there."

Addie was halfway up the stairs. "What's in the basement?"

"Who knows? I haven't gone down yet. It's too dark and it smells like someone died down there."

I trotted down the hall and stopped at the open basement door. It creaked as I started to close it.

I froze when I heard another sound. A moan?

Who could be down there?

I held my breath and listened. I heard a soft scraping sound. Like shoes against concrete. Footsteps?

Grabbing the doorframe, I leaned forward and peered down the stairs. Dark. So dark I couldn't see where the stairs ended.

I heard another muffled moan. So soft. As if from far away. More shoes scraping across the concrete floor.

"Hey—is anyone there?" I tried the light switch. I clicked it once, twice, three times. Nothing happened.

"Peter? Is that you?" I called. My voice sounded hollow in the heavy darkness of the stairwell. "Peter?"

"What? Are you calling me, Danielle?" Peter shouted from the kitchen. "Mom and I are unpacking!"

Okay. So it wasn't Peter.

I leaned farther into the darkness. "Dad? Are you home?" I called. My voice cracked. "Dad? Is that you down there?"

I listened hard. Silence now.

And then I heard a sigh. Long and low.

More scraping. A soft *thud*.

And then a whisper . . . so soft and distant . . .

A whisper . . .

"Peter . . . we're waiting . . . Peter . . ."

CHAPTER 3

"Who's there?" I called softly. "Who is it?"

Silence now.

"Did someone call my brother's name?"

Silence.

"I'm coming down there!" I threatened.

Silence.

I listened hard for another few seconds. Then I slammed the basement door shut. I pressed my back against it and struggled to catch my breath.

There's no one in the basement, I told myself. *You didn't hear that.*

All old houses make noises—all kinds of creaks and groans and sighs.

And whispers.

Everyone knows that.

I told myself I was just freaked out about moving, about moving into this huge, creepy house. I told myself that I was just hearing things.

But I had to find out for sure. So I took a deep breath, pushed away from the door, turned, and started to pull it open once again.

"Hey!" I cried out when the door wouldn't budge. "Hey!"

I twisted the heavy brass doorknob and tugged. Then I twisted it the other way. I took another deep breath and tugged with both hands, groaning loudly as I pulled.

Stuck. The door was completely stuck now.

"Danielle." Mom's voice startled me. I jumped. She staggered past, struggling under the weight of a big moving carton. "Did Addie leave already?"

"Uh . . . no," I replied. I opened my mouth to tell Mom about the whisper in the basement but decided against it. She would just tell me to take ten deep breaths and calm down. "Addie is still upstairs," I said. "I haven't started the house tour."

I hurried to join her.

I found Addie at the end of the hall outside my parents' room. She had her arms crossed in front of her and was staring hard at a framed photograph on the wall.

"Do you believe that's the first thing my parents hung up in the new house?" I said, a little breathless from running up the stairs.

Addie squinted harder. "What *is* it?"

"It's Peter's old teddy bear," I replied.

"But . . . *why*?" Addie asked.

"You know. They think everything Peter does is adorable." I rubbed a finger down the glass over the photograph. "Peter started wearing glasses when he was really tiny. He had some kind of eye muscle defect, and so he had to wear these tiny glasses. Everyone called him the Little Professor. Adorable, right?"

"Adorable," Addie echoed.

"Well, one day Peter toddles into my parents' room. He's put the glasses on the teddy bear. He holds up the bear, and he says, "Look! Now Teddy can see how cute I am!'"

Addie laughed.

"Okay. It's kind of amusing," I said. "But my parents went berserk, gushing about how wonderful Peter was. And they started crying their eyes out."

"Wow," Addie murmured.

"Do you believe it? They thought it was the cutest thing they ever saw. And then my dad took this picture of the teddy bear with the little glasses on so they'd never forget the moment."

Addie gazed at the photo for a few more seconds, then turned to me with a smile on her face. "I think it's a sweet story, Danielle."

I stuck my finger down my throat and made loud gagging sounds.

"I think you're jealous," she said.

I exploded. "Who, me? Jealous of that creep? Could you possibly say anything stupider?"

She raised both hands in surrender. "Okay, okay. I didn't mean it. Show me your room."

I felt bad. I didn't want to fight with my best friend. Besides, Addie never fights with anyone. She will always back down and apologize rather than get into any kind of argument.

I showed her my room. I didn't realize how drab it was until I brought Addie into it. The walls were gray and the carpet was a darker gray.

Outside, the sun had disappeared behind heavy clouds, making the room even darker. The only color anywhere was Addie's bright clothes.

"I . . . I'm going to brighten it up a bit," I said. "You know. Put up a lot of posters and stuff."

I could see Addie struggling to think of something cheerful to say. "It's a nice room for holding seances," she said finally.

I laughed. "You're not still into that weird 'talking-to-the-spirits' stuff, are you?"

Before she could answer, I heard voices outside. Boys' voices.

I ran to the window and peered down to the front yard. The glass was so dust-smeared, I could barely see. But I recognized two guys from our class, Zack Wheeling and Mojo Dyson, jogging up the front walk.

"Hey! I don't believe it!" Addie exclaimed, right behind me. She moved instantly to the dresser mirror and began fixing her ponytail, checking herself out.

The truth was, she and I had major crushes on *both* those guys. "What are they *doing* here?" Addie asked. "Did you invite them or something?"

"No way," I said, leaning into the mirror, rubbing a dust smudge off my cheek and pushing my hair back into place.

By the time Addie and I came downstairs, Peter had already opened the door and was welcoming the two boys. "Is that your real name? Mojo?"

From halfway down the stairs, I could see Mojo turn red. That's just his thing. If you talk to him, he blushes. Some kids are like that. I guess they have really sensitive skin or something.

"No. It's not my real name," he told Peter.

"What's your real name?" Peter demanded.

Mojo turned a darker red. "Not saying."

Peter wouldn't quit. He never does. "Why not? Is it something really dumb? Like Archibald?"

Mojo and Zack laughed. "How'd he guess your real name, Archibald?" Zack said.

"Hi, Archibald!" Addie called.

The guys looked up and saw us for the first time.

"Hey," Zack said, giving us a quick, two-fingered salute. He always gave that salute. "What's up?"

"What are you guys doing here?" I asked. It didn't come out quite the way I meant it.

"We brought you a housewarming gift," Mojo said.

"But we ate it on the way over," Zack added, grinning. "Actually, it was two Snickers bars."

"We were kind of hungry," Mojo said.

"Nice," I sighed, rolling my eyes. "Well, this is it." I motioned with one hand. "Our new palace. It's—" Something caught my eye down the hall, and I gasped.

The basement door—it had been jammed shut. Stuck.

Now it stood wide open again.

I turned to Peter. "How did you get the basement door open?"

He frowned. "I didn't. I never touched it."

I stared at the door. "Weird."

"Are you guys going to the game next Friday night?" Addie asked. "Maybe we could hang out or something after?"

Before they could answer, Peter interrupted. "I got a new computer for my birthday. It's all hooked up. Are you into *Tomb Raider*? I have the new one. It's been totally upgraded. And guess what else I got? Next year's *NFL Football*."

Zach let out a little cry. "You've got the new *Tomb Raider*? Is it cool?"

Peter nodded. "Yeah. It's awesome. The graphics are unbelievable."

Mojo slipped an arm around Peter's shoulders. "You're my MAN! Where is it? Let's check it out."

The three boys pushed past Addie and me to get up the stairs to Peter's room. A few seconds later, the door slammed behind them.

Addie and I stood frozen in the front hallway, as if in shock. "What just happened?" Addie asked finally. "Was it something we said?"

"Peter strikes again," I said, rolling my eyes. "I'm serious. Is there any way I can become an only child?"

Two days later, I would feel *very* guilty for saying that.

Two days later, my nightmare started with a knock on the front door.

CHAPTER 4

Sunday morning my parents were getting ready to leave on one of their short business trips. As usual, Mom packed the entire suitcase while Dad decided which neckties to bring.

I was leaning against the doorway to my parents' room, watching Mom pack. Yellow morning sunlight filtered through the window blinds, making stripes on the unmade bed.

Peter kept jumping up and down on the mattress, making their suitcase bounce. "Why can't I come?" he demanded. "Why don't you ever take me with you?"

Mom frowned at him. "There *is* a little thing called school tomorrow," she said softly.

"I can make up the work," Peter insisted. "Why can't I come? Why do I always have to stay home with Danielle? She'll only invite all her friends over and have a party, and tell me to get lost!"

"Whoa, Peter—" I shouted. "That is so untrue!"

Dad narrowed his eyes at me. "Are you having a party tonight?"

"Of course not," I told him, glaring at Peter. Then I added sarcastically, "I'm going to spend all my time taking good care of my sweet little brother."

"I can take care of myself," Peter grunted.

Dad tilted his head, the way he always does when he's thinking hard about something. "Danielle, are you sure you don't want Aunt Kate to come stay over?"

"No way!" I cried. "We don't need her. Really, Dad. I've taken care of Peter before, haven't I?"

"We have to go," Mom said, checking her watch. She slammed the suitcase shut and clasped it. "We'll call you from Cleveland," she told me.

"Hey, wait. You forgot my ties!" Dad cried.

A few minutes later, after hugs and kisses all around, and more promises to call and warnings to be careful, my parents backed down the driveway and headed for the airport.

I watched their car until it disappeared around the corner. Then I turned to Peter. "Help me clean up the breakfast dishes?"

"I can't," he said. "I have to go watch TV." He spun around and ran out of the kitchen.

I let out a sigh. It's going to be a long couple of days, I told myself. Peter is always at his worst when Mom and Dad are away and I'm in charge.

I started carrying the dishes to the sink. And that's when I heard the knock on the front door. Three sharp raps.

At first, I thought Mom and Dad had returned. They probably forgot something.

But why wouldn't they just open the door?

Three more sharp raps.

"Coming!" I shouted. I hurried down the long hall and pulled open the front door.

"Addie!"

She had a purple sweater pulled down over electric blue leggings. Her blond hair fell wild around her face. "I tried the doorbell, but I don't think it works," she said.

"It isn't hooked up," I told her. I stepped back so she could come in. The bright sunlight seemed to follow her into the house.

"My parents just left for the airport. I'm alone here with Peter the Great."

"Fun time," she said. She followed me into the living room.

"What's up?" I asked, gazing at the large book she held in her arms.

"I figured out what we can do, Danielle."

"Huh?"

"You know. For the talent show." She crinkled her nose. And then sneezed. "Is it dusty in here?"

"A little," I said. "My parents have been so busy

unpacking, there hasn't been time to dust. What's your big idea for us?"

"Hypnotism," Addie said. Her green eyes flashed with excitement. "I'm going to hypnotize you!"

I took a step back. "You're kidding, right? You don't know anything about hypnotism, and neither do I. Why would I ever let you hypnotize me?"

Addie groaned. "I don't mean I'm *really* going to hypnotize you. We're going to fake it. You know. Pretend. That's why I brought the book."

She held it up so I could read the title: *Hypnotism for Everyone*.

I squinted at her. "You're serious about this, aren't you!"

"This book will tell us how to make it look real," Addie said. "I'll pretend to put you in a trance. And then I'll have you go back, back, back in time, back to your previous lives."

I crossed my arms in front of my chest. "What previous lives?"

"We'll make up something," Addie replied. "It'll be great, Danielle! You'll tell some wild stories about living in the past. The audience will love it. They'll *believe* it!"

I stepped over to the living room window and felt the bright sunlight warm me. On the street, two boys sped by on bikes, chased by a big, yapping dog.

I started to turn back to Addie when something

caught my eye. A man. Half-hidden in the shadows of the twisted old maple tree at the bottom of our front yard.

Who is that? I wondered, feeling a flash of fear.

I squinted to see him better. He leaned away from the tree, and I could see that he wore a black raincoat over black slacks. I couldn't see his face. It was still hidden in the shadows. But I could see him staring, just standing there, hiding behind the gnarled tree trunk, staring up at our house.

Why was he staring at our house? What was he watching for? Who *was* he?

"What's wrong?" Addie asked, stepping up beside me.

"Uh . . . I'll be right back," I said.

My heart pounding, I crossed the room and made my way to the front door. I stuck my head out and squinted into the bright sunlight.

"Hello," I called to the man behind the tree. "Hey."

He didn't answer. A gust of wind made the brown leaves rustle over the ground. All of the old trees in the yard trembled and creaked.

I cupped my hands around my mouth and tried again. "Hello? Can I help you?"

No answer.

Without thinking, I pushed past the storm door and began running toward the tree. It had rained the day before, and my shoes sank into the soft, wet ground. The gusting wind made the dead, brown leaves dance around me.

I hugged myself against the autumn cold. "Hello?"

I stepped into the shadow of the maple tree—and gasped.

No one there.

The man was gone. Vanished.

I took a deep breath.

And two hands grabbed me roughly from behind.

CHAPTER 5

I cried out. And spun free.

"Danielle, what's your problem?" Addie asked.

"You—you scared me to death!" I told her breathlessly. "There was a man—here."

"Huh?" She looked past me to the tree. "What man?"

"I don't know. He—he disappeared. But look—" I pointed to the ground. Deep shoe prints in the wet dirt behind the tree.

"Maybe it was the mailman," Addie said. She put an arm around my shoulders and led me back to the house. "You've been so tense ever since you moved here, Danielle."

I closed the door behind us and bolted it. Addie headed back into the living room. But I had a sudden urge to get out of the house.

"Let's get our bikes and ride up to Summerville Park," I suggested.

Addie shook her head. "No. We have to rehearse.

We have to do this hypnotism thing."

I dropped down onto the couch. "Addie, *why* do we have to do this? Why do we have to be in the stupid talent show, anyway?"

She sighed and set the book down on the coffee table. "Because of Zack and Mojo, of course!"

My mouth dropped open. "Huh?"

"Danielle, those guys came over here, and they went right to Peter's room. They think a nine-year-old kid is more interesting than we are!"

She tossed the book aside and plopped down beside me on the couch. "Look. We've been in high school two years, and hardly anyone knows we're there. I want to be noticed. I want kids to say, 'Hey, there goes Addie. She and Danielle are really cool.'"

"But, Addie—" I started.

"Don't you want Zack and Mojo to think *we're* more interesting than Peter's stupid computer games?" she asked.

"Well, yeah. Sure." Once Addie gets worked up like this, there's no stopping her. "There's also a two-hundred-dollar prize, right?"

"Right."

"Let's do it," I said.

"Excellent!" She picked up the hypnotism book. "This is going to be a great act. We'll make it look so real that—"

"Just one thing," I said. "I'll do this crazy act only if I can hypnotize *you*!"

She stared at me. "*You* want to be the hypnotist?"

I nodded.

She thought about it for a few seconds. "Okay. Deal." She laughed. "I've got some *awesome* ideas about my previous lives!"

So we set to work. First we flipped through the book, reading the parts about how to put someone in a trance. It was all pretty much the way I'd seen it on TV and in movies.

"We need a coin," Addie said. "A big, shiny coin."

"I have a silver dollar on a chain," I remembered. "It'll be perfect."

I found the silver dollar in my jewelry box, and we started practicing with it. Addie sat on the couch, and I stood in front of her. I waved the silver dollar slowly back and forth in front of her and said in a soft, calm voice, "You're getting sleepy . . . sleepy. . . . Your eyelids are beginning to feel heavy. . . ."

Addie let her head fall back against the couch and started snoring really loudly.

"Very funny," I groaned. "I thought you wanted to be serious about this."

She opened her eyes and sat up. "Yes. I do. You're doing great, Danielle. That whole coin thing. The way you whispered everything. Terrific. I almost believed it myself."

"Well, let's practice taking you back in time," I

said. "First you have to be a little girl, you know. Then a baby."

"Goo-goo," Addie said in a tiny voice.

I raised the coin and began swinging it slowly again. "Watch the coin," I whispered. "Follow it closely."

"What are you doing?" a voice called from the doorway.

The chain fell from my hand. The coin rattled onto the living room floor and slid toward the door.

Peter darted into the room and grabbed it before I could reach it. "What's this, Danielle? What were you doing?"

"Hypnotizing me," Addie told him. "She's very good at it."

"I'm an expert," I said. "I can put anyone into a trance in seconds."

Peter stared hard at me. "You can really hypnotize people?"

"Of course she can," Addie said. "She can hypnotize anyone."

"Hypnotize me!" Peter demanded.

"No way," I said, reaching for the coin. "Addie and I are too busy."

He swung it out of my grasp. "Hypnotize me, Danielle. I won't give it back to you unless you hypnotize me too!"

"Peter, we're doing this for school," I said. "Give it back!"

Behind his red glasses, his dark eyes flashed excitedly. Waving the coin at me, he began to chant, "Hypnotize me! Hypnotize me! Hypnotize me!"

I grabbed for it again. Missed.

Addie jumped up beside me. "Okay. Let's hypnotize him," she said. "Why not?"

I turned to her. "Excuse me?"

"Go ahead. Put him in a trance. Turn him into a chicken or a puppy or something."

"Yeah! Turn me into a puppy!" Peter cried. He let out a loud cheer. "Go ahead. Hypnotize me. This is so cool!"

I grabbed the silver dollar away from him. "I'll do it if you promise one thing, Peter. After I'm finished hypnotizing you, you have to promise to leave Addie and me alone and not pester us."

"No problem," he said. "Where do I sit?"

I pushed him toward the couch. "Sit down there. Lean back. Get comfortable. You have to relax if I'm going to put you in a trance."

Peter leaped onto the couch. He bounced up and down several times on the cushion.

"What are you doing?" I snapped.

"This is how I relax," he said. Then he stopped bouncing, and his face grew serious. "Danielle, am I going to feel weird?"

"You won't feel a thing," I told him. "You'll be in a trance, remember?"

I knew exactly what I was going to do. I was going

to do my coin routine, swing it back and forth. Then I would pretend to put him in a trance.

Of course, Peter would say he didn't feel anything. It didn't work. And then I planned to tell him it was because he was in such a deep trance, he just didn't remember.

What a shame it didn't work out the way I had imagined.

CHAPTER 6

"Come on, sit still, Peter." I pushed him till his head rested on the couch back. "And don't talk."

Addie had wandered over to the front window. She sat on the window ledge with her arms crossed over her purple sweater, fiddling with her glass beads, watching us.

Outside, the sunlight faded in and out. Shadows seemed to reach up and swallow Addie.

I turned back to Peter. "Keep your eye on the coin," I said. Holding the chain high, I began to swing the silver dollar. "Follow the coin. . . . Follow it closely. . . ." I whispered.

Peter burst out laughing.

"What's so funny?" I snapped.

"You are," he said. "You're a total fake, aren't you?"

"Of course she isn't," Addie chimed in. "We both studied that hypnotism book." She pointed to the book on the table beside the couch. "We've been practicing for weeks, Peter."

Peter stared at the book. "Really?"

I sighed. "I can't hypnotize you if you keep laughing and asking questions."

Peter pushed his glasses up on his nose. "Well, what are you going to do to me when I'm hypnotized?"

"I'm going to make you remember things you've forgotten," I told him. "And then we'll see if you have any past lives."

"Cool," he said. He settled back. "Do it."

Addie flashed me a thumbs-up. I raised the silver dollar and turned back to Peter. "Watch the coin, Peter," I whispered. "You're getting very sleepy . . . very sleepy. . . ."

He didn't burst out laughing this time. He didn't say a word. His expression was solemn. He rested his head against the back of the couch, and nothing moved but his eyes. Back and forth . . . slowly, so slowly . . . back and forth.

"You feel so drowsy now, Peter. Your eyelids feel heavy . . . so heavy. . . . You can barely keep them open. . . ."

Perched on the window ledge, Addie shifted her weight. She seemed to fade deeper into the shadows.

"Sleepy . . . so sleepy . . . " I whispered. "Your legs are asleep. . . . Your arms are asleep. . . . Close your eyes, Peter. . . . Close them now."

Peter obediently closed his eyes. I expected him to burst out laughing, or shout "BOO!" or something.

Instead, a long breath escaped his throat, and his head slumped forward.

Addie laughed. "Your brother is such a good actor," she whispered.

I lowered the coin and stared at my brother. A smile crossed my face. It was totally cute how he was playing along, pretending to be hypnotized.

His eyes were shut tight. He was slumped on the couch, his head tilted forward. He was taking slow, steady breaths.

"When I snap my fingers, you will come out of the trance," I said. I snapped my fingers.

Peter didn't move.

I snapped my fingers again. "That's the signal for you to open your eyes," I said. "You will come out of the trance and feel totally normal."

Peter didn't move. As he breathed, so slowly and softly, his chin bobbed on his chest.

I snapped my fingers again. Then I hit my hands together in a sharp clap.

He didn't open his eyes. Or jump up. Or anything. In fact, his breathing seemed to get slower, softer.

"Okay, Peter. Cut the joke," I groaned.

"Yeah. Forget about it! Enough already," Addie said. "You're starting to scare us."

"This is so not funny, Peter," I said. I leaned over him and clapped my hands right in his ear.

He didn't react at all. Didn't flinch. Didn't move.

Addie and I frowned at each other. "Come on, Peter," I pleaded. "Get up. You promised you'd let Addie and me practice."

"It isn't funny," Addie said. "We know you're faking. We know you're not really in a trance."

Peter's head bobbed steadily on his chest. His eyes didn't open.

My throat suddenly felt tight and dry. My legs were trembling. "Peter, it's not a good joke," I said. "Stop it. Just stop it, okay? Open your eyes and get going!"

He didn't move. His steady breaths—whoosh . . . whoosh . . . whoosh—suddenly sounded deafening to me.

"What are we going to do?" I gasped.

"Tickle him," Addie suggested. "That'll wake him up!"

"Yes!" I cried. "Peter is totally ticklish."

I plunged both hands into his ribs and started to tickle. His head bounced around lifelessly. His eyes remained shut. His mouth dropped open, but he didn't laugh.

I tickled harder. Harder. I dug my fingers into his sides, so hard I knew I was hurting him.

"Wake up!" I screamed. "Peter, wake up!"

"Open your eyes, please!" Addie begged. She had her hands clasped tightly in front of her as if praying. I saw tears in her eyes. "Please, Peter, please!"

31

And then I had my hands on both of his shoulders, and I was shaking him. Shaking him. Shaking him.

And screaming. Screaming without even hearing myself.

"He won't wake up! What are we going to do? What are we going to DO?"

CHAPTER 7

I shook Peter frantically, screaming his name. His head bobbed limply on his shoulders. His mouth hung open, his tongue falling from side to side.

He suddenly seemed so frail and tiny.

"Peter, please! Peter!"

I suddenly pictured him as a baby. He was such a cute baby with that red hair and tiny freckles all over his face. I pictured him as a toddler, walking unsteadily, peering out at us through his tiny eyeglasses.

"Peter, wake up! I'm sorry! I'm so sorry!"

What have I done?

I gasped when his eyes opened. Slowly, like a doll's eyes when you tilt her straight up. He blinked. He shut them again.

"Peter! Peter! Are you awake?"

Addie and I were both leaning over him, screaming at him.

His eyelids slowly raised. He gazed up at us with

a blank, glassy stare. His mouth closed slowly, and he swallowed noisily.

I let go of his shoulders and dropped back a step. "Peter?"

A low groan escaped his open mouth. A sound I'd never heard before. An animal groan from deep inside him. Not a human groan.

He shook his head hard, as if trying to clear his mind. Then he gazed up at Addie and me again, a glassy doll's stare.

Addie squeezed my hand. Her hand was wet and cold as ice. "He's okay, Danielle," she said in a trembling voice. "He's going to be okay."

I slid my hand from hers and swept it gently through Peter's hair. "Peter?" I whispered. "You okay?"

The reply came from deep in his throat. "Unnn-huh." A low grunt. He pulled himself up slowly, still blinking, and shook his head again.

A chill tightened the back of my neck. "Peter, I'm sorry," I choked out. "The hypnotism thing . . . it . . . it was just a joke. I didn't realize . . . " My voice caught in my throat.

"You're okay, right?" Addie asked him. "You feel okay?"

He shifted his weight on the couch and gazed around the room. "I guess," he said finally. And then he asked a question that sent a cold stab through my heart. "Where am I?"

"We—we're in the living room," I stammered.

He took off his glasses and rubbed his eyes. Then he squinted up at me. "The living room? Really?"

Addie uttered a cry. "Stop kidding around, Peter. It isn't funny. You're starting to scare us."

Peter swallowed again. He blinked several times and gazed around. His eyes finally locked on me. "You're Danielle?"

"Yes!" I cried. "Don't you remember me?" I turned to Addie, my whole body shaking in panic. "I don't think he's kidding. I really don't think he remembers," I whispered. "I think I ruined his memory or something."

"No, you didn't," Addie insisted. "You couldn't. You don't even know how to hypnotize someone, Danielle."

"But look at him!" I whispered through my gritted teeth. "He doesn't know where he is! He's totally lost!"

"Hey, you know Peter. He's faking it," she said. "I think he's playing a really cruel joke."

We both turned back to Peter. He stood up shakily and took a few steps, as if testing his legs. Then he stretched his arms over his head. He gazed from Addie to me, concentrating hard, as if trying to remember.

"Should I call Dr. Ross?" I asked him. "Peter? Do you think you need a doctor?"

He squinted at me. He was always so quick.

Mom calls him Motormouth. But now it took him a long time to answer. "I'm . . . fine," he whispered.

He rubbed his forehead and gazed around the room again. "You're Addie. Right?" he asked.

Addie nodded solemnly. "Yes. Right."

"Addie and Danielle," Peter mumbled.

"I think I'd better call Dr. Ross," I said. I reached for the phone beside the couch.

Peter grabbed my arm. "No. I'm fine. I'm okay. Really, Danielle." He let out a short laugh. "I'm just kidding. You know."

I stared hard into his eyes, studying him.

He made a face at me. He stuck out his teeth, crossed his eyes, and made his monkey face. The face that always cracks Mom and Dad up.

Then he laughed. "Stop staring at me like that. I'm fine. Really. I'm perfectly okay. What's wrong with you two?"

Addie and I exchanged glances.

"I'm fine. I'll show you!" Peter cried. He started jumping up and down on the couch cushions. Then he leapt to the floor and did a wild tap dance. "See?"

Addie and I both laughed. "I think he's definitely back to normal," Addie said.

I still felt shaky. "Peter, you remember where you are now? You remember our names?"

"Duh," he said.

"He's back to normal," Addie sighed.

Then his expression changed. "Did you really hypnotize me?" he asked suddenly. "I felt kinda weird for a little while. Kinda dizzy or something."

"I—I don't know what happened," I told him. "But I'm glad you're okay. You're not dizzy now, are you?"

He shook his head. "I feel great."

"Then you can go," I said. "Addie and I have to practice our act."

"Why can't I hang out with you?" he asked.

"Peter, you promised," I said.

"I'll be quiet. Really," he insisted. "You won't even know I'm here. Please please please?"

Addie rolled her eyes. "He's definitely back to normal."

I gave Peter a shove toward the front stairs. "Out of here. You promised you'd leave us alone if I hypnotized you. Now, beat it."

He grumbled some more. Then he headed up to his room, taking the stairs two at a time, slapping the banister loudly with each step.

I turned and saw that Addie was at the front door. "I'd better go," she said. "That was kind of weird. I know you don't feel like rehearsing our act now."

"I never want to hypnotize anyone again," I said, shaking my head. "Even if it's pretend."

"That's just it," Addie said. "It was pretend, Danielle. You couldn't have hypnotized your brother. You couldn't."

"Then what happened to him?" I asked.

Addie frowned. "I . . . I don't know," she murmured. "At least he snapped out of it. That was scary for a minute or two. Hey, I'll call you later." She hurried out.

I closed the door after her. Then I just stood in the hallway trembling. I couldn't get that horrifying picture of Peter out of my mind—sprawled there so lifelessly as I shook him and shook him.

"Get it together," I scolded myself. "Everything is fine now."

I took a deep breath, pushed that picture from my mind, forced myself to move. Gripping the banister tightly, I pulled myself up the stairs, then down the long hallway to Peter's room.

The door was closed. I leaned close and pressed my ear against the door.

Silence in there.

My heart began to race.

Why was it so quiet in there? Was he really okay? Peter was never quiet.

I raised my fist and knocked on the door, harder than I had intended. "Peter? It's me."

No reply.

"Peter?"

I pounded again. Still no answer. So I twisted the knob and pushed open the door. "Peter—?"

He was sitting in front of his computer with his back to me. The computer was on, the monitor screen flashing bright colors and the name of the game, *Tomb Raider*. No sound. He had a game controller gripped in one hand.

I took a few steps into the room. "Peter? Didn't you hear me?"

He turned slowly. The red and yellow lights from the monitor screen reflected eerily in his glasses. I couldn't see his eyes.

"Peter—?"

"Hi," he said finally.

The words *Tomb Raider* blinked on the screen in huge letters, red, then green, then blue. The colors washed over Peter's face.

"Are you feeling okay?" I asked.

"Yeah. I told you. I'm fine," he snapped. "How many times do I have to say it?"

"Sorry," I murmured.

"Can I just ask you a question, Danielle?"

"Yes, of course," I said. "What is it?"

"How do you play this game?"

CHAPTER 8

I gasped. *Tomb Raider* was his favorite game. Why couldn't he remember how to play it?

He sat there gazing at me, the colors dancing over his face, twisting the controller in his hand. "Do you know how to start it?" he asked softly.

I forced myself not to cry out. I held my breath. I tried not to panic.

I had never played the game, but I knew I could figure out how to get it started. Leaning over him, I moved the controller. After fumbling around for a minute or two, I got the game to start. I picked the beginner level, even though I knew Peter was an expert player.

Peter took the controller and started to play. I watched him, my heart pounding hard, my arms crossed tightly in front of me.

"Hey, this is too easy!" he cried. He moved the controller until the setup screen returned. "You jerk. You set it for Beginner," he growled. "I'm not a beginner. I've already beaten this game three times!"

He started the game again, leaning into the monitor. The colors danced over his face as if he were in the game.

He didn't even seem to remember that I was standing there. I tiptoed out of the room.

Is he okay or not? I asked myself.

Should I call Dr. Ross?

One minute he's asking me how to start a game he's played a million times. The next minute, he's an expert again. . . .

"What have I done? What have I done?" I repeated in a whisper.

I decided I'd better call the doctor.

My hand shook as I punched in the phone number and listened to the ringing at the other end.

After four rings, a taped message began. No one in the doctor's office. Of course. It was Sunday. I shut the phone off and tossed it onto the couch. As it hit the couch, it rang.

I jumped. What if it's Mom and Dad?

What do I tell them? That everything is fine? Or do I tell them what I did? Tell them how weird Peter is acting?

I stared at the phone. It rang again. Again.

Finally, my heart thudding, I grabbed it. "Hello?" My voice came out tiny and shrill.

"Hey, Danielle?"

"Who is this?"

"It's me. Zack."

I couldn't help myself. I burst out laughing. I guess I was so relieved that it wasn't my parents.

"What's so funny?" he asked. He sounded hurt.

"Nothing," I said quickly. "It's . . . been a little weird around here today." I dropped onto the couch. "What's up, Zack?"

"Did your parents go away?" he asked.

"Uh . . . yeah. They're on their way to Cleveland."

"Well, I thought maybe you and I could grab a hamburger or something."

Hel-lo. Zack was asking me out? How great was that? But why today of all days?

"I'd really like to," I said. "But I don't know. I'm in charge of Peter. I can't go out and leave him alone."

"Bring him," Zack declared. "He's pretty cool, your brother. Why don't you bring him?"

"Well . . . yes! Great! Hold on. I'll go ask him."

I dropped the phone and ran back up to my brother's room. He was still leaning over his computer, frantically playing the game.

"Peter, would you like to come have dinner with Zack and me tonight?" I asked, shouting over the game.

He kept playing for a few seconds, then put the game on pause. He turned slowly. "What?"

"Would you like to go to dinner with Zack and me?" I asked. "You know. Go to Burger Palace or something?"

"Cool!" he cried. He jumped to his feet. "When are we going? Now? I'm starving!"

I burst out laughing. That was the same old Peter! He'd do anything to hang out with my friends.

I had a big smile on my face as I hurried back to the phone to tell Zack we had a date.

Burger Palace was noisy and jammed with people, even though it was a Sunday night. The three of us found a booth in the back. Zack and I slid in on one side. Peter playfully tried to shove into the same side.

"Get over there!" I cried, pushing him out. "You're not funny."

He laughed and moved to the other side of the table. Then he picked up the menu—upside down—and pretended to read it.

Normally, Peter's stunts to get attention drive me crazy. But tonight I was so thrilled to see him acting like himself, I didn't care if he stood on his head on the table!

"This was an excellent idea," I told Zack. We started to talk about school and kids we knew. I realized I really liked Zack. I wondered if he really liked me too.

Of course, Peter kept butting into the conversation.

He had about a dozen dumb jokes that he insisted on telling.

But I didn't get tense about it. I sat back and enjoyed myself.

I felt so good. So relaxed.

So relieved.

I stayed in a good mood until the food came.

Then I stared across the table at my brother. I stared with growing horror as he picked up French fries and stuffed them into his mouth, then picked up his double cheeseburger.

"Peter—!" I gasped. "What are you doing?"

He gazed at me, chewing hard. "Huh? What's wrong?"

"You—you're right-handed," I said. "Why are you eating with your left hand?"

CHAPTER 9

Mom and Dad called a few minutes after we returned home.

"Hi." I knew it was them before I answered.

"We're in the car, on the way to the hotel," Mom said. "Is everything okay, Danielle?"

I opened my mouth to tell them that everything wasn't okay. Come home, quick. I accidentally hypnotized Peter and now he isn't the same. I cast some kind of spell on him, and he's acting totally weird.

But I couldn't tell them. I couldn't. Besides, I knew they wouldn't believe me. Who would believe a crazy story like that?

"Fine," I said. "Everything is fine, Mom."

We talked for a minute or so. I told her we went to Burger Palace for dinner. Mom said something, but I couldn't hear very well. The connection kept cutting out.

I told her Peter was up in his room doing homework for tomorrow. She didn't seem to hear me. "Peter is fine," I lied.

"Who?" The phone crackled with static.

"Peter," I repeated.

"I can't hear you," Mom shouted. "I'd better get off. We'll be home tomorrow night."

Then silence. The connection was lost.

When I clicked off the phone, I was shaking. I hate lying to my parents. But what choice did I have?

Peter will be normal again by the time they return home tomorrow night, I told myself. Mom and Dad will never have to know.

Late that night I couldn't sleep. I stared up at the cracks in my ceiling and thought about Peter. Maybe he's still hypnotized, I thought. Maybe if I go up to him and snap my fingers or something, I can bring him out of it.

Or maybe I can try to hypnotize him again and—

My mind spun. I couldn't stop thinking about it. I felt so helpless. I didn't know what to do.

I grabbed my pillow and pulled it over my face. I tried to shut out the dim moonlight from outside, shut out the ceiling cracks above my head, shut out my troubled thoughts.

Finally, I fell into a light, restless sleep. I slept until the whispers started. So soft and distant, at first I thought they were part of a dream.

Tiny voices, speaking so quietly. Sighing. Moaning.

I struggled to hear them. What were they whispering?

"Who's there?" I cried, my voice tight, clogged with sleep.

I swung my feet to the floor and clicked on the bedside table lamp. Was I dreaming? Or were the whispers coming from down the hall?

Shivering, I stood unsteadily. "Who—who's there?" I repeated.

Burglars? Had someone broken in?

"Who's there?"

I stumbled to the doorway and peered up and down the dark hall. No one. Peter's door was closed. No light from under it.

And then the whispers began again. "Peter . . . Peter . . . "

I gasped. Was someone calling my brother?

It couldn't be a burglar. A burglar wouldn't be calling Peter.

The whispers seemed to float up the front stairway.

I clicked on the hall light, tugged down the hem of my nightshirt, and ran to the top of the stairs. "Who is it?"

"Peter . . ."

"Please! Who's there?"

My heart thudding, I raced down the stairs, the wood cold on my bare feet. My hand fumbled on the wall, finally pushing the switch, and the living room lights flickered on.

I gazed around the empty room.

"Peter . . . we're waiting. . . ."

"Who's here? Is someone in here?" I didn't recognize my shrill, frightened voice.

Danielle, call the police! I ordered myself.

I started to the phone. But I stopped when I saw the door open. The door to the basement stairs. Wide-open again, even though I had carefully closed it before going to bed.

Shivering, I hugged my nightshirt around me. Slowly, I made my way down the hall to the open door.

"Peter . . ."

I grabbed the door and peered into the darkness of the basement stairs. "Who's there?" I shouted in a quivering voice. "Please! Who is it? Who?"

CHAPTER 10

"Peter . . . Peter . . ."

The whispers were so faint, so pleading. As if they were calling to him, begging him to come down.

Who was down there?

I took a deep breath, struggling to force my body to stop trembling. Then I reached into the stairwell and clicked on the basement light.

Darkness.

Oh. I remembered. The switch was broken.

"Peter . . . Peter . . ."

I grabbed the heavy metal flashlight off its hook on the wall. I clicked it on and sent a beam of white light down the stairs. The light bounced over the plaster basement wall below. The steps were steep and crooked, tilted one way and another.

I took another deep breath, then stepped into the stairwell. I swept the light down the stairs, then over the basement floor.

No one there.

The whispers stopped. Damp, heavy air floated

up to greet me, sour smelling and musty. I gripped the flashlight so tightly my hand ached.

"I—I'm coming down," I shouted.

Silence.

I'll stop at the bottom, I decided. If I see someone, I'll run back upstairs and call the police.

Gripping the flashlight in one hand, pressing my other hand against the cold plaster wall, I slowly made my way down. Step-by-step. The stairs groaned beneath my weight. I could feel thick dust collecting on the soles of my bare feet.

The light trembled over the basement wall. As I reached the last step, it cracked under my foot. I grabbed the wall to keep from falling.

Stopping to catch my breath, I stared into the circle of trembling white light, and listened.

Silence. Such a heavy silence. Heavy as the damp, stale air.

And then I heard a moan.

I gasped.

Should I turn and run back up?

"Anyone here?" I tried to shout, but the words escaped in a whisper.

I swept the beam of light around the basement. I could see a large, low-ceilinged room, cluttered with cartons, old wardrobes, a battered dresser and other furniture, a stack of folding chairs, cans and jars, old newspapers piled nearly to the ceiling. . . .

Then . . . then . . . *a human figure*! A figure standing

stiffly in an empty square of bare floor. He had his back to me. He wore a dark jacket, collar raised, over black pants. At first, I thought it was a mannequin or clothing dummy.

But then he moved.

Captured in the light, he turned slowly. A boy with long, black hair. He raised a bony hand and pointed at me with a slender finger.

"Ohhh," I whispered. The flashlight started to slip from my hand. And as the light swerved, I saw another figure. A girl standing stiffly beside him. She wore a dark T-shirt over baggy jeans. Her blond hair spiked out around her face.

A wave of panic made my legs tremble. I grasped the flashlight tightly. "Who—who are you?" I choked out.

My hand shook. In the quivering light, I saw another boy, short and chubby with his hands raised to his cheeks. And another boy, pointing another bony finger at me.

"*Peter . . . Peter . . .* " they chanted. The four of them. The four strange intruders in my basement.

"Who are you? What are you *doing* down here?" I screamed.

They moved forward. Huddled side by side, they took a step toward me. My light trembled over their faces. Their glowing, shimmering faces.

"No—!" I cried out as I saw why they shimmered so eerily.

Their skin . . . their hands and arms . . . their faces . . . covered by a thick goo. A shimmering, clear slime. Like a clear, wet gelatin.

Their hair glowed in the thick layer of slime. It stretched over their wide-open eyes. Over their entire heads. They were trapped inside it.

And as they opened their mouths to whisper my brother's name, the gelatin bubbled, then snapped back tight.

"*Peter . . . Peter . . .*"

Trapped inside their clear cocoons, they moved in unison, slowly like robots—like *zombies*—they took another step toward me.

"This isn't happening," I murmured out loud.

Their eyes stared coldly at me through the thick, wet layer of jelly.

I spun away. Started to run to the stairs.

But another figure caught my eye. Another dark figure, standing behind the four terrifying kids. Hunched over as if in pain. Standing so still . . .

My whole body shuddered in terror. The four shimmering kids took another slow step toward me. I raised the light to the boy hunched behind them. It washed over his pale face, his wide, staring eyes, his mouth open in a silent cry.

And I screamed in horror.

"PETER!"

CHAPTER II

"*Peter . . . Peter . . .*"

Chanting through the bubbling film that covered them, the four kids reached out for me. I saw their unblinking, lifeless eyes. Grasping hands.

Grabbing for me. Mucus-covered hands, bony fingers grasping . . .

"*Peter . . . Peter . . .*"

Behind them, Peter stood still, as if frozen to the spot. His dark eyes glared from behind his glasses, so sad and frightening at the same time.

I dropped the flashlight. It hit my bare foot, shooting pain up my leg. Then it clattered onto the hard floor, making the beam of light roll crazily over the wall.

I spun away with another scream. Spun away, grabbed the flashlight, and started to run.

Before I realized it, I was up the stairs. Their eerie chant rang in my ears: "*Peter . . . Peter . . .*"

I pictured their grasping hands, their eyes so dead, so dead behind the covering of slime.

Panting hard, I burst through the doorway. I slammed the door hard. Slammed it and pushed my shoulder against it.

And listened. Listened to my wheezing breaths, my thudding heartbeat.

And then I was running through the dimly lit living room. To the stairs. And racing up the stairs, my side aching, each breath feeling as if my lungs would burst.

Into my room. Into bed. Into the silent, safe darkness.

Safe?

I sat up, still trembling, trembling so hard my teeth chattered.

"It was a dream," I told myself, my voice shaking too. "Danielle, you're safe in your own bed. You never went downstairs. It was a dream. It had to be a dream."

I hugged myself hard, staring at the gray light washing in through the bedroom window.

All a dream . . .

Of course. A dream.

I stood up, still hugging myself. I'll prove it, I decided. I can prove it was all a dream. I will go into Peter's room, and he will be sleeping soundly, tucked in, sleeping peacefully in his own bed.

Peter safe and sound, asleep in his bed. Not in

the basement with those creatures from my nightmare.

I hesitated, gripped with fear. What if Peter wasn't asleep in his room?

What if he was down in the basement with the slime-covered kids?

What would I do then?

What *could* I do?

I took a deep breath and pressed my hand against my chest, as if trying to *force* my heart to stop racing.

Then I took a shaky step toward the hall. My legs felt so rubbery and weak. I was dizzy with fear. The floor tilted and rocked beneath me as I made my way slowly down the long hall toward Peter's room.

I stopped outside his door.

Said a silent prayer.

"Peter, please be in there. Please!"

I turned the knob and pushed open the door. I clicked on the ceiling light.

And blinking in the sudden bright light, I stared at his bed.

Empty.

Peter wasn't there.

CHAPTER 12

. I stared in horror at the tangled sheets and blanket. The empty bed.

I heard a sigh. And raised my eyes to the window.

"What are you doing in here?" Peter asked. He was perched on his window seat. His red hair had fallen down over one eye. He wasn't wearing his glasses. One pajama leg was rolled up nearly to his knee.

"Peter, you're here!" I cried happily. I dove across the room and tried to wrap him in a hug. But he dodged away from me.

"Why did you come in here?" he asked, brushing back his hair with one hand.

"I—I—" How could I answer that? "I wanted to make sure you were okay. Why aren't you in bed?"

He shrugged. "Couldn't sleep."

I studied his face. "So you've just been staring out the window?"

He nodded.

"And you weren't down in the basement?" I asked.

"The basement?" He frowned, as if thinking hard about it.

"Were you?" I demanded. "Were you in the basement, Peter?"

"No. Of course not," he said sharply.

And then he startled me. He reached out suddenly and grabbed my wrist.

"Danielle," he whispered through gritted teeth. He squeezed my wrist hard and brought his face close to mine. "Danielle, don't forget me. Please—*don't forget me!*"

The next morning, I dressed for school in a hurry. I gazed out the window as I pulled on a baggy gray sweater over a pair of black straight-legged jeans. It was a cloudy day. Cold, gray light poured into my bedroom, making long, dark shadows over the floor.

Despite the gray, I felt cheerful, eager to get downstairs to breakfast. It was a new day. A new start. My frightening nightmare about the strange, glistening kids was just that—a nightmare.

It's normal to have strange dreams when you move into a new house, I told myself.

And I assured myself that Peter would be okay

today. I guessed that the effects of my dumb spell would be over by now. I guessed that Peter would be his cheerful, talkative, pesty self again.

I guessed wrong.

He stumbled into the kitchen still in his blue striped pajamas. His hair was unbrushed. It stood straight up in back. He squinted at me through his glasses, as if he didn't recognize me.

"Hel-lo," I said. "Aren't you forgetting about a little something? Like school?"

He frowned and rubbed his cheek. "What day is it?"

"Monday," I said. "Here. Pick a cereal. Have your breakfast, then go up and get dressed."

I had pulled three boxes of cereal from the cabinet. But I knew Peter would choose Golden Grahams. That's the only cereal he ever eats.

He walked over to the counter and stared from box to box. "I can't decide," he said softly. And then he turned to me with a heartbreaking, sad, sad expression on his face. And he whispered, "Danielle, which one do I like?"

I bit my bottom lip to keep from crying. "You really don't remember?"

He shook his head.

I picked up the box of Golden Grahams and poured him a bowl. A few minutes later, we sat across from each other at the kitchen counter, gulping down our cereal in silence.

He's lost his memory, I realized, watching him eat with his left hand again. He's forgetting everything. It's much worse today.

What am I going to do? Mom and Dad will be home tonight. And when they see what I've done to my poor brother . . .

A knock on the kitchen door interrupted my terrifying thoughts.

I heard a familiar shout. And saw Addie's smiling face through the window. I pulled open the door and dragged her inside. She was wearing a bright yellow V-neck top over a red T-shirt, and green spandex leggings. "Oh, Addie, I'm so glad to see you!" I exclaimed.

She blinked. "Uh-oh. What's wrong?"

I pointed to Peter at the counter. He had his spoon halfway to his mouth, but he was staring at Addie. Probably trying to remember who she was.

Addie's smile faded quickly. "He isn't any better? He isn't back to normal?"

I shook my head. "He—he's forgetting everything. His memory—"

Addie squeezed my hand. "You must have really hypnotized him, Danielle. By accident."

"I guess," I said. "But I really can't believe that waving a coin back and forth—"

"You must feel so awful," Addie interrupted.

My mouth dropped open. I couldn't hold back. A

wave of anger swept over me. "It was all your idea!" I screamed. "You brought the stupid book. You told me to go ahead and hypnotize my brother!"

"But—but—" Addie sputtered.

"Oh, wait!" I cried. "And something else. I was thinking about this all last night. After I hypnotized Peter and he wouldn't wake up, do you remember what you said to him?"

"Huh? Me?" Addie cried. "What? What did I say?"

"I remember it so clearly. You said, 'It's not funny. Forget about it. Enough already.' That's what you said, Addie. 'Forget about it!'"

Her green eyes flashed. "So? So what?"

"Well—that's what he did!" I screeched. "He forgot about it. He—]he listened to you, Addie. And when he woke up, he forgot just about everything!"

She let out an angry cry. "You're really blaming me? Because I said forget about it? It's all my fault? Danielle, have you gone crazy?"

"I—I don't know!" I wailed. "I don't know what happened, and I don't know what to do. I'm sorry, Addie. I really am. But I—I'm in a total panic. I'm so afraid!"

"Well, let's just try to undo it then," Addie said through gritted teeth. She stomped toward the living room. "Where's the book I left here?"

"Huh? Why? What are you going to do?" I asked, chasing after her.

"Since it's *all my fault*," Addie said bitterly, "I'm going to help fix things. We're going to hypnotize him again. Do exactly what you did yesterday. Then when he's under the spell, I'll tell him to *remember* everything. Then we'll bring him out of it, and he'll be fine."

I realized my heart was pounding. "Do you really think—?"

"Yes. Definitely," Addie said. She gave me a shove. "Hurry. Get the book. We'll be a little late to school, but no big deal. When we're finished, your brother will be his normal, adorable self."

"Peter, you're going to be okay!" I cried.

I turned to the kitchen counter. "Peter?"

He was gone.

"Where did he go?" I gasped.

Addie blinked hard, staring at the empty kitchen stool.

I spun toward the doorway—and saw that the basement door was open again. "Peter?" I ran out into the hall and looked down the stairs. "Peter? What are you doing?"

He was halfway down the stairs, walking so slowly in the dark, a step and then another step.

"Peter? Can't you hear me?" I screamed. "What are you doing? Where are you going?"

CHAPTER 13

Finally he turned back. He stared up at me. Even in the dim light, I could see the confusion on his face.

"Peter, come back up here," I demanded. "Hurry. Why were you going down to the basement?"

"I—I don't know." His voice was flat, faint, as if he were half-asleep. He obediently began climbing back up, slowly, his eyes locked on mine. It seemed to take him forever.

When he finally stepped back into the hallway, I slammed the basement door shut. I wished it had a lock. A chill ran down my back. I remembered those frightening kids in my dream, chanting his name over and over.

Or *was* it a dream?

Were there *ghosts* down there? Monster kids living in the basement? Zombies like in some horror movie?

Crazy thoughts. Really crazy.

But why was Peter heading down there?

I placed my hands gently on his shoulders and

guided him to the living room. "Addie and I are going to help you," I said softly. "You're going to be fine again."

I led him to the couch. I made him sit exactly where he sat the last time.

"Here's the coin," Addie said, handing it to me. "I found it in your room."

My hand shook so hard, I dropped it. It rolled under the coffee table. I bent to pick it up.

"What are you going to do?" Peter asked.

"I'm going to hypnotize you again," I said.

Peter squinted at me. "Again?"

"You're going to be fine," Addie told him, forcing herself to sound cheerful. "You're going to remember everything."

I climbed to my feet and held the chain up. The coin dangled in front of me, catching the light from the front window. *Please work!* I prayed silently. *Please let me return Peter to normal.*

"Sit back, Peter," I instructed. "Take a deep breath and relax." I began to swing the silver dollar gently back and forth.

Peter slumped back on the couch. His eyes followed the coin from left to right, right to left.

"You're starting to feel sleepy," I whispered. "So sleepy. You can hardly keep your eyelids open." I let the coin swing slowly. Peter's eyelids drooped. "You feel so sleepy . . . so sleepy. . . ."

I glimpsed Addie out of the corner of my eye. She

63

had a tight grin on her face. She flashed me a thumbs-up. "It's working," she whispered.

"No, it isn't," Peter said.

"Huh?" I gasped.

"I don't feel sleepy at all. You're just making me dizzy, swinging that dumb coin back and forth." He started to stand up.

"No, Peter—" I protested. "Let's keep trying. Please—?"

He shook his head. "It isn't working, Danielle. You don't know how to do it."

I turned to Addie. "I'm doing everything the same. What's wrong? Why isn't it working?"

She sighed. "I'm really sorry. Maybe we should go to school."

"Yes," Peter agreed, pushing his glasses up on his nose. "School."

The coin fell from my hand. I didn't bother to pick it up. "I'll get my backpack," I said.

Can Peter handle school? I wondered. Should I take him to Dr. Ross instead?

I turned toward the hall, and uttered a sharp cry when I saw the basement door—*wide-open again*.

"What is going on around here?" I sighed. I totally lost it. I ran down the hall. Grabbed the door—and slammed it as hard as I could. Then I hurried upstairs, grabbed my backpack, and tore out of the house.

"Hey, wait up!" I called to Addie and Peter, waving

to them. But they had started walking without me, and they were already a block ahead.

The sun was still hidden behind low clouds. The air felt heavy and wet, as if a storm were brewing.

As I started to jog, I heard soft thuds behind me. I turned and saw a figure moving rapidly toward me.

It took me a few seconds to recognize him—the man in the black raincoat. The man all in black. The one who had been staring at our house, spying on us through the front window.

Shadows hid him as he trotted under the tall trees along the street. I couldn't see his face. But keeping in the shadows, he came toward me quickly.

I froze in panic for a second. Then I spun away from him and took off.

The backpack bounced hard on my shoulders. My shoes slipped on the wet grass.

I glanced back and saw him gaining on me. His black raincoat flapped loudly behind him.

"Hey—!" he bellowed angrily. "Hey, you—!"

Who is he? Why is he chasing me? I wondered.

I didn't stop to ask. I raced across the street.

Peter and Addie were only half a block ahead of me now. And the tall brick elementary school came into view ahead of them.

If I can catch up to them, maybe I'll be safe, I thought.

But then I heard a *snap*. My backpack strap flew up. The backpack fell off my shoulder. Hit the ground and bounced in front of me. I nearly stumbled over it.

I dove for it.

Frantic now. Frantic to get away.

Away from the flapping black raincoat. The outstretched arms. The evil face hidden in darkness.

I saw the man lurch into the street. Closing in. Closing in on me.

I grabbed the backpack. Too late.

He was steps away from me.

I was caught.

CHAPTER 14

The blare of a car horn made me jump.

I turned in time to see a large blue van roar into the intersection. The man in black jumped back. He disappeared for a second behind the blur of blue.

It was all the time I needed. I scooped up my backpack and ran.

A few seconds later, I caught up to Addie and Peter. Addie caught the distressed look on my face. She stopped. "Danielle, what's wrong?"

I turned back and pointed. "Th-that man—" I sputtered breathlessly.

My mouth dropped open. He was gone. Vanished.

"Never mind," I said quickly. I didn't want to upset Peter. He was already in such bad shape.

Addie and I led him up the wide stone steps to the elementary school. There were no other kids in sight. We were really late.

I stopped at the door and placed a hand on his shoulder. "You sure you'll be okay?"

He nodded.

I hesitated. Could I leave him here? Was I doing the right thing?

"I'll be okay." He reached for the door handle.

I squeezed his shoulder. "Well . . ." I glanced down the street, feeling a chill of fear, expecting to see the man in the black raincoat waiting for me. But the street was empty.

"I'll meet you right back here after school," I told Peter. "Wait for me right here, okay?"

He nodded. He went inside.

Addie and I watched him through the windows in the door, until he disappeared around a corner.

"He's still not right," I said, biting my bottom lip. "When Mom and Dad get home tonight . . ."

"They'll know what to do," Addie said.

"But they left me in charge, Addie. They left me in charge, and I messed up."

Addie forced a smile. "Hey, look on the bright side, Danielle."

"Huh?" I stared at her. That was so typical Addie. Always cheerful no matter what. Always working hard to cheer everyone else up. "What's the bright side?" I asked.

She thought for a moment. "I don't know," she

answered finally. "I guess you should just try not to think about it. I mean, come on. Peter will be okay. What's the worst thing that could happen?"

Later in the lunchroom, I sat at a table against the back wall, staring at my tray. Why did I take all this food? I wondered. My stomach feels as if it were made of lead. I can't eat a thing.

I heard a chair scrape against the floor. I looked up as Zack dropped down across from me. He ripped apart his brown paper lunch bag and unwrapped a sandwich. "Want to trade?" He poked the sandwich in my face. "It's tuna fish."

"No thanks," I murmured.

"Mom knows I hate tuna fish. So she packs a tuna fish sandwich every day."

"Help yourself to mine," I said, shoving the tray across the table. "I'm not hungry."

"What happened to you in Chem class?" he asked, grabbing the pizza slice off my tray. "You totally messed up."

I shrugged. "Yeah. I guess. I just . . . I couldn't remember the assignment. I studied it. It just all went out of my head."

The truth was, I barely heard a word anyone said to me all morning. All I could think about was my poor brother. Was he okay? What was I going to tell my parents when they returned home tonight?

I suddenly realized Zack had been talking. He was gazing at me, waiting for a reply.

"What?" I asked. "I'm sorry. I—"

"After school," he said. "I'm an ace in chemistry. You know. We could go over the chapters for the test."

"Uh . . . I'd like that, Zack. But I'd better not. My parents are still away. I have to take care of Peter."

Zack pushed his lips out in an exaggerated pout. "Peter can amuse himself while we study."

I felt terrible. Zack was being so nice. I was beginning to think he really liked me. But I couldn't spend time with him while Peter was still so messed up.

And I couldn't explain to Zack what I had done to my brother.

"I—I can't," I said. "Maybe tomorrow we can—"

"Yeah. Maybe," Zack grumbled. He stuffed the rest of my pizza into his mouth. "Do you want those pretzels?"

The afternoon dragged by. I couldn't concentrate. Couldn't think. I kept picturing Peter on his own at school, sitting in class in a total trance, unable to remember anything.

Maybe he made it through the day okay, I kept telling myself. Maybe he snapped out of it. When I meet him at his school, he'll be his jolly old self again.

It's possible, isn't it?

I couldn't wait to find out. I cut my last class. It was only gym, so it was no big deal. I waved to Addie on my way out of the high school, signaling that I'd call her later. Then I made my way to Peter's school, two blocks away.

It had rained hard during the day. Water had puddled along the curbs and street corners. A gusty breeze sent water dripping down from the swaying trees. The storm clouds were finally parting, allowing narrow beams of sunlight to filter down.

I jogged all the way to the elementary school, my shoes splashing up rainwater. The cool, moist air felt soothing on my hot cheeks.

I reached the school at exactly three o'clock, in time to hear the clang of the final bell. Inside the building I heard cheers, the scrape of chairs, slamming locker doors. A few seconds later, kids came streaming out of their classes.

I waited at the bottom of the front stairs. Crossing my arms in front of me, I kept my eyes on the double doors, eager for my brother to appear.

The doors banged open, and kids came charging out. Laughing, shouting, shoving each other, they swarmed around me as they made their way to the street.

Maybe Peter will be laughing and shouting too, I told myself. The way he always has in the past.

When Peter didn't appear in the first stampede of kids, I felt my neck muscles tense. Where was he?

I knew that Mrs. Andersen's class was second from the door. Peter was always one of the first ones out of the building.

Relax, Danielle! I scolded myself. It's not even ten after three yet. Don't hit the panic button too soon.

Car doors slammed. Bike chains clattered as kids pulled them free of the bike racks. A bright silver Frisbee whirred past my head.

The school doors banged open again, and a group of girls in Scout uniforms stepped out. They were followed by several little kids, being led by parents or nannies.

I checked my watch. Three-fifteen.

"Okay, Peter," I muttered. "Let's get going."

What was he doing in there? Probably hanging out with friends, forgetting all about me.

The laughter and shouts had faded. Most of the cars and school buses had pulled away with kids inside. A few more kids straggled out. Two boys hopped down the stairs, tossing a small plastic football back and forth.

"Hey—!" I called out. One of them looked a lot like Peter. But it wasn't.

I let out a long sigh and checked my watch again. Three twenty-three.

"Come on, Peter. Give me a break!" I groaned.

I couldn't help it. Fear started to tighten my throat. My stomach suddenly felt like lead again.

Where *is* he? I *told* him to meet me on these steps.

Very quiet now. The doors were closed. One last kid came wandering out, holding a Game Boy up in front of his face. He was concentrating so hard on the game, he tripped and fell down the stairs.

"Peter . . . Peter . . . " I repeated his name under my breath.

I didn't know whether to feel frightened or angry. I decided I had no choice. I couldn't stand out here all afternoon. I had to go in and get him.

My legs trembled as I climbed the stairs.

Stay calm, Danielle, I scolded myself again as I pulled open the door. He's either goofing with his friends. Or else he's talking with Mrs. Andersen, probably showing off, trying to impress her.

Mrs. Andersen was Peter's favorite teacher ever. He never stopped mentioning her. It was always "Mrs. Andersen said this," and "Mrs. Andersen said that." I think Mom has actually been getting a little jealous that Peter is so crazy about Mrs. Andersen.

The long front hall was empty. My shoes made a hollow sound as I walked toward Peter's classroom.

It's always strange going back to your old school. When I went here, the place seemed enormous. But now, the classrooms all appeared so tiny, the desks and tables so low to the ground. The water fountain was practically down at my knees!

I turned the first corner, and Mrs. Andersen's room came into view. I stepped up to the door, my heart pounding a little harder, and poked my head in. "Peter—?" No.

I uttered a disappointed sigh.

Mrs. Andersen sat at her desk, her head bowed, writing rapidly on a stack of papers. She looked up as I stepped into the room and narrowed her eyes at me. "Yes?"

She was a young woman with wavy blond hair, round, blue eyes, and a nice smile. She wore a pale blue sweater-vest over a white top. As I came closer, I could see why Peter liked her so much. She was really awesome looking!

She kept her pen poised over the papers as she watched me approach.

"I'm Danielle Warner," I said.

She didn't appear to recognize the name. "Can I help you, Danielle?" she asked. She had a soft, little-girl voice. She sounded more like a kid than a teacher.

"I was hoping to find my brother, Peter, in here," I said.

Her smile faded. "Peter?"

I nodded. "But I guess he already left. Did you see him leave? Was he with some of his friends?"

Mrs. Andersen lowered the pen to the desk. She squinted at me. "What is your brother's name? Did you say Peter?"

"Yes. Peter Warner. He was supposed to meet me out front. I've been waiting since the bell rang and—"

"Well, I think you have the wrong classroom," she interrupted.

I stared at her. "Excuse me? You're Mrs. Andersen, right?"

"Yes, I am," she said softly.

"Then this is the right room," I replied. "You're Peter's favorite teacher. He doesn't stop talking about you."

She stood up. Her expression became stern. "I'm really sorry, Danielle. But you've made a mistake. *I don't have anyone named Peter Warner in my class.*"

CHAPTER 15

My mouth dropped open. I stared at her. "You're kidding, right? You are Peter's favorite teacher. You know Peter, right?"

She bit her bottom lip and shook her head. "No. I'm sorry. I—"

"Red hair!" I shouted. "Bright red eyeglasses. Never stops talking. You know. Peter!"

"Danielle," she said softly. "Why are you shouting at me? Your brother is not in my class. Maybe you mean Mr. *Anders*. Sometimes people get us mixed up since our names are so similar."

"No!" I cried. "I'm not mixed-up. Peter is in your class, Mrs. Andersen. I *know* he is."

She sighed and raised her eyes to the door, as if searching for help. "You need to try the office," she said softly. "Mrs. Beck can help you find Peter. She'll know whose class he's in."

I stared at her, breathing hard. I had my hands pressed against my waist. My brain was spinning.

Mrs. Andersen . . . Mrs. Andersen . . . Peter talked about her constantly.

No way I had the name wrong.

"Mrs. Beck," she repeated. She motioned to the door. "You'd better hurry if you want to catch her. She leaves early on Mondays."

"Oh . . . okay," I said softly. I turned and made my way out of the classroom. The little desks . . . the chalkboards so low on the wall . . . the water fountain nearly down on the floor . . . it all suddenly appeared unreal. As if I were back in another nightmare.

I made my way toward the front office. My shoes thudded loudly, echoing in the empty hall. Two teachers walked by, laughing softly about something.

I stopped at the office. The door was closed. The lights were off.

"Mrs. Beck already left," one of the teachers called to me. They disappeared around a corner.

I stared through the glass into the dark office. "Peter, where are you?" I murmured.

I walked through the halls, making a complete circle of the building. I looked into every classroom I passed. No sign of my brother.

Did he go home without me? I wondered.

Did he forget he was supposed to meet me? Did he go out a side door and walk home by himself?

Yes. That had to be the answer. Just thinking it

made me feel a lot better.

I hurried outside and practically leaped down the front steps. I ran all the way home.

He's already home. I know it. The little creep is already home.

I burst into the house and heaved my backpack to the floor. "Peter, are you here?" I called breathlessly.

No reply.

I raced down the hall toward the kitchen. "Peter? Are you home?"

No sign of him in the kitchen. I checked the den. The dining room. "Peter? Hey, Peter?"

I stopped and listened.

Silence.

Then I heard a sound that sent a shiver down my back.

A moan. A low moan. Like an animal in pain.

"Peter? Is that you?" I followed the sound to the front stairs. I grabbed the banister.

Another moan, followed by a high-pitched howl.

Gripping the railing tightly, I pulled myself up the stairs. "Peter? Is that you? I'm coming."

I reached the top, my heart thudding, and hurried down the hall to his room. The door stood open. I dove into the doorway—and gasped. "Peter?"

He was pacing back and forth in the middle of the room. He still had his jacket on. His eyes were nearly shut.

"Peter—?"

He had his hands shoved deep in his jeans pockets. He kept moaning to himself, moaning like a sick animal, shaking his head as he paced.

Why were his eyes closed like that? Why was he making those horrible sounds? What was he doing?"

"Peter, stop!" I cried. "Stop! Can you hear me? What are you doing?"

He moaned again, his eyes still nearly shut.

I could feel my throat tighten in fear. "You were supposed to meet me," I said. "Will you stop doing that? What is *wrong* with you?"

Finally, he stopped pacing. He turned toward me. His eyes opened slowly. He studied me for a long moment, his face filled with confusion.

When he finally spoke, his words came out in a hoarse growl: "Who are you? What are you doing in my house?"

CHAPTER 16

I gasped. A wave of nausea rolled up, tightening my throat. I suddenly felt so sick, I clapped a hand over my mouth to keep from hurling.

"Peter, don't you remember me? *Don't* you?"

He narrowed his eyes at me. "Get out of my house."

"I'm your sister!" I cried.

Poor Peter. I had to do something.

"Peter, just stay here in your room," I said. "You'll be okay. I promise."

He stared blankly at me through his glasses. I could tell that he had no idea who I was.

I spun away and ran down the hall. My mind was racing. What could I do? Who should I call?

I ran into my parents' room and frantically ransacked their desk drawers until I found their phone book. My hands were shaking so badly, I could barely turn the pages.

My stomach was lurching again. I found Dr. Ross's

number and quickly punched it into the phone.

It rang three times before a woman answered. "Doctor's office."

"I've got to speak to Dr. Ross," I said breathlessly. "It—it's an emergency."

"I'm sorry," she replied. "He's away at a conference this week. If you'd like to leave a message, I could—"

"No thanks!" I cried. I clicked off the phone.

Who else? Who else?

Aunt Kate. She lives in the next town. Aunt Kate is a sensible, practical woman. She's always calm. She always knows what to do.

I punched in her number. "Please be there," I murmured. "Please . . ."

The phone rang and rang. I let it ring at least ten or twelve times before I finally gave up.

"Now what?"

Who can I call? There's *got* to be someone!

I shut my eyes and tried to think. A loud knock on the front door made me jump.

"Who is that? Addie?"

The knocking repeated, louder this time.

I tossed down the phone and made my way quickly down the stairs to the front door.

Maybe Addie can think of someone who will help me, I told myself.

I pulled the door open.

Not Addie.

I stared in terror at the man in the black raincoat.

"Wh-what do you want?" I asked.

"Gotcha," he whispered.

CHAPTER 17

He lowered his head toward me like a bird about to attack a worm. He had a short black beard and mustache, and wavy black hair that fell over his forehead. He glared at me with round, black eyes.

His gaze was so cold, I felt a chill run down my back. Then he raised his eyes to look behind me into the house. "Are your parents here?" His voice was soft and scratchy, as if he had a sore throat.

"No," I said.

Why did I say that? How stupid! Why did I tell him my parents weren't home?

"I mean, they'll be home really soon. Sorry. I have to go." My heart pounding, I moved to close the door.

But he pushed past me, nearly bumping me aside. He was in the house!

He stood in the entryway, still glaring at me with those tiny black eyes. "You ran from me this morning. . . ."

"Y-yes," I replied. "I didn't know—I mean . . . who are you? What do you want?"

"Sorry if I frightened you," he said in that scratchy voice. "I'm a reporter. For the *Star-Journal.*"

"Huh? A reporter?"

I suddenly felt very foolish.

A newspaper reporter? But why had he been chasing me? And why had he been spying on our house?

He's lying, I thought. Why did I open the door without looking first? Why did I let him in the house? Why was I so stupid?

He glimpsed himself in the hall mirror and pushed back his wavy black hair with one hand. "I'm thinking of doing a story about your house," he said.

I studied him, trying to figure out if this was some kind of joke. "Are you selling something?" I asked. "Insurance or something? Because if that's what you're trying to do—"

He raised his right hand. "No. I'm a reporter. Really." He fumbled in his back pocket and pulled out a worn brown wallet. He flipped it open to show me a card that had his photo on it and said PRESS at the top.

"I found some old articles at the newspaper office. A big stack of yellowed papers hidden away in a corner cabinet. In the old articles, they call this house *Forget-Me House.*" His eyes burned into mine.

I stared hard at him. "Huh? Why?"

He shrugged. "I'm not sure. According to the papers I found, the house makes people forget."

My heart started to pound. "Forget what?"

"Forget themselves," he replied. "One by one, one at a time, the people who live here forget everything. And then . . . then . . . they are forgotten too. Forgotten forever."

I wanted to scream, but I held it in. I pictured Peter up in his room. Peter didn't remember me. He couldn't remember his own sister.

The reporter leaned closer, narrowing his cold eyes at me. "Has anything strange happened to you?"

My breath caught in my throat. "N-no," I choked out. I didn't want to tell him.

I had to think. Had to figure this out.

He studied me. "Are you sure? Have you seen anything strange? Heard anything? Is anyone in your family acting weird?"

"No!" I cried. "No! Please—you have to leave!"

"I'm sorry. I didn't mean to scare you," the reporter said. "It's just a bunch of old newspaper stories. Probably not true."

He stepped back, shifting his black raincoat on his shoulders. "I see I've upset you. I'll come back. I'll come back when your parents are home."

I heard a noise and turned to the stairs. "Peter— is that you?"

Silence.

When I turned back, the reporter was gone.

I stood staring out at the street, trying to stop my

head from spinning. My mind whirred with questions.

Was he telling the truth? Did those old articles explain what was happening to Peter?

Was it possible that I never hypnotized my brother? That Peter's strange behavior wasn't my fault at all? That it was all the house's fault?

Forget-Me House . . .

I remembered Peter's desperate plea. *"Danielle, don't forget me. Please—don't forget me!"*

"One by one, the people who live here forget everything."

The reporter's words repeated in my ears.

"They forget everything. Then they are forgotten too."

"But that's *crazy!*" I muttered. "Crazy." I realized my whole body was shaking. I turned back into the house and closed the front door behind me.

To my surprise, Peter stood right behind me.

"Get *out!*" he screamed. His eyes were wild. His red hair stood straight up. His body was tensed, as if ready to attack. "Get out! Get out of my house!"

I didn't have time to reply.

He leaped at me—and wrapped his hands around my throat.

"Get out! Get out!"

"Peter, no!" I shrieked. His hands tightened, cutting off my words.

"Peter, stop! You're choking me! I . . . can't . . . breathe. . . ."

CHAPTER 18

He opened his mouth in an animal growl. His fingers tightened around my throat.

I dropped to my knees, struggling to free myself. I wheezed as I struggled to take in air.

I grabbed his arms and tried to pull his hands off me. But he was suddenly so strong, so strong.

"Can't breathe!" I gasped. "Please!"

I staggered to my feet. Frantically grabbed him around the waist. And falling forward, stumbling, choking, I slammed him into the wall.

His hands slid off me. He uttered a startled cry.

I shoved him out of the way and burst out the front door. Sucking in breath after breath, I jumped off the front stoop and kept running. Down the front lawn, leaping over a coiled garden hose my dad had left there. Over the sidewalk, onto the street.

I ran. Not thinking. Not feeling anything. My throat aching, throbbing.

Peter . . . Peter . . . Peter . . .

His name repeated in my mind like some kind of

terrifying chant. I couldn't stop it. I heard his name each time my shoes thudded on the pavement.

Peter . . . Peter . . . Peter . . .

My brother had become a wild animal. A wild animal in a rage.

Why was he suddenly so angry? Was it because of what the reporter had told me? Because he was forgetting everything? Losing himself?

Was Peter in a total rage because of what the house was doing to him?

I ran through an intersection without stopping, without seeing anything. I heard a car horn honk. I heard an angry shout.

"Danielle, you've got to think clearly," I scolded myself. But how *could* I think clearly? My own brother didn't remember me. And now he had nearly strangled me.

I kept running.

I can't go home, I told myself. It isn't safe. It isn't safe with Peter there.

But I *have* to go back! I argued with myself. I'm in charge. I'm responsible for Peter. I can't just leave him there all alone, prowling around like a lost animal.

It was nearly dinnertime. My parents were on their way home. They would be back in an hour or two.

And then what?

How could I explain to them what had happened?

Would they blame me for Peter? Would they believe me about the reporter's story? Could they *do* anything to save my poor brother?

Without realizing it, I had run to Addie's house. I rang the bell and pounded on the door at the same time. "Addie, are you home? Addie—?" I called in a high, shrill voice.

After a few seconds, the door swung open. Addie gaped at me. "Danielle? What's wrong? You look horrible!"

"I—I—" I couldn't talk. I stumbled past her, into the front room. The TV was on. A local newscast.

Am I going to be on the news too? I suddenly wondered. Talking about how my poor brother went crazy because we live in *Forget-Me House*?

"Danielle—?" Addie placed a hand on my trembling shoulder. "What is it? It's cold out. You don't have a jacket or anything?"

I shook my head, still struggling to catch my breath. "I just ran," I finally choked out. "I had to run. Peter!"

Addie narrowed her green eyes. "Peter?"

"Yeah," I rushed on. "I don't think he was ever hypnotized. I think it's something else. Something much more scary."

"Oh. Right. Peter!" Addie stared at me. "Is he still acting weird?"

I nodded. "He—he tried to choke me."

She gasped. "Where are your parents? They're not back yet?"

I glanced at the clock above the TV. Nearly six. "Soon," I said. "They should be home soon."

"Do you want to wait here until they get back?" Addie asked.

I sighed. "I guess." I dropped onto her couch. I shut my eyes and buried my head in my hands.

And saw them. The eerie, slime-covered kids in the basement. I saw their sad faces. Heard them chanting my brother's name. And suddenly I knew. I knew who they were.

They were the forgotten ones.

They were the victims of *Forget-Me House*.

And now the forgotten kids were calling for Peter.

I jumped to my feet and let out a shrill scream. "Nooooo!" And without even realizing it, I was running again. Out the door and down Addie's front yard.

I heard Addie calling to me. But I didn't stop or look back.

Once again I ran without seeing, my mind a blur. I ran the whole way home.

What would I find there?

Would my brother try to attack me again? Would he still be a wild, raging animal?

I fought back my fear. I knew I had no choice. I had to be there. I had to save Peter. I had to be home when Mom and Dad returned. To warn them. To explain to them.

As I turned the corner onto our block, I heard a sharp animal cry. A dog bark. Without slowing down, I turned and saw our neighbor's large gray German shepherd racing after me.

"No, boy! Go home! Go home!" I pleaded. Why was he acting like this?

And what was his name?

Why couldn't I remember his name?

Running hard, the big dog barked a warning, its tail wagging furiously. It caught up to me easily. And then it jumped in front of me.

I stumbled over it.

It leaped up, panting hard, pushing its paws against my waist.

I screamed at him, "Go home! Please—down! Get down!"

Then I realized the dog only wanted to play.

"Not now. Please—not now." I grabbed its front paws and lowered them to the pavement. I petted the dog's head.

Why couldn't I remember its name?

"Not now, boy. Go home!"

I started running again, the dog yapping at my heels. I had the sudden hope that my parents' car would be in the driveway. Please, I thought, be there. Be home to help me. Maybe the three of us working together can do something to help Peter.

But . . . no car. The driveway stood empty. The front door to the house was wide-open, just as I'd left it when I ran from Peter.

My heart pounding, I started up the front lawn. And realized the dog was no longer at my feet. I turned and saw it at the curb. It gazed up at the house, uttering low, whimpering sounds. Its ears were down, tail between its legs, its whole body hunched, trembling.

It's terrified, I realized. The dog won't come up here. It's terrified.

Finally the dog lowered its gaze. It shook itself hard, and still whimpering, slinked away.

I had the sudden impulse to follow it. To run away. To find a place that was safe, a place that didn't make dogs tremble and cry.

But my brother was inside the house. And he was in trouble.

I had no choice.

I took a deep breath and went inside.

And as soon as I entered, I saw the basement door. Wide-open.

And I heard the whispered voices, harsh and raspy. The voices rising up from the basement.

But this time they weren't chanting my brother's name.

This time they were chanting my name, over and over.

"Danielle . . . Danielle . . . Danielle . . ."

I pressed my hands against my cheeks—and cried out in horror.

My face—it felt wet. Wet and sticky.

Frantically I clawed at the goo, tearing at it, pulling it, rubbing it off my face.

And all the while, the voices droned on: *"Danielle . . . Danielle . . . Danielle . . ."*

CHAPTER 19

"Noooo!" A cry of terror escaped my throat as I pulled the last of the slime away. "You're not going to get me. You're not going to get Peter."

Somehow I had to save Peter—if I wasn't already too late!

"Peter?" I choked out. My voice sounded tiny and hollow. I grabbed the banister and called up the front stairs. "Peter? Are you in your room?"

No reply.

I ran upstairs. Checked his room. Then mine. No sign of him.

"Peter?"

I hurried downstairs. I had no choice. A wave of cold dread swept over me as I approached the basement door.

The chanting had stopped. Silence now. A deep silence that rang in my ears.

It took all my strength to step into the stairwell and peer down to the basement. "Peter?"

I knew he was down there.

I knew I had to go down and bring him back upstairs.

"Peter, this is your sister. Danielle," I called down. "I know you don't remember me. But this is Danielle. I'm coming down now. I'm coming to help you."

I listened hard. No reply.

Then I heard a creaking sound. Very slow. A low grinding. Like a heavy door opening.

"Peter? Did you hear me? This is your sister. I'm coming down to help you."

I took a deep, shuddering breath. I spotted the long metal flashlight on the top step. I picked it up. A good weapon. I hoped I wouldn't need to use it.

"Peter, here I come."

My legs were shaking so badly, I had to take the stairs one at a time. I stopped every few steps and listened. Wind rattled the windowpanes at ground level. The only sound except for my shallow breaths.

Halfway down the stairs, I heard another creak. Then a soft, scraping sound. "Peter? Is that you? Can you hear me?"

No reply.

I forced myself down the rest of the way. Gripping the flashlight tightly in my right hand, I spun away from the stairs and gazed into the basement.

In the darkening evening light from the narrow windows above, I could see the clutter of junk, old furniture, stacks of old newspapers.

"Oh." My mouth dropped open as I turned to the far wall, the wall across from the enormous, time-blackened furnace, and saw the scrawled words.

Words at least a foot tall, scrawled in red paint. Still wet, dripping over the jagged, cracked stones.

DON'T FORGET ME.

Still wet. Just painted. Dark red paint. Red as blood.

DON'T FORGET ME.

And before I got over the shock of seeing that—I saw Peter.

I blinked once. Twice. Not quite believing.

Yes. Peter. In a doorway to a smaller room beyond the furnace.

Peter, bathed in a strange, silvery light. His back to me. His hair still on end. His shirt untucked over baggy jeans. Peter, not moving. Caught in the eerie light, standing so still in the tiny back room.

I opened my mouth to call to him. But no sound came out.

My cold, wet hand slid over the metal flashlight. I gripped it tighter. And took a trembling step toward him. And then another.

Stepping around the clutter of junk in the center of the room. The painted words, the dripping, blood-red words still in view at my side.

DON'T FORGET ME.

"Peter? Can you hear me?"

He didn't answer. Didn't move.

"I'm coming to help you. I am your sister. Danielle. Do you remember me? Do you?"

I stopped just outside the low doorway to the back room. And realized that Peter was leaning down into another opening. A dark opening. At first, I thought it was some kind of hole in the basement wall.

But as I blinked it into focus, I realized that Peter was standing in front of a tall trapdoor. A door that had raised up from the basement floor.

A door that led—where?

Leaning into the black opening, he took a step down.

"Nooooo!" I screeched. "Stop! Listen to me! Turn around! Peter, turn around!"

He froze. He didn't move.

I screamed again. I begged him to turn around.

And then, slowly . . . so slowly . . . he took a step back from the dark opening. He took a step back and then . . . slowly . . . bathed in the eerie light, turned to face me.

And as he turned, I uttered a sick cry. My stomach heaved. My knees buckled.

And I stared at him in horror.

Stared at the thick layer of mucus over his face. The clear gelatin that covered his hair, his face, his eyes!

His mouth!

The thick layer of goo glistened wetly under the silvery light.

And as I gaped in horror, unable to speak, unable to move, Peter opened his mouth. The gelatin bubbled over his mouth.

And I heard his muffled word!

"*Good-bye.*"

CHAPTER 20

"Stop!" I screamed. "Where are you going? What are you doing?"

But he didn't seem to hear me.

The thick jelly bubbled over his mouth. His eyes stared out from behind the shimmering layer of goo.

Then he turned and stepped into the darkness.

"Stop! No—stop!" I pleaded. I took off, racing to him, my shoes sliding on the dusty, concrete floor.

He lowered himself into a black pit beyond the trapdoor.

As I ran, I reached out to him, stretched out my arms to grab him and pull him back.

But the trapdoor snapped shut with a thundering *bang*.

Dust flew up all around me.

I covered my eyes, waiting for it to settle. I could taste it in my mouth, feel it in my lungs.

Then, forcing my eyes open, I dropped to my knees. I reached for the door to pry it up. To open it and free my brother.

But the basement floor was solid and smooth. I couldn't see the door. I couldn't see any trace of a door.

Frantically I slid my hands over the floor, searching . . . searching.

"Peter, where are you? Where did you go?"

No door. No door. Not the tiniest crack in the floor. I uttered an angry cry. I slapped the floor with both fists, sending up another cloud of dust.

"Don't worry, Peter. I'll get you out of there," I said, struggling to my feet.

As I ran to the stairs, I rubbed the thick dust from my hands onto my jeans. The floor seemed to tilt and sway beneath me. The walls spun wildly.

My brain whirring, I hurtled forward. Pulled myself up the groaning basement stairs. Into the kitchen.

I grabbed the phone off the wall.

I'll call the police. I'll call the fire department. They can open the trapdoor. They can get Peter out of there.

I raised my hand to dial 911. But I stopped as yellow light swept over the kitchen from outside.

Twin beams of yellow light. Headlights.

I heard the crunch of tires over gravel.

"Yes!" I ran to the back window. "Yes!"

Mom and Dad were home. "Yes!"

I tore open the kitchen door and ran out, screaming, waving both hands above my head wildly.

I leaped in front of the car. Into the wide rectangle of yellow light. "Mom! Dad! You've got to hurry! Help! You've got to help!"

I grabbed Mom's car door and tugged it open. "Hurry! Get out! There's no time!" I shrieked.

I saw their startled faces. I grabbed Mom's arm and started to pull her out of the car. But her seat belt was still attached. She let out a cry of protest.

The driver's door swung open, and Dad climbed out, frowning at me, his eyes darting from me to the house. "What's wrong? Danielle, what is it?" he cried.

"No time!" I wailed. "No time to explain! Hurry!"

Mom finally unsnapped her seat belt. She slid out of the car and stood unsteadily in front of me. "What's all the screaming? Is—is something wrong in the house?"

I grabbed her hand and tugged her toward the kitchen door. "It's Peter!" I cried. "He—he's in the basement. I mean—"

"Peter?" Dad squinted at me.

"Please! We have to hurry!" I shrieked. "Peter went down a trapdoor. It's a long story—but he's been acting so strange. Ever since you left! Come on! We have to go down there! Why are you just *standing* there?"

They stood side by side now, both staring hard at me.

"Danielle, *who* is in the basement?" Mom asked finally.

"Peter!" I screamed frantically.

"But *who* is Peter?" Dad asked.

"Huh?" My mouth dropped open. "Peter! My brother! What is *wrong* with you two? Hurry! We've got to get him out!"

They didn't move. Just stood there staring with such worried expressions on their faces.

Finally Dad came over and put his hands gently on my shoulders. "Danielle, please—calm down," he said. "What is this all about?"

"You know you don't have a brother," Mom said softly. "You know there's no one in our family named Peter."

CHAPTER 21

"Have you gone crazy?" I shrieked. "Of course I have a brother! Have you both gone totally crazy?"

Dad tightened his hold on my shoulders. "Danielle, please," he whispered. "Let's go in the house and talk about this quietly."

Mom sighed. "Your father and I have had a very long trip."

"But, Peter—!" I protested. "He's in the basement. We can't just leave him there."

Mom sighed again. "I knew we shouldn't have left her alone," she said to Dad.

Dad kept his eyes locked on mine. He shook his head. "Danielle, you used to make up imaginary friends when you were little. But you're fifteen now."

I pulled free from his grip. "I'm *not* making Peter up!" I cried. "I'm not! He's my brother! He's your *son!*"

Mom shut her eyes and held her hands over her

ears. "Please stop it. Please. I have a splitting head-ache."

"Can't we go inside and talk about this calmly?" Dad pleaded. "We'll sit down and have a cup of tea, and—"

"*How can I be calm?*" I wailed. "Peter is in horrible trouble—and you don't even remember him! Your own son! Your own son!"

I grabbed Dad's hands and pulled him toward the house. "Come down to the basement. I'll show you."

Walking with me, Dad slipped his arm around my shoulder. "It'll be okay, Danielle," he said softly. I saw him glance at Mom. "You can show us the basement later. Okay?"

He pressed his palm against my forehead. "Hmmm. It feels hot. I think you might have a fever. That would explain—"

"NO!" I shrieked. "I'm not sick! And I'm not crazy! You've *got* to remember Peter. You've got to!"

They led me into the house. They took me up to my room and forced a thermometer into my mouth. I didn't have any fever.

But they insisted I get into bed. Dad went downstairs to call Dr. Ross.

Mom kept clearing her throat tensely, crossing and uncrossing her arms, sighing loudly. All the while, she gaped at me as if I was some kind of alien from another planet.

I changed into my pajamas and sat on the edge of my bed. "I know what's happening here," I told her. "Peter is real. But you've forgotten him. Because this is *Forget-Me House*."

Mom narrowed her eyes at me. "Excuse me? This is *what*?"

"*Forget-Me House*," I repeated. "A man came here. He told me—"

"Someone was here?" Mom interrupted.

I nodded. "And he told me this would happen."

Mom sighed for the hundredth time. "I don't understand. A strange man came here? And he said you would start to imagine you had a brother?"

"I'm not imagining!" I cried. And then I totally lost it. I jumped to my feet. I grabbed Mom by the shoulders, and I started to shake her. "Listen to me! Listen to me! You've got to listen to me!"

Mom's eyes bulged in shock, in fear. "Danielle, stop! Let go!" she pleaded.

I heard footsteps. Dad rushed into the room. He uttered a startled cry. Then he pulled me off Mom. He wrapped his arm around my waist and guided me firmly back to my bed.

"Sit down, Danielle," he ordered. "Sit down and take a deep breath. Do I have to take you to the hospital?"

"She—she *attacked* me!" Mom whimpered, rubbing her shoulders. And then she added, "Like a wild animal."

"Dr. Ross will see us tomorrow," Dad told me. He stood between Mom and me, breathing hard, hands on his waist. He stood tensed, as if ready to protect Mom from another attack.

"She's completely out of control," Mom said, shaking her head. The tears in her eyes began to run down her cheeks.

"I—I'm sorry," I told her. "I didn't mean to hurt you. I only . . . " My voice trailed off.

They're not going to listen to me, I realized. They're not going to believe me.

They think I've gone crazy or something.

They really don't remember Peter.

What can I do?

I've got to wait, I decided. I've got to wait until everyone is calmer. Then I can sit down quietly with them and explain. Explain about the house. Explain what that reporter told me about this place.

I hunched myself on the edge of the bed, hands clasped tightly in my lap. My hair fell over my face, but I made no attempt to push it back.

"Sorry, Mom," I repeated. "Sorry I've been acting so insane. But we really need to talk. About Peter and about this house."

Mom and Dad exchanged glances.

"Of course, we'll talk," Dad said, sounding really forced and phony. "We'll talk about everything. You know, moving into a new house can be very, very stressful."

I wanted to argue with him, but I bit my tongue.

Mom wiped the tears off her cheeks. She suddenly appeared so tired, so old. "Let's discuss the whole thing in the morning," she said. She pressed her fingers against her temples. "When we're all calm and rested, and I don't have this splitting headache."

"Okay," I agreed.

"Yes, first thing in the morning," Dad added, nodding eagerly. "I know you'll feel a lot better about everything after a good night's sleep."

No, I won't! That's what I wanted to say. Instead, I murmured, "Yeah. Okay."

Mom started toward the door, then turned back to me. She forced a smile to her face. "Tell you what," she said. "I'll make your favorite—blueberry pancakes—for breakfast. How does that sound?"

"Great," I replied.

"Okay!" Dad said cheerfully. "Blueberry pancakes for breakfast. And we'll have a nice, long talk."

Dad put a hand on Mom's shoulder, and they hurried out of the room. They both seemed really eager to get away.

I know they're going to go downstairs and talk about me, I thought. About how crazy I am and how I totally lost it.

I'll set them straight in the morning, I decided. I'll take them down to the basement. I'll convince them that Peter is real. And together, we'll rescue my poor brother—from wherever he is.

I yawned loudly. All the tension, all the worry, all the *horror*—it made me feel so tired, so exhausted. I suddenly felt as if I weighed a thousand pounds. I couldn't raise my arms. I couldn't keep my eyes open.

"First thing in the morning!" I murmured to myself. "First thing . . . "

I fell into a deep, dreamless sleep.

Bright morning sunlight through my window startled me awake. I blinked hard, feeling dazed. Such a deep sleep. I groaned as I sat up. I didn't feel at all rested.

What kept me awake? I wondered. What was troubling me?

I gazed around the room, squinting against the bright light.

Something had upset me yesterday. But what?

What *was* it? What had me so worried?

I couldn't remember.

CHAPTER 22

I lowered my feet to the floor and climbed out of bed. I was still thinking hard, still trying to remember what had kept me awake for most of the night.

"Peter," I whispered finally. The word floated out as if from a distant place. "Peter."

Yes. Peter. Of course. Peter.

"Oh, no," I murmured. "Oh, no. Oh, no . . ." I had nearly forgotten him.

Peter was almost lost. Almost lost forever. And then I realized . . .

"I'm next."

"Peter . . . Peter . . ." Chanting his name so I wouldn't forget it, I hurried into the bathroom to shower. Then I pulled on an oversized blue sweater over black leggings.

As I made my way downstairs, I rehearsed what I was going to say to my parents. First I'd explain how strange Peter had been acting. How at first I thought it was because I hypnotized him.

Then I'd tell them about the reporter who came to

the door. And what he told me about the strange, frightening rumors about this house. I'd tell them why the house is known as *Forget-Me House*.

I'll be totally calm, I decided. I'll speak slowly and softly. They'll see that I'm not crazy. They'll believe me.

"Calm . . . calm . . ." I repeated to myself as I made my way down the back hall to the kitchen. But my heart started to pound. And my hands suddenly felt ice-cold.

"Calm . . . calm . . ."

I stepped into the kitchen.

And gasped in shock.

"Mom? Dad?"

I uttered a hoarse cry as I gazed around the dark, empty kitchen.

"Hey! Where are you?"

I clicked on the ceiling lights. My heart racing, I walked around the kitchen.

No sign of them. No breakfast dishes on the table or on the sink. No coffee cups. No cereal bowls.

"Mom? Dad? Did you leave?" I tried to shout, but my voice came out tiny and weak.

"That's impossible," I muttered to myself.

I hurried to the kitchen window and peered out. No car in the driveway.

Did they go to work? Did they just drive off?

They must have left a note, I decided. They always leave me endless notes on the refrigerator. I turned. Bumped my knee on a kitchen stool.

"Ouch!" I hopped across the kitchen on one foot. No. No note stuck to the fridge.

"Weird."

Rubbing my throbbing knee, I hurried upstairs to their bedroom. "Hey, are you two still asleep?"

I stepped into the room. Mom's nightgown lay crumpled on the floor beside their unmade bed. The suitcases from their trip had been emptied and stood open against the far wall. The light in their bathroom had been left on.

"Where *are* you?" How could they leave for work without even waking me up? And what about the blueberry pancakes? What about our serious talk?

What about Peter?

"They promised. . . ." I murmured as I headed back to my room to get ready for school. I suddenly felt so angry. And so hurt. "They promised. . . ."

The morning went by in a slow-motion blur. What did my teachers talk about? Did any of my friends talk to me? I couldn't tell you.

I shouldn't have come to school today, I told myself as I trudged like a zombie, a brain-dead zombie, from class to class. I should have stayed home. Called my parents. Called the police. Called *somebody* to come help me rescue Peter.

"Peter, I haven't forgotten you," I whispered

sadly. "Don't worry. I haven't forgotten."

But I kept repeating his name over. And I wrote it twenty times in my notebook in bright-red ink. Just to make sure he didn't slip away again.

At noon, I made my way into the lunchroom. Such a blur of faces . . . trays . . . laughing, talking kids.

Such a blur . . . such a dark blur . . .

Dark . . . darker . . .

"Huh?" Someone was shaking me.

Someone was squeezing my shoulders, squeezing so hard it hurt. Shaking me. Shaking me.

I blinked open my eyes. I struggled to see. "Addie—?"

She gripped my shoulders. Her face was bright red. She was breathing hard. "Danielle . . . Danielle, I—I couldn't get you to wake up."

I squinted at her, feeling dizzy, the lunchroom spinning.

"I shook you and shook you. You wouldn't open your eyes. I was so scared."

She dropped into a chair across the table from me. Her face was drenched in sweat. "I was so worried," she said, shuddering. "You—you passed out or something."

"I'm fine," I whispered. I cleared my throat. "Really. I feel perfectly fine. I guess I just . . . dozed off for a minute."

She lowered her gaze to the tabletop. "You're

okay? Well . . . where's your lunch?"

"Huh?" I stared down at the table too. "Oh. Uh . . . I think I brought one. I . . . I don't remember where I put it."

She squinted at me. "You're sitting here with no lunch?"

I shrugged.

Addie tugged at a strand of her hair, twisting it around one finger. "Well, do you feel like eating? You can share my lunch." She shoved the brown paper bag across the table toward me.

"I'm . . . not too hungry," I said.

"Didn't you see me waving to you in the auditorium during that boring assembly this morning?" she asked. "Why didn't you come over?"

"I didn't see you," I said. "I—I'm not too together today, Addie."

She rolled her eyes. "As if I couldn't see that? What is your problem, Danielle? When Mrs. Melton asked you to pass out the test papers, you just stared at her as if you didn't understand English."

I blinked. "I did? Really? I don't remember."

Addie squeezed my hand. "You sure you feel okay?"

"I'm not okay," I confessed, my voice breaking with emotion. "I'm not okay. I'm so worried, Addie. About Peter. He-he disappeared in the basement. And when my parents got home, they wouldn't believe me. They said that—"

"Wait. Wait." Addie made a time-out sign. "*Who* disappeared? *Who* disappeared in the basement?"

"Peter," I said. "He went into a trapdoor, and it closed, and then—"

"Who?" Addie looked totally bewildered. "Danielle, who is Peter?"

What happened next?

Did I try to explain to Addie? Or did I jump up from the table and run out of the lunchroom?

Did I stay in school and go to classes that afternoon? Did I wander around the school grounds until the final bell rang? Did I bolt out of the building at lunchtime with Addie calling after me and run all the way home?

I don't know. My mind was a blank.

When Addie couldn't remember Peter, something inside me snapped. I guess my fear took over.

I don't remember what happened next. My memory vanished in a swirl of terrified thoughts and cold panic.

Somehow I found myself on the front stoop of our new house. The afternoon sun was lowering itself behind the trees. I saw a squirrel scampering across the gray tiles of our roof.

I tried the front door. Locked. I had forgotten to take my key.

Mom was probably home. She usually gets home in the middle of the afternoon. I tried the doorbell. I pressed it hard. Pressed it again. Then I remembered it wasn't hooked up.

So I raised my fist and pounded on the solid wood door.

Please be home, I thought. *Please be home, Mom. We've got to save Peter. We've got to save him before everyone forgets!*

I pounded some more, harder. Until my fist ached.

Finally, the door swung open. My mother stuck her head out. She squinted at me. "Yes?" she asked. "Can I help you?"

"Huh? It's *me*!" I cried.

Mom squinted harder. "I'm sorry. What can I do for you, miss?"

CHAPTER 23

"It's me! It's ME!" I shrieked. "I'm your daughter!" I grabbed the storm door and jerked it open all the way.

Mom gasped. Her face tightened with fear. "Daughter? I don't understand. What daughter—?"

"*Let me in!*" I screamed. "You *can't* forget me! You can't! And you can't forget Peter, either!"

I lowered my shoulder and shoved her hard, out of the way.

She cried out and stumbled back into the entryway.

I hurtled into the house. The storm door slammed behind me.

"Get out!" Mom screamed. "What do you want? Get out of my house!"

"No! You come with me!" I shouted breathlessly. I grabbed her around the waist and pushed her roughly into the back hall.

"Let go of me!" she wailed. She squirmed and struggled. She grabbed my arms and tried to pry them off her. "Who are you? What do you want?"

My heart pounded so hard, my chest felt about to explode. "You're coming to the basement," I said through gritted teeth. I gave her another hard shove. "I'm going to prove to you—"

"Do you want money?" she demanded. "Is that it? You want money? Okay. I don't have much in the house. But I'll give you what I have. Just . . . don't hurt me. Please—don't hurt me."

She looked so terrified, I dropped my hands. I let her go. "Mom!"

She backed away, her eyes wide with fear. "Money?" she whispered. "Is that what you want? If I give you money, will you go?"

"I don't want money!" I screamed. "I want you to remember me! And Peter!"

"Okay, okay." She trembled in fear. "I remember you. Yes. I do. I remember you. Is that good?"

She's terrified of me, her own daughter, I realized.

I could feel tears welling in my eyes. But I knew I had no time to waste.

She's not going to believe me, I saw. She's not going to recognize me. She's too frightened to listen to me, to let me prove anything to her.

What can I do? What?

I spun away from her. And lurched down the hall to the basement door. "Peter—I'm coming!" I called down the stairs. I jumped into the stairwell and began racing down, taking the stairs two at a time.

"Peter, I haven't forgotten you. I'm coming!"

I heard footsteps above my head. My mother running across the floor. And then I heard her on the phone, her voice trembling, shrill, so frightened. My own mother, desperately calling the police.

"Yes. A strange girl. She broke into the house. She's acting very crazy. I—I think she's dangerous. Yes. Send someone. Right away."

CHAPTER 24

"I'm not a strange girl," I said out loud.

I wanted to run back upstairs and argue with her. *Plead* with her to believe me. *Beg* her to remember me.

But I heard a creaking sound. On the other side of the basement.

I turned away from the stairs and made my way toward the little room in back. Late afternoon sunlight slanted in from the basement windows, sending long, orange stripes across the cluttered floor.

"I'm coming, Peter," I called, my voice hollow, ringing off the stone walls. "I'm here."

At the entrance to the backroom, I stopped with a gasp.

The trapdoor—it was creaking open. Slowly. Stone grinding against stone.

I could see only blackness beneath it. A dark pit that appeared to stretch down forever.

Slowly, slowly, the door lifted. As it opened, the

blackness seemed to spread across the floor, over the room. Shutting out the sunlight, shutting out all light.

And then, out of the darkness, a thin, silvery figure appeared.

He seemed to form in front of my eyes, shimmering wetly against the opening trapdoor.

I cried out when I recognized my brother. He stood so stiffly, trapped inside the thick layer of mucus. His hair, his face, his entire body wrapped tightly in that wet, clear covering.

He staggered toward me stiffly, and then raised one arm, motioning to me. Behind the thick goo, I could see his glasses, and behind them, his eyes, staring out at me so blankly.

"Peter—!" I choked out.

He was almost colorless. Entirely gray. I could practically see through him.

He motioned with the one hand. And his mouth opened slightly. Opened, then closed, forming a bubble in the jelly so tight over his face.

Opened, then closed. And then I heard a single word: "Danielle!"

I took a step toward him. But my legs were trembling so hard, I nearly fell.

"Danielle . . ." he repeated, the name bubbling in front of his mouth. "Come, Danielle." He stretched his gray hand to me.

I froze. "Huh?" His hand grazed mine, sticky and wet, and so cold, cold as death.

"Come," he said, the word muffled behind the bubbling slime.

"N-no—!" I gasped. I pulled back.

"They've forgotten you too," he said. As he reached for me, the thick gelatin over his arm stretched with him. "Danielle, you are a Forgotten One now. You must come with us. Come."

Peter took a slow, heavy step away from the open trapdoor. And behind him I saw another figure. A girl, pale as my brother, covered in the wet, sticky goo. She climbed up silently from the pit, her lifeless eyes locked on me.

Behind her another gray kid. And then another.

The forgotten kids.

They climbed out one by one, moving in slow motion, stepping out of the dark pit and circling me.

I tried to break away. But they locked hands and formed a tight ring around me.

"*Come with us. . . .*" they moaned. And the moan became an ugly chant. "*Come with us. . . . Come with us. . . . Come with us. . . .*"

"You are forgotten too," Peter said. "You are one of us."

"*Come with us! Come with us! Come with us!*"

Peter grabbed me with his cold, sticky hands. "Come with us, Danielle."

The circle of kids tightened around me.

Peter pulled me, pulled me hard toward the black pit. I could feel a chill of cold air from below. The sour odor of decay floated up to me.

My stomach lurched.

Peter pulled me closer. Down, down, down to the foul blackness . . .

"Come with us. . . . Come with us. . . . Come with us. . . ."

And as the darkness closed around me, I opened my mouth in a scream of horror. "NOOOOOOOOOOO!"

CHAPTER 25

Still screaming, I broke loose.

With a hard, desperate tug, I tore myself from my brother's sickening grasp. I lowered my shoulders, and with another cry, with scream after scream bursting from my lungs—I tore through the ring of chanting kids.

And hurtled toward the stairs. The foul smell floated with me, heavy and rank. The cold mucus stuck to my hands. My brother's words repeated in my whirring mind: *"They've forgotten you too. . . . They've forgotten you too. . . ."*

No, I'm not! I told myself as I forced my trembling legs up the stairs. I'm not forgotten! I'm not!

"I'll *make* Mom remember!" I shouted down. "Somehow, I'll make Mom remember, Peter!"

I reached the top of the stairs, my chest heaving, my lungs aching.

I slammed the basement door shut and started down the back hall.

The floor spun beneath me. The walls appeared

to close in until I felt as if I were running through a dark, narrow tunnel.

What can I do? I asked myself. The whole house seems to be closing in on me. As if I don't belong here anymore.

How can I prove that I'm telling the truth? How can I make Mom remember us?

As I reached the front stairs, a figure jumped out to block my way.

"Dad!" I screamed. "You're home! Please—tell Mom—!"

"Who are you?" he demanded angrily. "You'd better get out of this house. The police are on their way."

"No, Dad—listen!" I pleaded.

"Get out—now!" he shouted.

"No! I live here!" I screamed. "It's my house too! You have to remember us! You have to!"

He dove for me. Tried to capture me.

I dodged to the side. Fell onto the steps. Landing hard on my knees and elbows. Pain shot through my whole body. But I ignored it. Ignored it and scrambled up the stairs on all fours.

At the top, I climbed to my feet. And stared down the long hall.

What can I do? How can I make them remember?

My room! I decided. I'll show them my room. Maybe that will remind them who I am. Maybe that will force them to remember.

I took a few steps—and then stopped.

I stared at the doors on both sides of the hall. Which room is mine? Which one?

"Oh nooooo," I moaned.

My room. I didn't remember my room.

I'm forgetting too. I'm forgetting everything.

Sick with horror, I sank against the wall.

"I'm lost," I murmured. "I give up. I'm lost."

Then something down the hall caught my eye.

I stared at it. Stared at it, forcing myself to remember what it was.

And suddenly, I had an idea.

CHAPTER 26

A rectangle of yellow light fell over the framed photograph on the wall. The photograph of Peter's teddy bear wearing the eyeglasses gleamed as if in a spotlight.

"Yes!" I cried, staring hard at it.

I knew it had something to do with Peter. I didn't remember exactly what. But I knew it was important to my parents.

I tore down the hall, reached up with both hands, and started to pull the photo off the wall.

"What are you doing?" a voice screamed angrily. "Put that down!"

"Get out of this house!"

Mom and Dad came bursting down the hall, their faces red with fury.

"She's up here, Officer!" Dad shouted downstairs. "We have her trapped in the hall!"

The framed photo stuck against its wire. I struggled to pull it free.

"What are you stealing, young woman?" Mom demanded. "Let go of that!"

"Are you crazy? Coming in here like this?" Dad cried.

He grabbed my arm. "Get away from there, miss. The police are here."

A blue-uniformed police officer, tall and blond, hands tensed at his sides, moved into the hallway.

"Here she is," Mom called to him, pointing to me. "She's crazy! Crazy! She just broke in and—and—"

The officer moved toward me menacingly. "Young lady, you'd better come with me," he said softly, blue eyes narrowed on me coldly.

He reached out to grab me.

I tugged the photograph free. My hands were shaking so hard, I nearly dropped it.

I spun around. And raised the photo high.

I held it up to my parents. And I screamed: "NOW TEDDY CAN SEE HOW CUTE I AM!"

CHAPTER 27

I watched Mom and Dad freeze. They stood like open-mouthed statues.

Will they remember? I asked myself. I gripped the frame tightly, held it up as if holding on to life . . . holding on to everything I knew.

Will they remember?

No.

They don't remember.

They're just standing there. Staring at it. Staring at me as if I'm crazy.

No . . . no . . .

And then I saw a single tear run down Dad's cheek.

Mom uttered a cry. And I saw her eyes glisten with tears. "Peter . . . " she whispered.

"Peter . . . " Dad echoed. He stared hard at me. "Danielle!"

He remembered!

"Oh, Danielle," he cried. His voice broke. "I'm so sorry."

And then the three of us were wrapped in a tearful hug.

"You remember!" I cried, still gripping the photograph tightly. "You remember us!"

"Danielle, please—forgive us!" Mom said, pressing her tear-stained cheek against mine.

The police officer shook his head. "What's going on here?" he demanded. "Do you know this girl?"

"Yes," Dad told him. "She's our daughter. We—we can't explain, Officer. We won't be needing you now."

"She—she didn't break in?"

"No," Dad told him. "You can go. Sorry for the trouble. We made a terrible mistake."

The policeman headed away, grumbling to himself, muttering and shaking his head.

"Peter," I choked out. "We have to hurry. We have to get Peter."

I led them down to the basement. "He-he's in the little back room," I told them.

But no.

The room stood empty. Bare, concrete floor. Stone walls. No trapdoor. No opening that led to an endless, black pit.

We're too late, I realized. He's gone.

Mom and Dad stared at me, bewildered. "Where is he?" Mom whispered. "You said—"

"Gone," I murmured. "Lost."

I couldn't stand it. I felt about to explode.

I realized I still had the teddy bear photo. I raised it high, as high as I could reach. "Peter, we remember you!" I screamed. "We remember you! We remember you!"

Silence.

The longest silence of my life.

And then the floor shook, and I heard a low, rumbling sound.

The rumble became a loud groan. The floor raised up . . . up. . . . The trapdoor slowly, heavily creaked open.

We all gasped as Peter stepped forward.

"We remember you!" I cried. "We remember!"

The thick mucus covering dropped from his body, fell off in chunks, rained to the floor, and then melted.

Peter stepped forward, blinking, testing his arms, his legs, stretching.

And then we were hugging. Celebrating. Celebrating the greatest family reunion of all time!

Later I was in Peter's room, helping him unpack some cartons and put the stuff away. It felt good to be doing something useful, something normal.

I kept glancing at the photo of the teddy bear with its eyeglasses. We had set it up on top of the dresser. The bear smiled down at us, as if it too was happy about being remembered.

"Tell me again about how you hypnotized me," Peter said, stacking comic books on a shelf.

"I *didn't* hypnotize you," I answered. "I only thought I did. I thought everything was my fault. But it was never me. It was the evil in this house. But we defeated this house. Thank goodness we defeated it!"

Peter thought about it a while. "I just don't understand how—" he started.

But Mom interrupted, calling from downstairs. "Addie is here!"

I pushed a carton away and hurried down to meet her. "Hi! I'm so glad to see you!" I cried.

She laughed. "Well . . . I'm glad too!"

I led her into the living room. "Everything is back to normal," I told her. "My brother is perfectly fine. And I'm okay. And everything is great! I'm just so *happy*!"

Addie let out a relieved sigh. "I'm so glad to hear it, Brittany. I was so worried about you."

I stared at her. "Excuse me? What did you call me?"

She stared back at me. "Brittany, of course."

My brother poked his head into the room. "Hi, Addie. What's up?"

She grinned at him. "What's up with you, Craig?"

I gasped and grabbed Addie by the shoulder. "What did you call him? Craig? You called us Brittany and Craig?"

Addie frowned. "Of course. What's your problem, Brittany? I should know your names, shouldn't I? I've known you two ever since you moved here with your aunt and uncle."

My mouth dropped open. I gaped at her in horror.

Addie laughed. "Come on. You didn't *really* forget your own names! You're joking, right? *Right?*"

THE NIGHTMARE ROOM
LOCKER 13

CHAPTER I

"Hey, Luke—good luck!"

Who called to me? The hall was jammed with kids excited about the first day of school. I was excited, too. My first day in seventh grade. My first day at Shawnee Valley Junior High.

I just *knew* this was going to be an awesome year.

Of course, I didn't take any chances. I wore my lucky shirt. It's a faded green T-shirt, kind of stretched out and the pocket is a little torn. But *no way* I'd start a school year without my lucky shirt.

And I had my lucky rabbit's foot in the pocket of my baggy khakis. It's black and very soft and furry. It's a key chain, but I don't want to ruin the good luck by hanging keys on it.

Why is it so lucky? Well, it's a *black* rabbit's foot, which is very rare. And I found it last November on my birthday. And after I found it, my parents gave me the new computer I wanted. So, it brought me good luck—right?

I glanced up at the red-and-black computer-printed

banner hanging over the hall: GO, SQUIRES! SUPPORT YOUR TEAM!

All of the boys' teams at Shawnee Valley are called the Squires. Don't ask me how they got that weird name. The banner made my heart race just a little. It reminded me that I had to find the basketball coach and ask when he was having tryouts.

I had a whole list of things I wanted to do: (1) check out the computer lab; (2) find out about the basketball team; (3) see if I could take any kind of special swimming program after school. I never went to a school with a swimming pool before. And since swimming is my other big sport, I was pretty pumped about it.

"Luke—hi!"

I spun around to find my friend Hannah Marcum behind me, looking as cheerful and enthusiastic as always. Hannah has short coppery hair, the color of a bright new penny, green eyes, and a great smile. My mother always calls her Sunshine, which totally embarrasses both of us.

"Your pocket is torn," she said. She tugged at it, ripping it a little more.

"Hey—get off!" I backed away. "It's my lucky shirt."

"Did you find your locker assignment yet?" She pointed to a group of kids studying a chart taped to the wall. They were all standing on tiptoe, trying to see over each other. "It's posted over there. Guess what? My locker is the first one outside the lunchroom. I'll be first for lunch every day."

"Oooh, lucky," I said.

"And I got Gruen for English," Hannah gushed. "He's the best! He's so funny. Everyone says you can't stop laughing. Did you get him too?"

"No," I said. "I got Warren."

Hannah made a face. "You're doomed."

"Shut up," I said. "Don't say things like that." I squeezed my rabbit's foot three times.

I pushed my way through the crowd to the locker chart. This is going to be an *excellent* year, I told myself. Junior High is *so* not like elementary school.

"Hey, man—how's it going?" Darnell Cross slapped me a high five.

"What's up?" I replied.

"Check it out. You got the *lucky* locker," Darnell said.

I squinted at the chart. "Huh? What do you mean?"

I ran my eyes down the list of names until I came to mine: Luke Greene. And then I followed the dotted line to my locker number.

And gasped.

"No way!" I said out loud. "That can't be right."

I blinked a few times, then focused on the chart again.

Yes. Locker 13.

Luke Greene . . . . *#13*

#13.

My breath caught in my throat. I started to choke.

I turned away from the chart, hoping no one could see how upset I was.

How can this be happening to me? I wondered. Locker 13? My whole year is *ruined* before it begins!

My heart pounded so hard, my chest ached. I forced myself to start breathing again.

I turned and found Hannah still standing there. "Where's your locker?" she asked. "I'll walk you there."

"Uh . . . well . . . I can deal with it," I said.

She squinted at me. "Excuse me?"

"I can deal with it," I repeated shakily. "It's Locker thirteen, but I can handle it. Really."

Hannah laughed. "Luke, you're such a superstitious geek!"

I frowned at her. "You mean that in a nice way—right?" I joked.

She laughed again and shoved me into a crowd of kids. I wish she wouldn't shove me so much. She's really strong.

I apologized to the kids I stumbled into. Then Hannah and I started down the crowded hall, checking the locker numbers, searching for number 13.

Just past the science lab, Hannah stopped suddenly and grabbed something up from the floor.

"Hey, wow! Look what I found!"

She held up a five-dollar bill. "Mmmmm—yes!"

She raised it to her lips and kissed it. "Five bucks! Yay!"

I sighed and shook my head. "Hannah, how come you're always so lucky?"

She didn't answer that question.

It seemed like a simple question, but it wasn't.

And if she had told me the answer, I think I would have run away—run as far as I could from Shawnee Valley Junior High, and never come back.

CHAPTER 2

Let's skip ahead two months. . . .

Seventh grade was not bad so far. I made some new friends. I made real progress on the computer animation piece I had been working on for nearly two years. And I actually won a spot on the basketball team.

It was early November, about two weeks into the season. And I was late for practice.

Guys were already on the floor, doing stretching exercises, bouncing basketballs to each other, taking short layups. I crept to the locker room, hoping no one would notice me.

"Luke—get dressed. You're late!" Coach Bendix shouted.

I started to call, "Sorry. I got hung up in the computer lab." But that was no kind of excuse. So I just gave Coach a nod and started jogging full speed to the locker room to get changed.

My stomach felt kind of tight. I realized I wasn't looking forward to practice today. For a little guy, I'm a pretty good basketball player. I've got a good outside shot and pretty fast hands on defense.

I was so excited to make the team. But I wasn't counting on one problem—an eighth grader named Stretch Johannsen.

Stretch's real name is Shawn. But everyone in the world calls him Stretch—even his parents. You might wonder how he got that name. But if you saw him, you wouldn't wonder.

Stretch had some kind of a growth spurt last year in seventh grade, and he became a big blond giant practically overnight. He's taller than anyone in the high school. He has shoulders like a wrestler and long arms. I mean, *really* long arms, like a chimpanzee. He can reach halfway across the gym!

And that's why everyone started calling him Stretch.

I think a better name for him would be *Ostrich*. That's because he has long skinny legs, like bird legs, and a huge chest that's so wide it makes his pale, blue-eyed head look as tiny as an egg.

But I would never try my nickname on him. I don't think I can run fast enough. Stretch doesn't have much of a sense of humor. In fact, he's a pretty mean guy, always trash-talking and shoving people around—and not just on the basketball floor.

I think once he got over the shock of being a giant, he decided to be really impressed with himself.

Like being a giant is some kind of special talent or something.

But don't get me started. I'm always analyzing people, thinking too hard about them, about everything. Hannah is always telling me I think too much. But I don't get it. How do you stop thinking?

Last week after a practice, Coach Bendix said nearly the same thing. "You've got to play on instinct, Luke. There isn't time to think before every move."

Which, I guess, is another reason why I ride the bench. Of course, I'm only in seventh grade. So, unless another giant forward tries out for the Squires, I'll probably get to play next year—after Stretch graduates.

But for now, it's really embarrassing not to get to play. Especially since my parents come to every game to cheer me on. I sit on the team bench and watch Mom and Dad up in the gym bleachers, just staring at me. Staring . . .

It doesn't make you feel great.

Even the time-outs are painful. Stretch always comes trotting over to the team bench. He wipes the sweat off his face and body—and then throws the towel onto me. Like I'm some kind of towel boy!

During one time-out late in the first game, he took a long gulp of Gatorade and spit it onto my uniform shirt. I looked up and saw my parents watching from the bleachers.

Sad. Really sad . . .

Our team, the Squires, won our first two games, mainly because Stretch wouldn't let anyone else handle the ball. It was great to win—but I was already starting to feel like a loser. I wanted to play!

Maybe if I have a really strong practice today, Coach Bendix will try me out at guard, I told myself. Or maybe even as a backup center. I laced up my shoes and triple-knotted them for luck. Then I shut my eyes and counted to seven three times.

Just something I do.

I straightened my red-and-black uniform shorts, slammed the gym locker shut, and trotted out of the locker room and onto the floor. Guys were at the far end, taking three-point shots, everyone shooting at once. The balls bounced off each other, bounced off the hoop. The backboard rang out with a steady *thud thud thud*.

Some of the shots actually dropped in.

"Luke, get busy!" Coach yelled, motioning me to the basket. "Get some rebounds. Make some shots. Get loose!"

I flashed him a thumbs-up and ran to join the others. I saw Stretch leap up and make a high rebound. To my surprise, he spun around and heaved the ball at me. "Luke—think fast!"

I wasn't expecting it. The ball sailed through my

hands. I had to chase it to the wall. I dribbled back to find Stretch waiting. "Go ahead, man. Shoot."

I swallowed hard—and sent up a two-handed shot.

"He shoots—he *misses!*" Stretch shouted. Some guys laughed.

My shot bounced off the rim. Stretch took three fast strides, reached up his long arms, and grabbed the rebound in midair. He tossed it back to me. "Shoot again."

My next shot brushed the bottom of the net.

"He shoots—he *misses!*" Stretch repeated, as if that was the funniest thing anyone ever said. More loud laughter.

Stretch took the rebound and tossed me the ball. "Again," he ordered.

Everyone was watching now. I sent up a one-handed layup that almost dropped in. It rolled around the rim, then fell off.

"He shoots—he *misses!*"

I could feel sweat rolling down my forehead. Why can't I get lucky here? I asked myself. Come on, Luke—just one lucky shot. I slapped my left hand rapidly against the leg of my shorts seven times.

Stretch bounced the ball to me. "Go, champ. You're O for three. You got a streak going!" More laughter.

I shut my eyes for a second. Then I sailed this

one high—and gasped as it sank through the hoop.

Stretch grinned and shook his head. The other guys all cheered as if I'd just won the state junior high tournament.

I grabbed the ball and dribbled away from them. I didn't want to give Stretch a chance to ruin my victory. I knew he would keep me shooting till I was one for three hundred!

I turned to see if Coach Benson had watched my shot. He leaned against the wall, talking to two other teachers. He hadn't seen it.

I dribbled across the floor, then back toward the others. Then I made a big mistake.

A *really* big mistake. A mistake that ruined my life at Shawnee Valley Junior High.

"Hey, Stretch—think fast!" I shouted. And I heaved the ball at him as hard as I could.

What was I *thinking*?

I didn't see that he had bent down on one knee to tie his sneaker lace.

I froze in horror—and watched the ball fly at him. It hit him hard on the side of the head, knocked him over, and sent him tumbling to the floor.

"Hey—!" he cried out, stunned. He shook his head dizzily. I saw bright red blood start to flow from his nose.

"Stretch—I'm sorry!" I shrieked. "I didn't see you! I didn't mean—!"

I lurched forward, running to help him up.

"My contacts!" he cried. "You knocked out my contacts."

And then I heard a soft squish under my shoe.

I stopped. Lifted my foot. Stretch's contact lens lay flat as a pancake on the gym floor.

Everyone saw it.

Stretch was on his feet now. Blood rolled down his lips, his chin.

He didn't pay any attention to it. He had his eyes narrowed on me. He lumbered forward, clenching and unclenching his giant fists.

I was doomed.

CHAPTER 3

Stretch reached under my arms and lifted me up. He was so huge and strong, he picked me off the floor like I was a ventriloquist's dummy.

"Whoa. It was an accident," I whispered.

"Here's *another* accident!" he said. When he talked, he spit blood in my face. He tightened his grip under my arms.

He raised me higher and gazed up at the basket. Is he going to make a three-point shot with me? I wondered.

Yes. He is. He's going to slam dunk me!

Behind me, I heard shouts. A whistle blowing. Running footsteps.

"Take it outside, Stretch!" I heard Coach Bendix shout.

Huh?

Stretch slowly lowered me to the floor. My knees started to buckle, but I managed to stay on my feet.

Stretch rubbed a hand across his bloody nose, then wiped it on the front of my jersey.

"Take it outside," Coach repeated, edging between us. "Let's pair up, everybody. One on one. Stretch—you and Luke."

"No way," Stretch muttered.

"He's your backup," Coach said, poking Stretch in the chest with his whistle. "You've got to teach Luke. I'm putting you in charge of Luke's development."

Stretch snickered. "Development? He doesn't have any development!"

"Go to my office. Get some tissues and stop that nosebleed," Coach instructed Stretch. "Then take Luke to the practice court behind the playground. Show him some moves. Teach him something."

Stretch stared at the floor for a few seconds, as if thinking it over. But he knew better than to argue with Coach Bendix. He nodded at me. "Let's go, Champ."

What choice did I have? Even though I knew it was pain time for me, I turned and followed him outside.

It was late afternoon, pretty cold to be outside in basketball shorts and a sleeveless jersey. Since it was November, the big, red sun had already lowered behind the houses across the street from the playground.

I shivered.

Stretch didn't give me much of a chance to get

ready. He pounded the ball hard on the asphalt court and came racing at me like a stampeding bull.

I tried to slide to the side. But Stretch lowered his shoulder and slammed it hard into my gut.

"Ohhh." I groaned and slumped back.

"Defense!" he shouted. "Get your hands up, Champ! Get ready. Here I come again!"

"No—wait—!" I pleaded.

The ball thundered in front of him as he drove into me again. This time he kept his body up straight. The force of the collision sent me sprawling to the asphalt.

"Defense!" he shouted. "Show me something. Block me. At least slow me down a little!"

Groaning again, I climbed to my feet. I felt as if I'd been hit by a truck.

Stretch dribbled around me, circling me, his eyes locked angrily on me. His nosebleed had stopped, but he still had dried blood caked under his nose.

I rubbed my chest. "I . . . I think I broke a rib," I whispered.

With a wild shout, he slammed into me again. This time I flew back—and smashed into the thick wooden post that held up the backboard.

"You're going to pay for those contacts, Champ," he called, hulking over me so I couldn't stand up, dribbling the ball inches from my feet.

"Yeah. Okay," I said, trying to rub the pain from my chest. "I said I was sorry."

"You're gonna be more sorry," he said. He bounced the ball hard against my bare leg. "Get up."

I didn't move. "It was an accident," I insisted. "I really didn't see you bend down. Really."

He picked at the caked blood under his nose. "Get up. Let's go. I'm supposed to teach you something." He laughed really loud. I'm not sure why. Then he swept a huge hand back through his short white-blond hair and waited for me to stand up. So he could teach me more lessons.

I climbed shakily to my feet. I felt so dizzy, I had to grab the wooden post. My head ached. My ribs ached.

"Can we . . . uh . . . play a different game?" I asked weakly.

"Yeah. Sure," he said. "Hey—think fast!"

He was standing so close, and he heaved the ball so hard, it felt like a cannonball as it shot into my stomach.

I stumbled back. And let out a sharp gasp.

And then realized I couldn't breathe.

I struggled hard to suck in some air.

No . . . no air . . . I . . . can't . . . get . . . air. . . .

I saw bright yellow stars. The yellow darkened to red.

Pain shot through my chest. The pain spread, growing sharper, sharper.

I was down on my back now, staring up at the

sky, staring up at the dancing red stars. I wante[...] scream. But I had no air.

Can't breathe . . . can't breathe at all. . . .

The stars faded away. The color faded fr[...] sky.

All black. All black now.

And as I sank into the blackness, I he[...]

A beautiful, soft voice from far, far a[...] my name.

An angel, I realized.

Yes. Through the blackness, I heard an angel calling my name.

And I knew that I had died.

CHAPTER 4

"Luke? Luke?"

The blackness lifted. I blinked up at the afternoon sky. The voice was closer now. And I recognized it.

"Luke?"

My chest ached as I took a deep breath.

Hey—when had I started to breathe again?

I lifted my head and saw Hannah running across the basketball court. She wore a blue windbreaker, unzipped, and it flapped up over her shoulders like wings. Her red hair glowed in the late afternoon sun like a halo.

Not an angel. Just Hannah.

She turned angrily to Stretch as she ran past him. "What did you do to Luke—*kill* him?"

Stretch giggled. "Probably."

Hannah dropped onto her knees beside me. Her windbreaker fell over my face. She tugged it away. "Are you alive? Can you speak?"

"Yeah. I'm okay," I muttered. I felt like a jerk. A helpless jerk.

Stretch walked up behind Hannah. "Who's she?" he sneered at me. "Your *girlfriend*?"

Hannah spun around to face him. "Hey—I've seen *your* girlfriend!"

Stretch's mouth dropped open. "Huh? Who's that?"

"Godzilla!" Hannah declared.

I tried to laugh, but it made my ribs hurt.

The next thing I knew, Hannah was on her feet, shoving Stretch's shoulders with both hands, forcing him to back up. "Ever hear of picking on someone your own size?" she demanded.

Stretch laughed. "No. Tell me about it." He backed away from her and raised his big, meaty fists. He grinned and started dancing like a fighter. "Come on. You want a piece of me? You want a piece of me?" Imitating someone in a movie, I guess.

"One on one," Hannah challenged.

Stretch tossed back his head and laughed. His blue eyes rolled around in his tiny head. "You want a piece of me?"

"Freestyle shooting," Hannah said, tearing off the windbreaker. She tossed it to the side of the court. "Come on, Stretch. Twenty shots each. Any kind of shot." She stared up at him. "You'll lose. Really. You'll see. You'll lose to a *girl*!"

His smile faded. "You're on the girls' basketball team—right?"

Hannah nodded. "I'm the center."

Stretch started to dribble the ball slowly in front of him. "Twenty shots? Layups or three-point?"

Hannah shrugged. "Any kind. You'll lose."

I climbed to my feet and went over to the side of the court to watch. I still felt a little shaky, but I knew I was okay.

Stretch didn't hesitate. He raised the ball and pushed up a one-handed shot from half-court. The ball hit the backboard, then the rim—and dropped in. "One for one," he said. He ran to retrieve the ball. "I'll keep shooting until I miss."

He missed his next shot, an easy layup from under the basket.

Hannah's turn. I crossed my fingers and counted to seven three times.

"Go, Hannah!" I cheered, holding up my crossed fingers.

Hannah sank a basket from the foul line. Then she drove under the basket and shot another one in from underneath.

My mouth dropped open as she sank eight more baskets without a miss. "Wow. Go, Hannah!"

Stretch just stood there looking dumb. I couldn't tell what he was thinking. His face was a total blank.

"Ten for ten!" Hannah declared. She bounced the ball to Stretch. "You go. Just to keep it interesting."

Hannah glanced at me, grinned, and flashed me a thumbs-up.

Stretch wasn't smiling anymore. He had a grim,

determined look on his face as he drove in close to shoot. He dropped four straight baskets, then missed one from in front of the foul line.

He muttered something under his breath and bounced the ball to Hannah.

Hannah sank eight more in a row. She turned to Stretch. "Eighteen for eighteen!"

But he was already jogging back to the gym, a scowl on his face.

"I'm not finished!" Hannah called after him.

Stretch turned back to me. "Hey, Champ—maybe you should take a lesson from your *girlfriend*. Or maybe you should play on her team!" Shaking his head, he disappeared into the school.

A strong wind began to blow across the playground. It was dark as evening now. I picked up Hannah's windbreaker and reached out to hand it to her. But she took another shot. "Nineteen." And then another. "Twenty. Yay! I win!"

I gaped at her. "Hannah—you never miss! How do you *do* that?"

She shrugged. "Just lucky."

I shivered. We started jogging back to the school. "Ask me how lucky I am," I muttered. "I made a new enemy today. A *huge* enemy!"

Hannah stopped and grabbed my arm. "Hey—I totally forgot why I was looking for you. I wanted to tell you the coolest news!"

I held the school door open. "Yeah? What?"

Hannah's green eyes flashed. "You know those photos I took of my dog? I sent them to a magazine in New York. And guess what? They paid me *five hundred dollars* for them. They're going to publish them—and do a big story about me! Isn't that so totally cool?"

"Wow. Totally," I said.

And that's when I decided my luck had to change.

Why should Hannah have all the luck? I can be lucky, too, I told myself.

It's all attitude. That's what it takes. The right attitude.

I changed into my street clothes. I made my way upstairs to stop at my locker. Locker 13.

Basketball practice had run so late, the halls were empty. My shoes clonked noisily on the hard floor. Most of the lights had already been turned off.

This school is creepy when it's empty, I decided. I stopped in front of my locker, feeling a chill at the back of my neck.

I always felt a little weirded-out in front of the locker. For one thing, it wasn't with all the other seventh-grade lockers. It was down at the end of the back hall, by itself, just past a janitor's supply closet.

Up and down the hall, all the other lockers had been painted over the summer. They were all a smooth, silvery gray. But no one had touched locker 13. The old, green paint was peeling and had large patches scraped off. Deep scratches crisscrossed up and down the door.

The locker smelled damp. And sour. As if it had once been filled with rotting leaves or dead fish or something.

That's okay, I can deal with this, I told myself.

I took a deep breath. New attitude, Luke. New attitude. Your luck is going to change.

I opened my backpack and pulled out a fat, black marker. Then I closed the locker door. And right above the number 13, I wrote the word LUCKY in big, bold capital letters.

I stepped back to admire my work: LUCKY 13.

"Yessss!" I felt better already.

I shoved the black marker into my backpack and started to zip it up. And that's when I heard the breathing.

Soft, soft breaths. So soft, I thought I imagined them. From inside the locker?

I crept closer and pressed my ear against the door.

I heard a soft hiss. Then more breathing.

The backpack slipped out of my hands and thudded to the floor. I froze.

And heard another soft hiss inside the locker. It ended in a short cry.

The back of my neck prickled. My breath caught in my throat.

Without realizing it, my hand had gripped the locker handle.

Should I open the door? Should I?

CHAPTER 5

My hand tightened on the handle. I forced myself to start breathing again.

I'm imagining this, I told myself.

There can't be anyone breathing inside my locker.

I lifted the handle. Pulled open the door.

"Hey—!" I cried out in shock. And stared down at a black cat.

The cat gazed up at me, its eyes red in the dim hall light. The black fur stood up on its back. It pulled back its lips and hissed again.

A black cat?

A black cat inside my locker?

I'm imagining this, I thought.

I blinked hard, trying to blink the cat away.

A black cat inside locker 13? Could there be any *worse* luck?

"How—how did you get in there?" I choked out.

The cat hissed again and arched its back. It gazed up at me coldly.

Then it leaped from the locker floor. It darted over

my shoes, down the hall. Running rapidly, silently. Head down, tail straight up, it turned the first corner and disappeared.

I stared after it, my heart pounding. I could still feel its furry body brushing against my leg. I realized I was still gripping the locker handle.

My head spun with questions. How long had the cat been in there? How did it get inside the locked door? Why was there a black cat in my locker? Why?

I turned and checked out the floor of the locker. Just to make sure there weren't any other creatures hiding in there. Then, still feeling confused, I closed the door carefully, locked it, and stepped back.

LUCKY 13.

The black letters appeared to glow.

"Yeah. Lucky," I muttered, picking up my backpack. "Real lucky. A black cat in my locker."

I held my lucky rabbit's foot and kept squeezing it tightly all the way home.

Things are going to change, I told myself. Things have got to change. . . .

But in the next few weeks my luck didn't change at all.

One day after school I was on my way to the computer lab when I ran into Hannah. "Where are you going?" she asked. "Want to come watch my basketball game?"

"I can't," I replied. "I promised to install some

new modems for Mrs. Coffey, the computer teacher."

"Mr. Computer Geek strikes again!" she said. She started jogging toward the gym.

"Did you get your science test back?" I called after her.

She stopped and turned around with a grin on her face. "You won't believe it, Luke. I didn't have time to study. I had to guess on every question. And guess what? I got a hundred! I got them all right!"

"That's excellent!" I called. I'd studied for that test for a solid week, and I got a seventy-four.

I made my way into the computer lab and waved to Mrs. Coffey. She was hunched over her desk, sorting through a tall stack of disks. "Hey, how's it going?" she called.

The computer lab is my second home. Ever since Mrs. Coffey learned that I can repair computers, and upgrade them, and install things in them, I've been her favorite student.

And I have to admit, I really like her too. Whenever I don't have basketball practice, I check in at the computer lab to talk with her and see what needs to be fixed.

"Luke, how is your animation project coming along?" she asked, setting down the disks. She brushed back her blond hair. She has the nicest smile. Everyone likes her because she always seems to enjoy her classes so much.

"I'm almost ready to show it to you," I said. I sat

down in front of a computer and started to remove the back. "I think it's really cool. And it's going much faster now. I found a new way to move pixels around."

Her eyes grew wide. "Really?"

"It's a very cool invention," I said, carefully sliding the insides from the computer. "The program is pretty simple. I think a lot of animators might like it."

I set down my screwdriver and gazed across the room at her. "Maybe you could help me. You know. Show it to people. Get it copyrighted or something."

"Maybe," she said. She stood up, smoothing the hem of her blue sweater over her jeans. She came up behind me and watched as I removed the old modem. "You're really skillful, Luke. I think you're going to make a lot of money with computers some day."

"Yeah. Maybe," I replied awkwardly. "Thanks." I didn't really know what to say. Mrs. Coffey is so awesome. She is the only teacher who really encourages me and thinks I'm somebody.

"I can't *wait* to show you my animation," I said.

"Well . . . I have some big news," she said suddenly. I turned and caught the excited smile on her face. "You're the first person to hear it, Luke. Can you keep a secret?"

"Yeah. Okay," I said.

"I just got the most wonderful job! At a really big software company in Chicago. I'm leaving school next week!"

The next afternoon I couldn't check in at the computer lab. I had to hurry to the swimming pool behind the gym.

Swimming is my other big sport. I spent all last summer working with an instructor at our local pool. He was fast enough to make the Olympic tryouts a few years ago. And he really improved my stroke and showed me a lot of secrets for getting my speed up.

So I looked forward to the tryouts for the Squires swim team. I couldn't wear my lucky swimsuit because it didn't fit anymore. But I wore my lucky shirt to school that day. And as I changed for the pool, I silently counted to seven three times.

As I left the locker room, I heard shouts and laughter echoing off the tile pool walls. Feeling my heart start to race, I stepped into the steamy air of the indoor pool. The floor was puddled with warm water. I inhaled the sharp chlorine smell. I love that smell!

Then I bent down and kissed the top of the diving board. I know. It sounds weird. But it's just something I always do.

I turned to the pool. Three or four guys were already in the water. At the shallow end I saw Stretch. He was violently splashing two other guys. He had them cornered at the end of the pool. His big hands slapped the water, sending up tall waves over them. They pleaded with him to give them a break.

Coach Swanson blew his whistle, then shouted

for Stretch to cut the horseplay. Stretch gave the two guys one more vicious splash.

Then he turned and saw me. "Hey, Champ—" he shouted, his voice booming off the tiles. "You're early. Drowning lessons are next week! Ha ha! Nice swim trunks. Are those your *girlfriend's*? Ha ha!"

A few other guys laughed too.

I decided to ignore them. I was feeling pretty confident. About twenty guys were trying out. I knew there were only six spots open on the team. But after all my work last summer, I thought I could make the top six.

We all warmed up for a bit, taking easy laps, limbering up our muscles, getting used to the warm water. After a few minutes, Coach Swanson made us all climb out and line up at the deep end of the pool.

"Okay, guys, I've got to get to my night job by five, so we're going to keep this simple," the coach announced. "You have one chance. One chance only. You hear the whistle, you do a speed dive into the pool. You do two complete laps, any stroke you want. I'll take the first six guys. And two alternates. Any questions?"

There weren't any.

Everyone leaned forward, preparing to dive. Stretch lined up next to me. He elbowed me hard in the side. "Give me some room, Champ. Don't crowd me."

Okay, so he'll come in first, I figured, rubbing the pain from my side. That leaves five other places on the team.

I'm good enough, I told myself. I know I am. I know I am. . . .

The whistle blew. All down the row, bodies tensed, then plunged forward.

I started my dive—and slipped.

The pool floor—so wet . . .

My feet slid on the tile.

Oh . . . no!

I hit the water with a loud *smack*.

A belly flop! No kind of dive.

Struggling to recover, I raised my head. And saw everyone way ahead of me.

One unlucky slip . . .

I lowered my head, determined to catch up. I started stroking easily, forcing myself to be calm. I remembered the slow, steady, straight-legged kick my instructor had taught me.

I sped up. I passed some guys. Hit the wall and started back.

I can do this, I told myself. I can still make the team.

Faster . . .

At the end of the second lap the finish was a furious blur. Blue water. Thrashing arms and legs. Loud breaths. Bobbing heads.

I tried to shut out everything and concentrate on

my stroke . . . ignore everyone else . . . and swim!

At last my hand hit the pool wall. I ducked under, then surfaced, blowing out water. I wiped my hair away from my eyes. The taste of chlorine was in my mouth. Water running down my face, I glanced around.

I didn't finish last. Some guys were still swimming. I squinted down the line of swimmers who had finished. How many? How many were ahead of me?

"Luke—you're seventh," Coach Swanson announced. He made a large check on his clipboard. "First alternate. See you at practice."

I was still too out-of-breath to reply.

Seventh.

I let out a long sigh. I felt so disappointed. I could do better than seventh, I knew. If only I hadn't slipped.

As I started to trudge back to the locker room, Stretch strode up beside me. "Hey, Champ!" He slapped my bare back with his open hand, so hard it made a loud *smack*. "Thanks for making me look so good!"

I got dressed quickly, standing in a corner by myself. A few guys came over to say congratulations. But I didn't feel I deserved it.

Across the locker room Stretch was still in his swim trunks. He was having a great time, smacking guys with his towel, really making the towel *snap* against their bare skin, laughing his head off.

I tossed my towel in the basket. Then I stepped up to the mirror over the sinks to comb my hair. A ceiling lightbulb was out, and I had to lean over the sink to see.

I had just started to comb my wet hair back— when I saw the jagged crack along the length of the glass.

"Whoa." I stopped combing and stepped back.

A broken mirror. Seven years bad luck for someone.

I reached into my khakis pocket and squeezed my rabbit's foot three times. Then I turned back to the mirror and began combing my hair again.

Something was wrong.

I blinked. Once. Twice.

A red light? Some kind of red glare in the mirror glass.

I squinted into the glass—and let out a cry.

The red glare was coming from a pair of eyes— two red eyes, glowing like hot coals.

Two angry red eyes, floating in the glass. Floating beside my reflection.

I could see my confused expression as I stared at the frightening red eyes . . . as I watched the eyes slide across the glass . . . slide . . . slide closer . . . until their red glow covered my eyes!

My horrified reflection stared out at me with the fiery, glowing eyes.

And I opened my mouth and let out a long, terrified scream.

CHAPTER 6

Over my scream I heard heavy footsteps behind me. And then I heard a voice—Stretch's voice: "Hey—get used to it!"

I spun around. He grinned at me. "Get used to it, Champ. That's your face! It makes other people scream too!"

"No!" I cried. "No! It's not! Don't you see—?"

Coach Swanson burst in behind Stretch. "Luke—what's wrong?"

"My eyes!" I cried. "Look! Are they red? *Are* they?"

Coach Swanson and Stretch exchanged glances.

"What is his problem?" Stretch murmured.

Coach Swanson stepped up close and examined my eyes. "What's wrong with you, Luke? It's just the chlorine from the pool. Your eyes will be okay in a little while."

"Chlorine? Huh? No!" I insisted. Then I glanced into the mirror. And saw my normal, brown eyes gazing back at me.

No glowing eyes. No red eyes burning in the glass like an evil movie monster.

"Uh . . . well . . ." I rubbed my eyes. They didn't burn or anything. They felt okay.

I turned back to Stretch and Coach Swanson. I didn't know what to say to them. They were both still staring at me as if I were nuts.

And maybe I was.

Black cats jumping out of my locker? Glowing red eyes in the mirror?

"Well . . . see you at practice," I said.

Stretch laughed. "Not if I see you first! Ha ha!"

I laughed too. It wasn't funny, but I wanted to sound calm again, normal.

As I followed them out of the locker room, I realized I was trembling.

Why were these strange things happening to me?

CHAPTER 7

After dinner I was supposed to go to the mall with Hannah. She wanted to buy me some computer software for my birthday. But she wanted me to pick it out.

That was really nice of her. But at the last minute I decided not to go.

I was still feeling weird from the swim tryouts. And I wanted to work on my animation project. If I worked really hard, I might be able to get it finished in time to show Mrs. Coffey before she left school.

I went up to my room and booted up the animation. But I couldn't concentrate. I kept staring at the four-leaf clover inside a block of clear Lucite I keep on my desk. And I kept jumping up and running to the mirror to check my eyes.

Perfectly normal.

Not glowing.

So what happened? What happened to me in that locker room? I asked myself. I tried to convince myself there was something wrong with the mirror.

The red glow was because of the way the light hit the crack in the mirror. Or something.

No.

That didn't make sense.

The phone rang a little before ten o'clock. And it was Hannah, sounding very breathless and excited.

"Luke—you should've come! You should've come!"

I had to hold the phone away from my ear, Hannah was shouting so loud. "Why? What happened?" I asked.

"I won it!" she declared. "Do you believe it? I won!"

"Excuse me? Hannah—what are you talking about?"

"You know the raffle at the mall? That huge red SUV? It's been on display there for a month? Thousands of people put tickets in the box. Thousands! And—and—I just happened to be walking by when they had the drawing tonight. And—"

"You *didn't*!" I shrieked.

"Yes! Yes! I won it! I won the SUV!"

"Wow!" I slumped onto my bed. I actually felt faint. My heart was pounding as if I had won!

"You should've seen me when they called out my name!" Hannah gushed. "I screamed. I just stood there and screamed!"

She screamed again, shrieked at the top of her lungs. A long, high, joyful scream.

"Hannah—that's so awesome," I said. I don't think she heard me. She was still screaming.

"My family is so happy, Luke. You should *see* them. They are *dancing* around the living room!"

"That's so great," I said.

Hannah lowered her voice. "I just feel bad about one thing, Luke. I was so crazed, I was so *berserk*, I forgot why I was at the mall. I forgot all about buying you a birthday gift."

I stood up. I picked up the block with the four-leaf clover inside and smoothed it between my hands. "That's okay," I told Hannah. "I just decided what I really want for my birthday."

"What's that?" she asked.

"I want *your* luck!"

Hannah laughed. She thought I was kidding. But of course I was serious.

"Are you going to school tomorrow?" she asked.

"Huh? Yeah, sure. Why not?"

"Tomorrow is Friday the thirteenth," she said. "I know how superstitious you are. I thought maybe you'd stay home and hide under the bed all day."

"Ha ha," I said. But I felt a cold tingle at the back of my neck. "I'll be there," I told Hannah. "I'm not totally wacko, you know."

But I'll wear my lucky shirt, I thought. And I'll take my four-leaf clover in my backpack. And I'll ask Mom to pack my lucky sandwich for lunch—peanut butter and mayonnaise.

"I have to go to school tomorrow," I told Hannah. "I have basketball practice after school."

"How's practice going?" Hannah asked.

I chuckled. "Not bad. So far, I haven't gotten any splinters from sitting on the bench!"

Hannah laughed. I could hear shouts and wild laughter in the background. "I've got to go!" she said, shouting over the racket. "My family is still celebrating my winning the SUV! Bye!"

She clicked off before I could reply.

That night I dreamed about locker 13.

In the dream I stepped up to the locker. Someone had taped a calendar to the door. I came closer and saw that Friday the thirteenth had been circled in red.

I started to rip the calendar off the locker door. But I stopped when I heard loud breathing. Hoarse wheezing sounds. Like someone was having trouble breathing.

I touched the locker door. And it was burning hot!

I screamed in shock and pulled my hand away.

Again, I heard the hoarse breathing from inside the locker. And then I heard a tiny voice cry out: "Please . . . get me out."

In the dream I knew I was dreaming. I wanted to lift myself out of the dream. But I was stuck there. And I knew I had no choice. I had to pull open the locker door and see who was in there.

"*Please . . . I want out. Get me out!*" the tiny, frightened voice called.

Even though I knew I was dreaming, I still felt so frightened. Real fear that makes you shake, whether you're awake or asleep.

I watched myself grip the door handle. Slowly— so slowly—I pulled the locker door open.

And I stared in horror at the figure huddled inside the locker. *Because it was ME!*

It was me inside the locker, hugging myself, trembling all over. It was me—and my eyes started to glow. My eyes glowed out from the dark locker, red as fire.

And as I stared at myself, stared at those ugly, evil red eyes, I watched my face begin to change. I watched hair grow out of my nostrils. Long braids of thick black hair, sliding out of my nose—down, down to the locker floor.

Beneath the shining red eyes, thick, black, twisted ropes of hair were pouring from my nose. Out of the locker. Piling onto the hall floor. Curling around me as I watched.

Yes. The long hair flowed from my nose and snaked around me as I watched in horror. Curled around me, covering me in warm, scratchy hair. Covering me like a big, furry coat, and then tightening. Tightening. Tightening around my chest. Tightening around my face. Wrapping me like a mummy. Wrapping me in my ghastly nose hair.

I woke up, one hand tightly wrapped around the Lucite block with the four-leaf clover. Gray morning sunlight seeped through my bedroom window. My room was so cold, cold as a freezer.

"Luke, what are you doing up there? You're late!" Mom's voice shattered the frozen silence.

"A dream," I murmured. A hoarse laugh escaped my throat. My eyes darted around the room. Normal. Everything normal.

"Hurry, Luke! It's really late." Mom's voice sounded so good to me.

I followed her order. I hurried. I got showered, dressed, ate breakfast, and arrived at school with about two minutes to spare. The halls were pretty empty. Most kids had already gone to their homerooms.

I glanced at the clock on the tile wall. Then jogged to the end of the back hall to toss my jacket into my locker.

But a few feet from my locker I stopped with a gasp.

What was that on the door to locker 13?

I crept closer.

A calendar?

Yes.

Someone had taped a calendar to the door. And . . . and today . . . Friday the thirteenth was circled in red.

"My dream!" I murmured.

That horrifying dream. It's coming true, I realized. I'm going to open the door, and it's going to come true.

CHAPTER 8

I stared at the calendar, at the number 13 circled in red marker.

Last night's dream played itself again through my mind. I shuddered. My legs and arms itched. I could practically feel the disgusting hair curling around my skin.

With an angry cry I ripped the calendar off the door and crumpled it in my hand.

Now I expected to hear the heavy breathing from inside the locker. And the tiny cries—my cries—begging to be let out.

But I didn't wait. "I'm not opening it," I said out loud.

No way am I going to allow the dream to come true.

I tossed the wadded-up calendar sheet to the floor. Then I spun around and began running to class. The hall was empty. My shoes thudded loudly on the hard floor as I ran.

I'll keep my coat with me, I decided. I'll just drag

it around with me all day. I don't need to open the locker.

The bell rang as I reached my homeroom door. Mr. Perkins looked up as I burst into the room. "Good morning, Luke," he said. "Running a little late this morning?"

"A little," I replied breathlessly. Unzipping my jacket, I started to my seat.

"Would you like time to go hang your coat in your locker?" Mr. Perkins asked.

"Uh . . . no. That's okay." I lowered my backpack to the floor and dropped into the chair. "I'll just . . . keep it."

A few kids were staring at me. Mr. Perkins nodded and turned back to the papers he was reading.

I took a deep breath and settled back against the chair. I rubbed the right sleeve of my lucky shirt seven times.

That dream is *not* going to come true! I told myself. No way! I won't let it.

Of course, I wasn't thinking clearly. How *could* that crazy dream come true?

If I had stopped for one second to think about it, I would have realized the whole idea was insane.

But today was Friday the thirteenth. And I *never* can think clearly on Friday the thirteenth. I admit it. I'm always a little crazy on that unlucky day.

I glanced up to see that Mr. Perkins had been reading the morning announcements. I hadn't heard a word he said. I pulled the four-leaf clover from my backpack, twirled it in my hand, and wished for good luck for the rest of the day.

At noon I found Hannah at a table against the back wall of the lunchroom. She was sitting all by herself, staring down at her brown lunchbag, which she hadn't opened.

"Hi. Whassup?" I dropped across from her.

"Hi," she said softly, without raising her eyes. "How's it going?"

"Well, pretty okay for a Friday the thirteenth," I said. Actually, the morning had flown by without any problems at all.

I expected Hannah to make some kind of joke about how superstitious I am. But she didn't say a word.

I pulled the sandwich from my bag and started to unwrap the foil. "My lucky sandwich," I said. "Peanut butter and mayonnaise."

"Yum," she said, rolling her eyes. She finally looked at me. She appeared tired. Her eyes were bloodshot, red, as if she'd been crying. Her hair was a mess, and her face was gray.

"How come you're wearing your coat?" she asked.

"Oh . . . uh . . . no reason," I said. "I was kind of cold."

She nodded glumly.

"Did you come to school in the new SUV?" I asked.

She shook her head. "We don't have it yet. Dad has to go fill out a lot of papers." She let out a long sigh.

I lowered my sandwich. "Are you feeling okay?" I asked.

She didn't answer. Instead, she sighed again and stared down at the table.

I poked her lunchbag with one finger. "What do you have for lunch?"

She shrugged. "Just some fruit. I'm not very hungry." She opened the bag, reached a hand in, and pulled out a bright yellow banana.

She struggled with the skin. Then finally peeled it open.

"Oh, yuck!" Her face twisted in disgust. She dropped the banana to the table.

Inside the skin, the banana was completely rotten. Just a soft pile of black mush. A horrible, sour smell—like ripe vomit—floated up from it.

Hannah shoved the banana away. "Sick. That's really sick."

"The skin is perfectly fresh," I said. "How could the banana be so rotten?"

"I think I have an apple," Hannah said glumly. She tore the bag apart and pulled out a red apple. She twirled it between her hands—then stopped with a gasp.

I saw the deep, dark hole on the side of the apple. And as we both stared at it, a fat, brown worm—at least two inches long—curled out from inside. And then another. And another.

The worms dropped from the apple, onto the tabletop.

"I don't *believe* this!" Hannah shrieked. She scraped her chair back so hard, it toppled over.

And before I could say anything, she was running from the room.

After school I looked for Hannah on my way to basketball practice. I was worried about her. She had acted so weird at lunch. Not like herself at all.

I reminded myself that it was Friday the thirteenth. And sometimes people act a little weird on this day.

But not Hannah. Hannah is the least superstitious person I know. She walks under ladders all the time, and she hugs black cats, and doesn't think a thing of it.

And why should she? Hannah has to be the luckiest person on earth!

Lockers slammed as kids prepared to go home. I started to the gym, then turned back. I don't want to carry my coat and backpack to the gym, I decided. I'm going to stuff them in my locker.

I hesitated as the locker came into view at the end of the hall. I read the words on the door: LUCKY 13. Of course I remembered my nightmare—and the calendar from my nightmare taped on the locker door.

But I had to open the locker. I didn't want to carry my stuff around with me for the rest of the year!

"Hey, Luke!" I saw Darnell Cross waving to me from the doorway to the science lab. "Are the Squires going to beat Davenport?"

"They're not so tough," I called back. "We could take them."

"You going to play?" Darnell asked. He grinned because he already knew the answer.

"As soon as I grow taller than Stretch!" I replied.

He laughed and disappeared back into the lab.

I stepped up to locker 13. I brought my face close to the door. "Anyone in there?" I called in.

Silence.

"Just checking," I said. I grabbed the door handle. I was feeling pretty confident. Friday the thirteenth was two-thirds over, and so far, nothing terribly unlucky had happened to me.

I squeezed my rabbit's foot for luck. Then I took a deep breath—and pulled open the locker.

CHAPTER 9

Nothing unusual inside the locker.

I realized I was still gripping the rabbit's foot inside my pocket. I let go of it and slipped my backpack off my shoulders.

I studied the locker carefully. A bunch of books and notebooks on the top shelf, where I had left them. My old gray sweatshirt lay crumpled on the locker floor.

No black cats. No one breathing or crying or shooting piles of hair from his nose.

I let out a long sigh of relief. Then I tossed the backpack on top of the balled-up sweatshirt. Shoved my jacket onto the hook on the back wall.

I started to slam the door shut when I spotted something at my feet.

My shoe kicked it and it rolled against the locker bottom, then bounced back.

A ball?

I bent down and picked it up. I raised it close to my face.

"Whoa." Not a ball. A tiny yellow skull, a little larger than a Ping-Pong ball.

It had an open-mouthed grin, revealing two rows of gray teeth. I ran my finger over the teeth. They were hard and bumpy.

I squeezed it. The little skull was made of some kind of hard rubber.

The eyes—sunken deep in the sockets—were red glass. They glowed in the hall lights, like tiny rubies.

"Where did you come from?" I asked it.

I turned back to the locker. Did the skull fall out of the locker? How did it get in there? Was someone playing some kind of Friday the thirteenth head game with me?

I decided that had to be the answer.

I rolled the skull around in my hand a few times. I poked my finger against the glowing, red glass eyes.

Then I tucked it into my pants pocket. I slammed the locker shut—and headed to practice.

"Look alive! Heads up. Look alive!" Coach Bendix was shouting.

I ran out of the locker room and grabbed a basketball off the ball rack. I began dribbling around the floor.

We were having one of Coach's free-for-all practices. That meant we had to keep moving, keep playing—run, dribble, pass, shoot, play defense. Do everything all at once in a big free-for-all.

I dribbled slowly across the floor, concentrating hard. Trying not to lose the dribble. I saw Stretch turn toward me. He stuck out both hands and moved forward, ready to block me.

I decided to try and fake him out. I dribbled left—and moved right. I edged past him easily. Moved under the basket. And sent up a shot that sailed across the gym and dropped in.

"Hey—one for one!" I cried happily.

"Lucky shot!" Stretch called.

I took the ball and moved back to the top of the key. I sent up a two-handed jumpshot. It soared over the rim—and dropped through the basket with a soft *swish*.

"Yes!" I pumped my fists in the air.

I didn't have long to celebrate. I turned and saw Stretch barreling toward me, dribbling hard, leaning forward with grim determination.

He's going to charge right over me, I realized. He's going to *flatten* me.

Guys backed out of his way as Stretch flew across the floor.

"Look out, Luke!" someone shouted.

I froze for a moment. Then I ducked to the left. Stuck out my hand and slapped the ball away from Stretch.

He made a wild grab for it. But I dribbled it out of

his reach. Then I spun around and sent a wild, high shot into the air. The ball hit the glass backboard—and sank through the net.

"Wow!"

"Way to go, Luke!"

"Three for three!"

The other players were in shock.

Stretch shook his head. "Feeling lucky, today? Think fast!" He pulled back his long arm—and heaved the ball at my chest with all his strength.

I caught it easily. Dribbled it three times. Shot—and dropped another basket.

Stretch scowled. "I don't believe this," he muttered, shaking his head.

I don't, either! I thought to myself. I've never shot four baskets in a row in my life!

I turned and saw Coach Bendix watching me. Was this my big chance? Stretch and another player were passing the ball back and forth, moving across the floor.

I shot forward. Intercepted Stretch's pass. Drove to the basket. And sent up an easy layup. "Two points!" I cried.

With an angry grunt Stretch reached for the rebound. But I pushed it out of his hands. Grabbed it. Spun. Shot again. "Two points!"

Stretch cried out angrily. He bumped me hard

from behind. I think he would have flattened me on the spot. But he saw that Coach Bendix was running over to us.

Coach slapped me on the back. "Way to go, Luke!" he boomed. "Way to show real improvement! I'm impressed. Keep it up, okay? I'm going to give you some playing time next Friday."

"Hey—thanks," I replied breathlessly.

I saw Stretch scowl. Saw his face turn an angry red.

I grabbed a ball and dribbled away. I wanted to shout and jump for joy. Had my luck finally changed?

It seemed that way. Suddenly I could pass and jump and shoot and play defense like I never could before! It was as if I was possessed or something! Possessed by an all-star athlete.

In the locker room after practice, Stretch ignored me. But other guys slapped me on the back and flashed me a thumbs-up.

"Lookin' good, Luke!"

"Way to go, man!"

"Go, Squires!"

I was feeling really happy. Like a new person. As I changed into my street clothes, I felt the little skull in my pants pocket. I pulled it out and gazed at it, smoothing my thumb over the hard rubber.

"Are you my new good-luck charm?" I asked it.

The tiny, red eyes glowed back at me. I kissed it, gave it a smack on top of its yellow head, and shoved it back into my pants pocket.

That skull is going everywhere with me, I decided. It's got to be lucky.

It's *got* to be!

As I walked home, I kept reliving my great basketball triumph. I pictured my long, perfect jump-shots again. And I saw myself stealing the ball from Stretch's hands, driving right past him, and scoring. Embarrassing him. Embarrassing Stretch again and again!

Wow! What a day!

It was a cold, gray afternoon. Dark clouds hung low over the nearly bare trees. It felt more like winter than fall.

A few blocks from home, I crossed a street—and heard a short cry.

A long, low evergreen hedge ran across the front yard on the corner. I stopped, gazing over the hedge. Had the cry come from the yard?

I listened hard. Down the block a car door slammed. A dog started to bark. The wind made a whistling sound through the phone lines overhead.

And then I heard it—another sharp cry—longer this time.

A baby? It sounded like a baby's cry.

"*Owwwww. Owwwwww.*"

I lowered my gaze to the hedge—and saw the creature making the shrill cries.

A cat. No. A small orange-and-white kitten.

It appeared to be stuck in the prickly brambles of the hedge.

"*Owwwww. Owwwwww.*"

Carefully I bent down and gently lifted the cat out with both hands. As I cupped my hands around it, it stopped crying immediately. But it was still breathing hard, its white chest moving rapidly up and down. I rubbed its head, trying to soothe it.

"You're okay, little kitten," I whispered.

And then I heard another cry. A loud shriek.

I looked up to see a large woman running at me angrily. Her face was bright red, and she waved her arms furiously.

"Oh, no," I muttered. I nearly dropped the cat.

Why is she so angry?

What have I done?

CHAPTER 10

"The kitten—!" she cried, shoving through a break in the hedge.

"I—I'm sorry," I stammered. "I didn't know. I—"

"Where did you find her?" the woman demanded, her face still bright red.

"In . . . in the hedge."

"Oh, thank you! Thank you!" the woman said. She took the kitten from my hands and raised it to her cheek. "Sasha, where did you go?"

I'm not in trouble, I finally realized. The woman is happy—not angry.

"Sasha has been missing for two days," the woman told me, pressing the kitten against her face. "I offered a reward and everything. I almost gave up hope."

I let out a long sigh of relief. "She was right there," I said, pointing. "In the hedge. I think she was caught in it."

"Well, she's fine now, thanks to you." Still pressing the kitten to her cheek, the woman pushed through the hedge and started to the house. "What is your name?"

"Luke."

"Well, follow me, Luke. I'll get your reward for you."

"Huh? Reward? No. Really," I started to back away.

"You saved Sasha's life," the woman said. "You did a wonderful thing. And I insist you take the reward I offered."

I saw that I had no choice. I followed her to her kitchen door.

A few minutes later she counted out five twenty-dollar bills and pressed them into my hand. "Thank you, Luke. You really did your good deed for today!"

A hundred dollars!

A hundred dollars reward!

My luck really is starting to change, I decided.

When I got home, a big surprise awaited me.

Mom had made my favorite dinner—meat loaf, mashed potatoes, and gravy. And a coconut cake for dessert!

"It's not even my birthday!" I exclaimed.

"I just felt like doing something nice for you today," Mom said. She brushed back my hair with one hand. "I know Friday the thirteenth is always a hard day for you."

"Not today!" I told her, grinning. "Not today!"

After my second slice of coconut cake, I went up to my room and started my homework. I spent about an hour writing out the answers to my science assignment.

It shouldn't have taken that long. But I kept taking out the twenty-dollar bills, counting them again, and dreaming about what I could buy with them.

After science I worked on my computer animation. I'd been having trouble with the last section. I couldn't get anything to move the way I wanted.

But tonight my good luck continued. I had no trouble at all. The images all slid together perfectly. I almost finished the project.

A little after nine I decided to give Hannah a call. She'd acted so weird at lunch that afternoon. I thought maybe she was sick or something.

I called to see if she was feeling better. But I could tell by the way she answered the phone that she still wasn't her old self.

I tried to cheer her up. I told her about my triumph at basketball practice. And about the hundred-dollar reward for finding the lost kitten.

"Very cool," Hannah said. But her voice showed no enthusiasm at all.

"And then Mom made all of my favorite things for dinner!" I exclaimed.

"Lucky," Hannah muttered.

"What's your problem?" I demanded. "What's wrong with you today?"

A long silence at her end.

Finally she said, "I guess I'm just in a bad mood. I fell off my bike on the way home this afternoon."

I groaned. "Oh, no. Are you okay?"

"Not really," she replied. "I scraped all the skin off my right hand. And I twisted my ankle pretty bad."

"Wow," I muttered. "Bad news."

"Especially since I have a basketball game tomorrow," Hannah sighed.

"Think you'll be able to play?" I asked.

"Maybe," she said glumly.

"Maybe I'll come watch your game," I said.

There was a long silence. And then Hannah said, "Luke, there's something . . . something I have to tell you."

"Excuse me?" I said. She was whispering, so low I could barely hear her.

"I really should tell you something. But . . ."

I pressed the phone tighter to my ear. "What? What is it?"

"Well . . ."

Another long silence.

"I can't," she said finally. I heard a click, and the line went silent.

The next morning my good luck came to an end.

CHAPTER 11

At least, I *thought* my good luck had ended.

When I arrived at my science class, I searched my backpack for the homework questions. Not there. I took everything out—every paper, every book, every pencil.

Not there. I had spent over an hour on that assignment last night. And I'd left it at home.

Now I was in major trouble. Miss Creamer didn't accept late homework. And homework counted for fifty percent of the grade in her class.

My stomach tightened with dread as she entered the science lab to begin class.

How could I be so stupid?

"Good morning, everyone," she began. "I have an announcement to make. It's about last night's homework."

The room grew silent.

"I have to apologize to all of you," Miss Creamer continued. "I gave the wrong assignment. Those weren't the right questions. I'm really sorry. You don't have to turn it in. Just tear it up and throw it away."

Cheers rang out. Some kids gleefully ripped their papers into shreds. A big celebration.

Yes! More good luck for me, I thought happily.

I was on a hot streak. Later, when Miss Creamer handed back last week's test, I had the only A in the class.

In the lunchroom I grabbed the *last* slice of pizza on the counter!

All the kids behind me in line groaned. Darnell came up and offered to pay me five dollars for it. But no deal.

After school I stopped by the computer lab to see Mrs. Coffey. She told me her plans had suddenly changed. She wouldn't be leaving school for another two weeks.

I cheered. That meant I had time to finish my computer animation project and show it to her before I left.

"Luke, I was talking about you to my friend who owns Linkups. You know—the computer store on Highlands? I told him about how you can do anything with computers, fix them, upgrade them. He said you might be able to come into the store on Saturdays and help out in the service department."

I gasped. "Really?"

She nodded. "He's a really nice guy, and he's always looking for people who can fix machines. He said he couldn't give you a real job since you're only twelve. But he could pay you five dollars an hour."

"Wow! I cried. "That's awesome! Thanks, Mrs. Coffey."

I practically flew down the stairs to the gym. I wanted to flap my arms and take off! So many great things were happening to me! I couldn't believe it!

Hannah's basketball game had already started when I stepped into the gym. I found a seat in the bleachers and glanced up at the scoreboard. The Squirettes were already losing ten to two.

What's going on? I wondered. How can Hannah's team be losing so badly? The team they were playing—the Bee Stingers from Elwood Middle School—were the worst team in the city!

I turned and glanced around the bleachers. There were only about twenty kids watching the game. And four or five parents, clustered together at the top of the bleachers.

"Go, Sharon!" one of the mothers yelled.

But the gym was pretty quiet. I guess because the Squirettes were playing so badly.

I leaned forward and tried to concentrate on the game.

Sharon McCombs, the tallest girl in the Shawnee Valley eighth grade, tossed the ball in. A pass. Then another pass, which was almost stolen by a Bee Stinger.

Hannah grabbed the ball. She turned and started

to dribble to the basket. After about three steps she tripped. The ball bounced away as she fell flat on her stomach.

A Bee Stinger grabbed it just before it went out of bounds. She dribbled all the way down the floor—and scored easily before Hannah had even picked herself up off the floor. Twelve to two.

I cupped my hands around my mouth. "Get 'em, Hannah!" I shouted.

She didn't look up. She was fiddling with the white bandage on her hand.

A minute later Hannah had the ball again. In close. She jumped and shot. And missed. Missed the net, the backboard. Missed everything.

I leaned on my hands and watched the game in silence. Hannah missed six or seven shots in a row. She tripped over the ball, hit the floor hard, and got a huge, bright red floor burn on her knee. Her passes to her teammates went wild. She kept losing the ball to the other team. Tripping over her own feet. Bumping into other players.

It was sad. She didn't look like Hannah at all.

The half-time score was Bee Stingers twenty-five, Squirettes five.

When the team came out to start the second half, Hannah sat down on the bench and didn't play.

What's going on? I wondered.

I climbed down from the bleachers and walked over to her on the bench.

"Luke, you came to a bad-news game," she said, shaking her head.

"What's wrong?" I asked. "You're hurt? From your bike accident yesterday?"

She watched the Bee Stingers score another basket. Then she turned to me. "No. It's not because of my accident," she whispered. Her eyes were dull, watery. Her skin was so pale.

"So, what is it?" I asked.

Hannah frowned. "It's all because I lost my good-luck charm," she said.

I gaped at her. "Huh?"

"It's what brought me all that amazing great luck," Hannah said. "I have to find it. As soon as I lost it, my luck changed."

My mouth dropped open. I realized my heart had started to pound.

"It's a tiny skull," Hannah continued. "A little yellow skull. I—I never went anywhere without it."

She tugged at the bandage on her hand. Then she raised her eyes to me. "You haven't seen it anywhere . . . have you, Luke?"

CHAPTER 12

My legs suddenly felt weak. I gripped the back of the bench and stared at Hannah. I could feel my face growing red.

I could feel the skull in my jeans pocket. I knew I should pull it out and hand it to her.

But how *could* I?

I needed the good luck, too. Hannah had enjoyed so much good luck for so long. Mine had just started. For the first time in my life, I was having a little good luck.

How could I go back to being a loser again?

Hannah's watery eyes locked on mine. "Have you seen it, Luke?" she repeated. "Have you seen it anywhere?"

My face burned. So many frantic thoughts whirred through my head.

I really needed that good-luck charm. Ever since I found it, my life had changed. I was a new person.

But Hannah was my friend. My best friend in the

whole world. She was always there for me when I needed her.

I couldn't lie to her—could I?

"No," I said. "I haven't seen it anywhere."

Hannah's eyes remained on me for a few seconds more. Then she nodded slowly and turned back to the game.

My heart was pounding hard now. I had a heavy feeling in the pit of my stomach. "Where did you lose it?" I asked.

She didn't reply. She cupped her hands around her mouth and cheered on her teammates.

I backed away from the bench. I felt like a total creep. I jammed my hand into my pocket. Wrapped my fingers around the rubber skull.

Give it back to her, Luke, a voice in my head urged. The voice of goodness. The voice of friendship.

But I knew I wasn't going to give it back. I was already trotting out of the gym and down the hall to the exit.

I need it a little while longer, I told myself. Just a little while.

Long enough to win the basketball championship. Long enough to get really good grades for the first time in my life. Long enough to impress my friends . . . to get on the swim team . . . to make a name for myself . . . long enough to be a *winner.*

I squeezed the little skull all the way home. I'll

give it back to Hannah in a couple of weeks, I told myself. Two weeks, that's all. Maybe three. And then I'll give it back to her. And she can have her good luck again. No harm done.

No harm done—right?

The phone was ringing when I stepped in the kitchen door. I tossed down my backpack and ran to answer it.

To my surprise, it was Mrs. Coffey.

"Luke, I'm glad I caught you," she said. "I have some really good news. You know my friend at the computer store?"

"Yes?"

"I spoke to him after you left the computer lab. And he said you could start work at his store on Saturday."

"That's great!" I exclaimed.

"But that's not my good news," Mrs. Coffey continued. "He has a friend who is putting together a show of computer animation. And his friend is very interested in seeing your work."

"Really?" I cried.

"He needs short pieces for his animation show right away," she said. "If he likes your piece, he said he will pay a thousand dollars for it."

"Wow!"

"Is it finished, Luke?" Mrs. Coffey asked. "Is it ready to show to him?"

I thought hard. "Almost," I said. "I need two more days on it. Maybe three."

"Well, try to hurry," Mrs. Coffey said. "I think he has most of the pieces he needs. He's going to be showing them all over the country. It would be a shame to miss out—"

"It sure would!" I interrupted. "I'll get right to work on it, Mrs. Coffey. And thanks. Thanks a lot!"

Excited, I hurried up to my room and turned on the computer. Maybe I can get some work done on it before dinner, I decided.

I heard Mom come in downstairs. I called hi to her and said I was working on my computer project.

A few minutes later the phone rang again. I heard Mom talking for a while. Then I heard her running up the stairs. She burst into my room, ran up behind me, and wrapped me in a big hug.

"Huh? What's that for?" I cried.

"That was Mario's Steakhouse on the phone," Mom said, grinning. "You know. Your favorite restaurant. You won, Luke! Remember that drawing we all entered the last time we were there? Well, you won it. They picked your card. You won dinner for the whole family. Twelve dinners! One a month for the next year!"

"Wow!" I jumped up from the computer. Laughing and cheering, Mom and I did a happy little dance around the room.

"I can't believe you won that drawing. That is so

terrific!" Mom exclaimed. "We're going to have to start calling you Lucky Luke!"

"Yeah. Lucky Luke," I repeated. "I like that. That's me. Lucky Luke."

I worked on my animation until nearly midnight. I stared into the glow of the monitor until I couldn't see straight, and the images became a fuzzy blur.

"Almost finished," I said, yawning.

I changed into pajamas, brushed my teeth, got ready for sleep. But just before I climbed into bed, I pulled out my lucky little skull for one last look.

I held it gently in my hand and studied it, rubbing my fingers over the smooth top of the skull. The tiny, red jewel eyes glowed brightly.

I rubbed my fingers over the hard, bumpy teeth. I twirled the skull in my hand.

"My little good-luck charm," I whispered.

I set it down carefully on my dresser, in front of the mirror. Then I turned out the lights and climbed into bed.

I settled back on my pillows, pulling the quilt up to my chin. I yawned loudly. The mattress creaked under me. Waiting for sleep, I stared into the darkness.

The curtains were pulled, so no light washed in from the street. The room was completely black, except for a faint red glow.

The glow of the two red eyes in the skull. Like tiny

match flames against the blackness.

And then I saw two more glowing spots of red light. Larger. Behind the tiny skull eyes.

Two circles of light in the mirror glass. Two flame-red circles, the size of tennis balls.

And as their light grew brighter, more intense . . . I could see a form in the dresser mirror.

Deep nostril holes . . . two rows of jagged, grinning teeth.

A skull. A red-eyed skull.

Not tiny. A huge, grinning, yellow-boned skull that *filled* the mirror!

Filled the mirror! And stared out at me with those fiery, flame-red eyes.

I sat straight up. Squeezed the quilt. And gaped in horror as the jagged teeth moved. The jaw slid open.

And the enormous skull mouthed the words . . . mouthed them so clearly . . .

"Lucky Luke."

CHAPTER 13

The giant, glowing skull leaned forward, as if to push out of the mirror. The jaw worked up and down. The red glow seemed to bathe the whole room in flames.

I opened my mouth in a horrified scream.

I screamed and then screamed again.

The ceiling light flashed on.

"Luke—what's wrong?"

Blinking in the sudden light, I saw my dad burst breathlessly into the room. His pajama shirt was twisted. One pajama pants leg rode up to his knee. His hair was tangled from sleep, standing straight up on one side.

"What is it?" he repeated.

"I—I—" I pointed to the mirror. My head spun with confusion. I couldn't find words.

"The skull—" I finally choked out.

Brushing back his hair, Dad crossed the room to my dresser.

I stared into the glass.

Nothing now.

Nothing in there, except the reflection of my room. As he came near, I could see Dad's worried face reflected in the glass.

"Is *this* what you were screaming about?" Dad asked. He picked up the little yellow skull and held it out to me. "This skull?"

"N-no," I stammered.

I was thinking hard, trying to figure out what I had seen.

It couldn't have been the reflection of the little skull I saw in the glass.

No.

The skull that loomed in the mirror was enormous, its eyes as big as basketballs!

Dad still squinted at me from the dresser, holding the little skull up in front of him.

"I guess I had a bad dream," I said softly, settling back onto my pillows. "It—it was so weird. I dreamed I saw a giant skull with flaming eyes. But . . . it was so real!"

Dad shook his head. "Well . . . if this little skull is giving you bad dreams, want me to take it away?" He started to the door.

"No!" I screamed.

I jumped out of bed to block his path. He looked startled as I grabbed the skull from his hand.

"It's . . . it's a good-luck charm," I said. "It's brought me a lot of good luck."

Dad frowned as he gazed at the little skull in my hand. "You sure, Luke? It doesn't look good to me. It looks evil."

"Evil?" I laughed. "No way, Dad. No way. Trust me."

He clicked off the light on his way out. A short while later, I fell asleep gripping the skull tightly in one hand.

A few days later I screamed my head off again.

CHAPTER 14

This time it was for fun.

A bunch of us were on our skates up on Killer Hill. It's actually Miller Hill. But we call it Killer Hill because it's up at the top where Broad Street scoops straight down—a steep, steep slope down three blocks to Miller Street.

Miller Street has the most traffic in Shawnee Valley. So the idea is, we come skating down Broad Street full speed. We come rocketing down the steep slope as fast as we can—and try to skate right through the traffic on Miller.

It makes all the car drivers totally crazy! You can always hear tires squealing, horns honking, drivers screaming as kids come skating right at them.

Yes. It's really dangerous. Most kids won't even *think* of trying it. But for a guy with my kind of good luck, what's the big deal?

It was a sunny, cold Sunday afternoon. Frost stuck to the tops of the cars. My breath smoked up in front of me as I skated to the top of Killer Hill.

I met Darnell up there. He was having trouble with the brake on one of his skates. Finally he just ripped the brake off and tossed it in a trash can. "Why do I need brakes?" he said, grinning at me. "They only slow you down."

Stretch and some of his pals appeared a few minutes later. Stretch was wearing some kind of yellow sweats. He looked like Big Bird on skates!

He lowered his shoulder and tried to bump me off my feet. But I skated away easily. And he didn't try again.

Things have been a little different between Stretch and me since I took his place on the basketball team. He's *my* backup now. He gets to play only when I'm tired and need a short rest. And I think he's in shock over it.

Stretch still tries to give me a hard time. But I don't think his heart is in it. He knows he's a loser. He knows he's not one of the lucky people—like me.

"You ready to skate?" Darnell called. He pulled on his helmet. Then he stood in the middle of the street, leaning forward, hands on his knees.

I gazed down the steep hill to the traffic below. Even though it was Sunday afternoon, cars and vans sped along Miller as if it were the afternoon rush hour.

I adjusted my knee pads. "Ready," I said. I moved beside Darnell.

Stretch skated in front of us. He grinned at me.

"How about a race?"

I shook my head. "You're too slow. Darnell and I don't want to have to wait for you down there."

"Ha ha. When did you get so funny, Champ?" Stretch reached into the pocket of his yellow sweats. He held up a ten-dollar bill. "Let's make it a real race. Ten bucks each. Winner takes all."

He stuck the money in front of my face. I shoved it away. "I don't take candy from babies," I said. "Keep your money."

Stretch gritted his teeth. His pale face turned an angry red. He leaned close. "You gonna race me or not?" he growled.

I squeezed the rubber skull in my pocket. I knew there was no way I could lose. "Okay," I said. "But I'm going to make it fair."

I pulled a wool scarf from my coat pocket and started to wrap it around my head. "Just to give you a chance, I'll skate blindfolded."

Stretch snickered. "You're joking, right? You're going to skate through all those cars blindfolded?"

"Don't do it, Luke!" a voice called.

I turned to see Hannah waving to me. She was hobbling up the sidewalk on crutches. Her right foot had a large, white bandage over it. "Don't do it!" she called shrilly.

I spun away from the guys and skated over to her.

"Hannah—what happened?" I asked, motioning to the crutches.

She sighed and leaned heavily on them. "It's my ankle," she said. "Remember when I fell off my bike? We thought it was just a sprain. But my ankle keeps swelling up like a water balloon. I had to have it drained three times."

"Yuck," I said, staring down at the bandage.

The wind fluttered her red hair. She shook her head sadly. "The doctors can't figure out what's wrong. I—I might need surgery. I don't know. And Mom says if it doesn't get better, I can't go on the junior high overnight on Wednesday."

"Wow. That's bad news," I murmured. Everyone looks forward to the overnight. The whole junior high goes to a campground by the lake, and everyone stays up and parties all night.

I couldn't take my eyes off Hannah's bandaged ankle. Is this my fault? I suddenly wondered. Did I really take away her good luck? Hannah has had nothing but bad luck ever since I found the skull. . . .

I'm going to give it back to her, I silently promised. Real soon. Real soon.

"You skating or not?" Stretch called. "Or are you just going to stand there and talk with your girlfriend?"

"I'm coming," I said. I started to wrap the scarf around my eyes.

"Luke, don't," Hannah insisted. "Don't do it blindfolded. It—it's crazy."

"No problem," I said. "I'm a superhero, Hannah. Cars will bounce right off me!"

I skated away from her.

"You're wrong!" she called. "Luke, listen to me. The good luck—it doesn't last forever!"

I laughed. What was she *talking* about?

I skated up beside Darnell and grabbed his arm to steady myself. I pulled the scarf over my eyes until I saw only black.

"You're crazy," he muttered. "You could get killed, man."

"No way," I declared. "I'm going to win twenty bucks from you two!"

I heard Stretch skate up beside me. "You're doing this for real?" he asked. "You're going to skate into all those cars blindfolded?"

"You going to talk or skate?" I asked him. "First one past Miller Street *without stopping* wins the money."

"Luke—don't be crazy!" Hannah called.

It was the last thing I heard before the three of us took off.

I leaned forward, skating straight and hard. I heard Stretch and Darnell beside me, their Rollerblades scraping the pavement.

As we picked up speed, I could hear the traffic on Miller. I heard a horn honk. Heard someone shout.

I skated down . . . down . . . laughing through the darkness.

CHAPTER 15

"Luke—loooook out!"

I heard Darnell's scream. I heard the squeal of tires. Horns honked.

I tossed back my head and laughed. I roared through Miller Street, the blade wheels whistling over the pavement.

Then, as I turned my skates and came to a slow stop, I ripped the scarf away. And saw Darnell standing on the curb on the other side of Miller. His mouth was open. He shook his head.

Stretch came skating around me. "You crazy jerk!" he shouted. "You were almost killed *three* times!"

I calmly held out my hand. "Money, please."

"You lucky jerk," Stretch muttered. He slapped the ten-dollar bill into my gloved hand. "You're crazy. Really. You're just plain crazy."

I laughed. "Thanks for the compliment! And the ten bucks!"

Grumbling to himself, Stretch skated back up to his friends.

Darnell waited for the traffic to clear, then skated over to me. He wiped sweat off his forehead. "You were almost killed," he said, his voice shaking. "Why did you do it, Luke?"

I grinned at him. "Because I can."

The weather turned warm for our overnight camp-out. Even though the trees were bare, the woods smelled fresh and sweet, almost like spring. High, white clouds dotted the bright blue afternoon sky. Twigs and dead leaves crackled and crunched under our feet as we hiked through the tall trees to the camping grounds.

I squeezed the small skull in one hand as I walked, weighted down by the heavy pack on my back. Some kids were singing a Beatles song. Behind me, a group of girls were telling really bad knock-knock jokes, laughing shrilly after each one.

Coach Bendix and Ms. Raymond, another gym teacher, led the way along the twisting path through the trees. I was about halfway back in the line of kids.

I turned and found Hannah beside me. She wore her blue windbreaker with the hood pulled up over her head. She was leaning on one crutch as she walked, struggling to keep up. "Do you have any water?" she asked.

I slowed down. "Your parents let you come? Is your ankle better?"

"Not really," she replied, frowning. "But I told them I had to come anyway. I wouldn't miss it. Do you have any water? I'm dying!"

"Yeah. Sure." I reached for the bottle of water in my pack. "Didn't you bring any?"

Hannah sighed. "My water bottle had a leak or something. It poured out and soaked all the extra clothes in my pack. Now I don't have a thing to wear."

I handed her the water bottle.

Leaning on the crutch, she pushed back the windbreaker hood, and I saw her face for the first time.

Her skin was covered with big, red splotches.

"Hannah, what's that?" I cried. "Your face—"

"Don't look at me!" she snapped. She turned her back and took a long gulp of water.

"But what is it?" I demanded. "Poison ivy?"

"No. I don't think so," she said, still facing away from me. "I woke up with it. Some kind of red rash. All over my body." She sighed. "I don't get a break."

She handed the water bottle back to me and pulled the blue plastic hood over her head. "Thanks for the water."

"Does it itch?" I asked.

She let out an angry cry. "I really don't want to talk about it!" She grabbed the crutch tightly, swung it hard in front of her, and hurried ahead of me,

217

dragging her bandaged foot over the dirt path.

She's having so much bad luck. I guess it's my fault, I thought, squeezing the skull in my pocket.

But *why* are all these terrible things happening to her? Why isn't there enough good luck for *both* of us?

I didn't have much time to think about it.

Behind me, I heard shrill, frightened screams. I saw kids running off the path. Screaming. Calling for help.

I spun around and headed toward them, the heavy pack bouncing on my back. "What's going on?" I cried. "What's wrong?"

More shrill screams.

And then I saw the two enormous brown snakes. Swinging down from a low tree limb. Blocking the path.

The same color as the tree, they twisted their long bodies, thicker than garden hoses, and snapped their jaws.

I didn't hesitate. I dived forward, stretching out my arms.

"Luke—what are you doing? Stay away from them!" I heard Coach Bendix shout.

The kids' frightened screams rang through the woods.

"Get away from them!" Coach ordered.

But I knew nothing could hurt me. I knew my good luck would keep me safe.

I shot my hands out. And grabbed both snakes, one in each hand.

I wrapped my fingers around their thick bodies. Then, with a hard tug, I wrenched them off the tree limb. And raised them high.

"Whoa!"

I didn't realize how *long* they were.

And how strong.

I let out a startled cry as both snakes wriggled loose. I saw the tiny, black eyes flash. Saw the jaws open.

Then both snake heads came crashing toward me, jaws snapping—snapping so furiously beneath the flashing eyes, snapping like bear traps.

CHAPTER 16

I felt a rush of air as they snapped—snapped—snapped their sharp-toothed jaws. Heads swinging wildly. Whole bodies swinging and shaking. Thick, white drool clinging to their pointed teeth.

Shrill screams rose all around me. I stared at the snapping heads, the glimmering, black eyes—until it seemed that the snakes were screaming, too.

And then—they flew from my hands.

Wriggled free with strong tosses of their heavy bodies. And plunged to the ground. Disappearing so quickly. Blending into the hard, brown dirt. Vanishing beneath the carpet of fat brown leaves, twigs, and fallen limbs.

As kids surrounded me, I stood hunched over, gasping for breath. I smoothed my open hands over my ears, my cheeks, my whole face.

I waited for the pain of the snakebites to spread over me.

But no. No sting. No throbbing. No pain.

They had snapped so close, I felt their breath on my skin.

But they hadn't bitten me.

"You're so lucky!" Coach Bendix was saying. He had a hand on my shoulder and was examining my face. "I never saw anyone so lucky. Why did you do it, Luke? Those snakes are deadly poisonous. Deadly! Why did you do it?"

I stared at him but didn't answer. I didn't know what to say.

How could I explain it to him? How could I explain to *anyone* what it felt like to be so incredibly, awesomely lucky?

All around, kids were cheering. Congratulating me. Talking about me, how brave I had been.

Leaning against a tree, I saw Hannah. She stood by herself, crutch under one arm. She was the only one not smiling, not cheering.

I saw the red blotches on Hannah's face. Watched as she transfered the crutch to her other arm. And saw her scowling at me, her eyes narrowed. She shook her head and scowled.

And in that moment, I realized that she was *jealous*. Jealous of my good luck.

Jealous that she was no longer the hero. *She* was no longer the lucky one.

Too bad, Hannah, I thought, watching her angry expression. I had felt sorry for her. I had felt really *guilty*, too.

But no more.

I've got the luck now, Hannah, I thought. *And I'm going to keep it*!

"Let's go, guys. We've got another game to win!" I cried. I gave Sam Mulroney a playful towel slap.

Locker doors slammed. Guys finished lacing up their basketball shoes.

"Did you *see* those Deaver Mills guys?" Mulroney asked, peeking into the gym through a crack in the locker room door. "They're *monsters*! They must feed those guys whole steaks five times a day!"

"Big doesn't mean good!" I said. "They look like cows! They're so slow."

"We'll dribble circles around them!" Jay Boxer said.

"Just feed me the ball!" I instructed them. "No matter where I am. Feed me the ball. I'll put it in. I'm feeling lucky today, guys. Real lucky!"

"Hey, Champ—" Stretch called, pulling on his jersey. "You're not a ball hog or anything—are you?"

Guys used to laugh when Stretch shouted insults at me. But not anymore. Everyone was on my side now. Everyone wanted to be on the *winner's* side.

"Hey, Stretch—what do they call *you*?" I shouted back. "A *bench* hog?"

Everybody laughed.

Stretch laughed too. Now that I was a winner, he was starting to be a little nicer to me. He even gave me some dribbling tips after one practice.

The guys all headed out to the gym. I could hear the shouts of the crowd in the bleachers. And the steady *thud* of basketballs on the floor as the Deaver Mills Lions warmed up.

"Time to kill me some Lions," I muttered. I finished lacing my sneakers.

Then I stood up. Started to swing my gym locker closed.

And slammed my left hand in the door.

"Hey!" I cried out in surprise as pain shot up my arm.

I shook the hand hard, trying to shake the pain away. My wrist throbbed. I moved my fingers, tilted my hand back and forth. It moved okay. Not broken.

But the hand was red and already starting to swell.

"No time for this," I muttered.

I slammed the locker shut with my right hand. And, still shaking my left hand, hurried out into the gym.

The crowd cheered as I ran onto the floor. I saw some of the Deaver Mills players whisper to each other and point at me. They knew who the star player was. They knew who was going to *wipe the floor* with them today!

We huddled close around Coach Bendix. "Take it slow with these guys," he instructed. "Feel them out. Get their rhythm. Let's rattle them, show them we can play defense."

"Just get me the ball!" I chimed in. "I'm going to be loose under the basket all day!"

We gave our team cheer and trotted out to the center of the floor. I searched the bleachers for Hannah. She said she would try to come to the game today.

I spotted her at the side of the bleachers, hunched in a wheelchair. Her bad foot was propped up, and it had an even bigger bandage over it.

I guess it isn't getting better, I thought. I felt a pang of guilt.

Poor Hannah.

I looked for my parents. Then I remembered they weren't coming today. They had to stay home for a furniture delivery.

I turned away from the crowd. I had a game to play. Time to get my game face on. No time to think about Hannah and her problems.

I went up for the opening jump. I tapped the ball to Mulroney, and the game was underway.

He dribbled to half-court, then sent a high pass to me.

"Whoa—!" The ball flew right through my hands and bounced out of bounds.

"Mulroney—too hard!" I called. "Who were you throwing at?"

He shrugged and started trotting to the Lions' basket.

"Get in there, Luke! Get going! Look alive!" I heard Coach Bendix shouting.

The Deaver guard came dribbling slowly toward me. I darted up to him, stuck out my hand to steal the ball—and missed.

He moved past me easily and sent up an easy layup for two points.

"Weird," I muttered. I shook my left hand. The pain had dulled to an ache, but the hand was pretty swollen.

I moved down the court. Caught a pass. Spun away from the Lion defender. Went in for an easy shot.

And missed!

"Huh?"

I heard the crowd groan. Startled voices all around.

Mulroney slapped me on the shoulder. "Take it easy, man," he said. "Play your game. Just play your game."

A few seconds later I drove in for a shot—and was fouled. I moved to the foul line—and missed both foul shots!

More groans and muttering from the bleachers. I saw Coach Bendix shake his head.

A bounce pass from Jay Boxer sailed right through my legs. Some of the Lions' players had a good laugh over that one.

Then I missed three more shots in a row!

Mulroney flashed me a thumbs-up. "No prob," he called. "Play your game, Luke! We'll get 'em!"

The Lions were winning twelve to four.

I took another pass and moved under the basket. I

leaped high for a slam dunk.

My arm hit the rim hard. I cried out in pain. And watched the ball sail over the backboard.

"Whoa. This isn't happening," I muttered, picking myself up off the floor. "No way."

At the other end of the floor I grabbed a rebound off the backboard. I dodged past a huge Lion player. Dribbled away from him easily. Picked up speed. Brought the ball onto our side of the court.

Eyed the basket. Prepared to stop short and put up a three-pointer.

And tripped. Felt one sneaker bump the other. Tripped over my own shoe.

And watched the ball sail into a Lion's hands as I stumbled. I fell forward onto my stomach. My arms and legs were out flat on the floor. "OOOF!"

I heard startled gasps from the bleachers. And laughter.

Yes. Some people were laughing at me.

"What is going on?" I cried.

I forced myself to my feet. Shook off the pain.

"This isn't happening. It can't be!"

I reached into the pocket of my uniform shorts. Reached for my good-luck skull.

Fumbled in the pocket. Searched both pockets.

"Hey—"

No. No. No way.

The skull was gone!

CHAPTER 17

Fumbling frantically in both pockets, I began running for the team bench. "Time out! Time out!" I screamed.

Had the skull fallen out of my pocket?

I squinted hard, searching the gleaming, polished floor.

No sign of it.

"Time out!" I pleaded.

I heard a whistle blow on the sidelines.

I had to find it—now! I couldn't play without it.

My eyes swept over the floor. I began to run full speed to the bench.

I didn't see the huge Lions player—until we collided.

I plowed right into him. Caught him flat-footed. He let out a startled, "Oof." And we cracked heads.

"Yaaaiiii!" I let out a scream of agony as blinding red pain shot around my head. The red shimmered to gold. Brighter, brighter . . . bright as the sun.

I felt my legs giving out. Felt myself collapsing, crumbling into a deep, deep, bottomless darkness.

I woke up to pinpoints of yellow light. They flickered high above me. Each time they flashed, a wave of pain rolled over my forehead, down the back of my neck.

I blinked hard. Blinked until I realized I was staring up at the lights on the gym rafters.

I lay on my back on the gym floor, one knee raised, my hands flat at my sides. I squinted up at the high rafters—until faces blocked my view.

Players' faces. And then a few worried-looking adults. And then Coach Bendix's face, looming over me, bobbing over me like a parade balloon.

"What—?" One word escaped my throat. My dry throat. So dry, I couldn't swallow.

"Stay still, Luke," Coach ordered, speaking softly. His dark eyes peered down into mine, studying me. "You've had a bad concussion. Don't try to move. We're sending you to the emergency room."

"Huh? No!" I gasped.

I rolled onto my side. I lurched to my feet. The floor tilted from side to side, as if I were on a rocking boat.

"Don't move, Luke." Coach reached for me.

But I staggered out of his grasp. Stumbled through the circle of people that had formed around me.

"No. No hospital!" I croaked.

I had to find that skull. That was all I needed, and then I would be okay again.

The skull . . .

I stumbled over someone's shoe. Staggered toward the locker room. The gleaming wood floor swaying beneath me.

"Luke—come back!"

No. No way. I shoved open the locker room door with one shoulder. And sliding a hand against the lockers, moved to the back row. Lurched to my gym locker. Pulled open the door so hard it slammed against the frame.

"Where is it? Where?"

I frantically pawed through my street clothes. Searched and then tossed everything onto the floor.

"Where? Where?"

Not in my khakis pockets. Not in my shirt pocket. Not in my sweatshirt.

The locker floor? No. Nothing down there.

Stumbling over the pile of clothes on the floor, I lurched back down the row of gym lockers. Ran through the gym, out the doors, and up the stairs. Into the long, empty hall.

My sneakers squeaked on the hard floor as I ran. The walls and ceiling appeared to close in on me, then slide back into place.

To my locker. To locker 13.

It took me three tries to get the combination right. But finally I unlocked it and flung open the door.

And jammed my hand into one coat pocket, and then the other.

"Where is it? I have to have it! Where? Where?"

And then a long, happy sigh escaped my parched throat as my hand closed around it.

Yessss!

I was so happy!

I had the skull in my hand. I squeezed it tightly. So happy. So happy.

I pulled it out of the coat pocket. Raised it in front of me. Raised it close to examine it.

And let out a cry of horror.

CHAPTER 18

The eyes. They were dark. Not red, not glowing.

And the face had *changed*! The bump-toothed grin was gone. The open mouth was curled down in a fierce, angry scowl.

"No—it's impossible!" I gasped.

I held the skull up to the light. The red jewel eyes were gone! The deep, round sockets were empty. The skull scowled down at me, dark and menacing.

What does this mean? I wondered. How did this happen?

Before I could think about it clearly, I glimpsed something in the open locker. A soft glow. A slow moving light, growing larger as if moving closer.

The light split into two. Two circles of red light. Down low. Very low, near the locker floor.

I gripped the skull tightly in my fist and stared as the red lights glimmered closer. The whole locker shimmered. The dark walls reflected the two lights. Brighter . . . bright as fire now.

Two red eyes, I realized. Two glowing eyes floating from the blackness of locker 13.

I jumped back as a black cat stepped silently out, as if floating. A black cat with fiery, red eyes. The same black cat as before?

It pulled back its lips, bared pointed, white teeth, and hissed at me.

My back hit the wall. I blinked against the brightness of those two circles of red light.

And as I trembled in horror, squeezing the skull, squeezing it so tightly my hand ached—the cat rose up off the floor.

And melted into another form.

Melted and grew taller. Taller . . . The cat became a human figure, dressed all in black, wrapped in a broad, black coat down to the floor, its face hidden in the darkness of a black hood.

Hidden. All hidden . . . except for the eyes—those horrifying, fiery eyes.

"Wh-who are you? What do you want?" I startled myself by crying out those words. I didn't think I could speak.

My whole body trembled. I pressed myself against the wall to keep from falling to my knees.

The hooded figure stepped silently away from the open locker. A hoarse rasp burst out from under the hood, a whisper like the crackle of dead leaves: *The luck has run out, Luke.*

"No!" I gasped.

A bony hand swung out from the sleeve of the black coat—and swiped the skull away from me.

"No!" I cried in protest. "No! No!"

The luck is over.

"Who are you?" I shrieked in a tight, terrified voice. "Wh-who? How did you get in my locker? What do you want?" I screamed in total panic.

The luck is over.

"It can't be!" I cried. "It can't be! I need it!"

"*Over . . .*" the hooded figure rasped. "*Over . . . over . . .*"

The red eyes glowed from under the hood. The bony hand held the tiny skull in front of the broad black coat.

"I need that luck!" I wailed. "I need that skull!"

And I grabbed it back. Grabbed it out of the bony hand.

"I need it! I *have* to have it!"

I raised the skull in front of me. Stared hard at it.

What was *wrong* with it? Something wriggling on it . . . wriggling in my hand . . . crawling over my palm . . .

"Ohhhh." I let out a moan as I saw. The skull was covered . . . crawling . . . crawling with hundreds of maggots!

CHAPTER 19

The skull fell from my hand and bounced across the floor. I frantically shook my hand, scraped it against the wall, brushing the disgusting maggots off my skin.

Under the black hood the red eyes glowed brighter. *"You enjoyed a lot of good luck, Luke,"* the figure said in his hoarse croak. *"But the luck has ended. And now you must pay for it."*

"Huh? Pay?" I felt my throat tighten. I stared at the fiery eyes, trying to see a face, trying to see who was speaking to me from under that hood.

"Luke—I'm so sorry!" a voice called.

I turned to find Hannah wheeling herself rapidly down the hall, leaning forward in her wheelchair, turning the wheels with both hands.

"Hannah—? What—?" I couldn't find any words.

"I'm so sorry," she repeated. As she wheeled herself closer, I saw tears brimming in her eyes, rolling down her red-blotched face.

"Sorry?" I repeated, my head spinning in confusion.

"He made me do it!" she wailed. "You have to believe me, Luke. I didn't want to. Really! But he made me!"

She grabbed my hand. Squeezed it tightly. Her hand was as cold as ice. Tears rolled down her cheeks.

"*Very touching!*" the hooded figure rasped coldly.

"Hannah—he made you do *what?*" I asked.

"He—he made me give you the skull!" Hannah stammered, still squeezing my hand.

"Huh?" I let out a startled cry. "You *gave* it to me? But I thought I found it. I thought—"

"I had the good luck for a long time," Hannah said, wiping her wet cheeks with both hands. "Remember when I had so much good luck? Then it ran out. The skull went dark. And he forced me—he forced me to pass the skull on to you!"

I stared at her in disbelief. "But who is he?" I cried. "How can he do this?"

"*Haven't you guessed?*" the hooded figure boomed. The red eyes glowed like two angry suns. "*Haven't you figured it out yet, Luke? I am the Fate Master. I decide who has good luck and who has bad!*"

"No," I whispered. "That's . . . crazy."

"It's the truth," Hannah said, her voice breaking. "He controls me. And now you."

"*Luke,*" the evil figure whispered, lowering himself toward me. "*Did you really think you could have all that good luck without paying for it?*"

"I didn't want to give the skull to you," Hannah whispered, holding on to my arm. "I gave you a chance to hand it back to me, remember? Remember during my game? I asked if you had seen it?"

I nodded sadly, feeling my face grow hot.

"I knew you had it. Why didn't you give it back then?" Hannah demanded. "I gave you a chance to return it. I didn't want you to keep it."

"*Too late for that now!*" the Fate Master rasped. "*Now you are BOTH mine!*"

"No way!" I protested. "I don't believe any of this! This can't be happening! It—it's some kind of bad joke!"

"It's not a joke," Hannah whispered. "Look at me." She pointed to her red-blotched face, her bandaged foot, the wheelchair.

"No!" I insisted. "It won't happen to me! I won't let it! I'll—I'll make my own luck!"

The bulky, black coat shook as the Fate Master uttered a hoarse laugh. It sounded more like dry coughing than laughter. "*Young man, do you really think you can go up against FATE? I control EVERYTHING that happens! Do you really think you can defy FATE?*"

"I don't care what you say!" I screamed. "I'm not going to be some kind of slave! You can't control me! You can't!"

The Fate Master sighed. The red eyes faded inside the hood. *"Do I really have to prove myself to you? Okay. So be it."*

He leaned closer. So close that I could see into the hood. I could see that he had no face! Just two glowing eyes floating in blackness.

"Luke—that concussion you had in the gym?" he rasped. *"I'm afraid it's much worse than you thought. Feel your ears."*

"Huh?" My hands shot up to my ears. I felt wetness.

Warm wetness.

I lowered my hands. My fingers dripped with blood.

My ears were bleeding!

I felt the warm blood pour down my earlobes, trickle down the sides of my face.

Frantically I pressed the palms of my hands against my ears.

"That won't stop the bleeding, Luke," the Fate Master whispered. *"That blood won't clot. It's just going to keep pouring out. Bad luck, I'm afraid. Very bad luck."*

"No—please!" I pleaded. "Make it stop!"

The eyes flared. *"Do you believe in me now? Do you believe that you belong to me?"*

"Okay," I said. "Okay. I believe you."

"*Your fate is in my hands—both of you. You must pay for the good luck you had. You must suffer bad luck now—*"

"No—please!" I begged. "I need more time. Things are just starting to go right for me. The basketball team . . . my animation . . . the swim team . . . I'll do anything. I need more time!"

"*NO MORE TIME!*" The hoarse rasp echoed off the tile walls. Angry flames shot out from the blackness of the hood.

"But—" I started, shrinking back beside Hannah.

"*I control you!*" the Fate Master boomed. "*I decide your luck from now on! Do you want me to go easy on the two of you? DO you?*"

"Y-yes," I stammered. "I'll do anything. Anything!"

The Fate Master was silent for a long moment. The eyes faded, as if retreating into the distance, then glowed brightly again. "*If you want me to go easy on you both,*" he said finally, "*here's what you have to do. . . .*"

CHAPTER 20

"Pass the skull on to another," the Fate Master ordered.

"Huh? You—you want me to give it to someone else?" I stammered.

The eyes sparked beneath the hood. *"Pass it to that big kid, the one called Stretch. I've had my eye on him. I will give him good luck for two months. Then I will claim him as mine."*

"No, I can't do that!" I protested. "It isn't right! It isn't—"

The Fate Master uttered a furious growl. *"Then you will suffer bad luck your whole life. You and everyone in your family!"*

I shivered in fear. My mind spun. I felt the warm blood start to trickle from my ears again.

Could I do it? Could I trap Stretch the way I had been trapped?

I felt Hannah tug my arm. "You have to do it, Luke," she whispered. "It's our only chance. Besides, Stretch has been asking for it—hasn't he? He's not a

239

friend of yours. He's an enemy. Stretch has been asking for it all year."

True. Stretch wasn't my friend. But could I be responsible for ruining Stretch's life? For turning him over to the Fate Master?

Hannah gazed up at me from the wheelchair with pleading eyes. "Do it," she whispered. "Save us, Luke. Do it."

I turned to the Fate Master. "Okay," I choked out. "I'll do it."

The eyes flashed, from red to sunlight yellow. The big coat opened and appeared to fly up. It raised itself over me like giant bat wings. Floated over me . . . then floated down.

I felt myself covered in a heavy darkness.

I couldn't move. It spread over me . . . blacker . . . blacker.

I felt so cold. So cold and lost. As if I had been buried, buried deep in the cold, cold ground.

And then I blinked and saw pinpoints of light. Flickering white lights that grew brighter, so bright I had to squint.

It took me a while to realize I was back in the gym. Back on the gym floor. A crowd huddled around me. Tight expressions, worried faces.

Someone leaned over me. A face came into focus. Coach Bendix stared down at me, the whistle hanging from his neck.

"Coach—?" I tried to speak, but the word came out a whisper.

"Don't move, Luke," he said softly. "You've had a concussion, but you're going to be okay."

"A concussion?"

"Lie still," he instructed. "An ambulance is on the way."

A concussion?

It didn't happen! I realized.

The hooded figure with the glowing eyes. The Fate Master stepping out of locker 13. Taking away my good luck. Ordering me to pass the skull to Stretch.

It didn't happen!

It was a dream. A nightmare caused by my concussion.

I jumped to my feet. The floor swayed beneath me. The bleachers appeared to tilt to one side, then the other.

I saw Hannah in her wheelchair at the side of the bleachers.

She's still in the gym! I told myself happily. We never left the gym. It didn't happen. None of it happened.

I felt so happy. *So free!*

Before I even realized it, I was running. Running to the door.

"Luke! Hey—Luke! Stop!" I heard Coach Bendix calling to me.

And then I was out the gym doors. And racing through the dark, empty hallways. Running full speed.

So happy. And so eager to get away from there! Away from the school. Away from my nightmare.

Did I stop at my locker?

I must have stopped there because I had my jacket on when I burst outside. Into the frosty night air. I saw a tiny sliver of a moon high in a purple-black sky. I stopped for a second to breathe in the cold, fresh air.

Then I ran across the teachers' parking lot to the bike rack. I'd ridden my bike to school. And now I planned to put the pedal to the metal—to race all the way home.

"Yes!" So happy. I felt so happy, I could have *danced* all the way home.

I jumped on my bike. Grabbed the handlebars.

Whoa. Something wrong. A scraping sound.

I climbed off and glanced down. A flat tire. No. *Two* flat tires.

"Oh, wow," I murmured. How did that happen?

No big deal. I'll get the bike tomorrow, I decided. I started to jog across the parking lot, heading to the street. My sneaker felt loose. I squatted down to tie the shoe lace—and it ripped between my hands.

No problem, I told myself. I have plenty of shoelaces at home. I started walking, turned onto the sidewalk, crossed the street. Behind me I could hear shouts and cheers coming from the gym. I guessed that the game had started up again.

"Go, Stretch!" I murmured.

As I made my way down the next block it began to rain. Softly at first. But the wind picked up, and then the rain started coming down in sheets.

I zipped my jacket and leaned into the wind. But the rain drove me back, wave after wave of freezing water.

I heard a crackling sound nearby—and saw jagged, white lightning streak across the front yard across the street. A deafening boom of thunder shook the ground.

I pressed forward. Trees creaked and nearly bent sideways in the torrents of wind and rain. I couldn't move. I ducked under a broad-trunked tree for safety.

But a loud *crack* of lightning sent a tree branch crashing to my feet.

"Ohh!" I cried out. A close call!

I jumped over the fallen branch. Sharp pieces of the limb scratched my arm as I struggled to race away. Another jagged bolt of lightning crackled a few feet in front of me, sizzling over the wet grass.

Squinting through the downpour, I saw smoke snake over the lawn. The grass was burned black where the lightning had spread.

The wind shoved me backward. Sheet after sheet

of rain washed over me. I choked. Struggled to breathe.

And then . . . just beyond the rain . . . just beyond the heavy waves of dark water . . . I saw two glowing lights . . . two red eyes . . . like dark headlights . . . Two evil eyes, moving with me, watching me.

The Fate Master.

It wasn't a dream. I suddenly knew that my flat tires—the storm—the lightning, the pounding rain—it was all a show. A show of strength.

I staggered up my driveway. Slipped on the wet gravel. Sprawled facedown on the soaked stones.

"Nooooo . . ."

I struggled to my feet. Stumbled onto the front stoop.

A deafening, shattering crash made me spin around. I saw one of the oak trees in front of the house split in half. It appeared to move in slow motion. One half shivered but stayed upright. The other half of the broad, old tree came crashing onto the roof of the house.

Windows shattered. Roof tiles came sliding down.

I covered my head with one hand. And pushed the doorbell. Frantically pushed the bell. "Let me in! Mom! Dad!" I pounded on the front door with both fists.

Where were they?

The lights were all on. Why didn't they open the door?

A crash of thunder made me jump and cry out. Above the front stoop rainwater poured like a waterfall over the sides of the gutters. Waves of rain rattled the living room window and battered the bricks of the front wall.

"Let me in!" I screamed over another roar of thunder. I pounded the front door until my fist ached.

Then I heard a window slide open. I turned to our neighbor's house. Through the curtains of rain, I saw Mrs. Gillis poke her head out the bedroom window. She shouted something. But I couldn't hear her over the roar of rain.

"They're not home!" I finally heard her shout. "They had to go to the hospital, Luke."

"What? What did you say?" My heart jumped. Had I heard correctly?

"It's your dad. He fell down the stairs. He's okay. But they took him to the emergency room."

"No!" I cried. I beat my fists against the door. "No! No! No!"

The Fate Master was putting on a show for me. He was showing me who was boss. Giving me a little taste of what the rest of my life could be like.

"Okay!" I shouted, cupping my hands around my mouth. Water pounded me, washed over me, battered me against the house. "Okay—you win!" I screamed. "I'll do it! I'll do whatever you say!"

And I did.

The next morning I gave the skull to Stretch.

CHAPTER 21

I found Stretch at his locker before school started. Giving him the yellow skull was the easiest thing in the world.

Stretch was leaning into his locker, searching the shelf for something. His backpack stood open on the floor. I pulled the skull from my jeans pocket—and dropped it into his backpack.

He didn't see anything. He didn't even know he had it.

"Hey, Stretch—how's it going?" I asked, trying to sound calm, natural. As if I hadn't just done something terrible to him. Something that would ruin his life forever.

"Yo—hey, Champ!" He slapped me a hard high five, so hard my hand stung. "How's your head, man? It looks as ugly as ever!" He laughed.

I stared at him. "My head?"

"That was a nasty collision," he said. "Your head must be hard as a rock. You feeling okay?"

"Yeah. Not bad," I replied.

Stretch snickered. "Well, thanks for letting me get some playing time." He started to close up his backpack.

I stared at the backpack, picturing the skull inside it. The skull I had passed on to Stretch. The tiny, red eyes were probably glowing again. Stretch was going to have a lot of good luck for a while. But then . . .

"Maybe you and I can practice together later," Stretch said, slamming his locker shut. "I can give you some more pointers. Make you look like you know what you're doing!"

"Yeah. Maybe," I said.

Stretch's expression turned serious. "Actually, you're not bad, man," he said. "I mean it. You are so improved. I mean, you're almost pretty good! Really."

I don't believe this! I thought. Stretch is actually paying me a compliment.

I shrugged. "It was just luck," I muttered.

Just luck. Ha ha.

"No way!" Stretch insisted. "Luck had nothing to do with it, man. It was hard work and skill. No kidding. It isn't luck. You're good!"

I swallowed hard. I suddenly felt like a total creep.

Stretch was being so nice to me. And what had I done to him? I just gave him a life of bad luck, a life of slavery to the Fate Master.

"Whoa. Forgot my science notebook," Stretch groaned. He dropped his backpack to the floor and turned to unlock his locker.

I stared down at the backpack, feeling dizzy, feeling sick.

What am I going to do? I asked myself. What am I going to do?

My bad luck continued all day.

I answered the wrong questions on my algebra test and got an F. Miss Wakely warned me that I'd have to do extra work if I didn't want to fail the course.

At lunch the milk in my milk carton was lumpy and sour. I didn't notice until I had gulped down a big mouthful. Then I nearly puked my guts up in front of everyone.

After lunch I started to comb my hair in the boys' room—and a huge clump came out on the comb. I gasped in horror and tugged out another clump of hair.

I'm going to lose all my hair! I realized.

As I hurried out of the bathroom, I caught my shirt on a nail and ripped one sleeve off. I was so upset, I bumped into Miss Wakely from behind. Her coffee cup flew out of her hand, and scalding hot coffee splashed all over her.

I found Hannah after school. She came rolling slowly down the hall in her wheelchair. Her foot was still bandaged. Her face was still covered in red blotches. And I saw that one of her eyes was swollen shut.

"Hannah—I've got to talk to you!" I cried.

"Did you pass it on?" she asked in a loud whisper.

"Huh?"

"I've lost my voice," she whispered. "Did you pass the skull on to Stretch? We've got to change our luck. I can barely see. My skin itches like crazy. I can barely talk. I—I can't go on like this, Luke."

"I've got to find the Fate Master," I said.

Hannah grabbed my torn shirtsleeve. "You've got to do what he said. You've got to obey him. It's our only chance."

"How do I find him?" I asked.

"He will find you," Hannah whispered. "He appears in places of bad luck. You know—broken mirrors, wherever the number thirteen is written."

"Come with me," I said. I led the way to my locker. I waved to some guys heading to the pool for swim team practice. I wanted to be with them. But this was more important.

"We've got to talk to the Fate Master," I told Hannah. "Maybe he'll come through my locker again."

Hannah groaned in pain as she wheeled herself behind me. "My foot hurts so much!" she whispered.

"He promised to end the bad luck," I said.

I turned the combination lock, then pulled open

my locker door. A burst of sour air choked the hall. I gagged, then held my breath.

"Look—" Hannah choked out. She pointed to the floor of the locker.

It was littered with dead birds. A pile of brown-and-gray sparrows, all dead and decaying.

"He left us a present," I murmured. "Where is he? Is he going to appear?"

We didn't have to wait long.

A few moments later I saw the glow of the red eyes at the back of the locker. And then the dark figure stepped over the pile of dead birds and floated out, hunched beneath the black hood.

"Have you done what I asked?" he rasped, the fiery eyes burning into mine. *"Have you given me a new slave?"*

"Yes," I replied, avoiding his stare. "That was our deal, right? And now will you stop torturing us? Will you end our bad luck as you promised?"

The hood bobbed up and down. *"No,"* he said softly.

Hannah and I both uttered cries of protest.

"Did you really think you could make a deal with the Fate Master?" he boomed. The open coat floated up like bat wings. *"I don't make bargains with anyone! I don't make promises! You will take whatever Fate dishes out!"*

"You promised—!" Hannah shrieked.

The evil figure snickered. *"First you enjoy good*

251

luck. Then you must pay for it. You cannot break the pattern. You should know that. You should know that you cannot bargain with Fate! You will pay for your good luck for the rest of your life!"

"No! Wait—! Wait!" Hannah pleaded, reaching up from the wheelchair, grasping at the black cloak, grasping frantically with both hands.

But the Fate Master spun around, swirling the foul air. He stomped heavily on the dead birds as he strode back into locker 13.

In a second he had vanished.

Dead birds littered the floor of the hall, the floor of my locker.

I turned to Hannah. Her shoulders heaved up and down. Loud sobs escaped her throat. "He promised. . . ."

"It's okay," I said softly. "I didn't keep my promise, either."

I pulled the yellow skull from my jeans pocket.

Hannah gasped. "You didn't give it to Stretch?"

I squeezed the skull in my fist. "Yes, I gave it to him. But I took it back before Stretch even saw it. I couldn't do it. Stretch was too nice to me. I—I couldn't. I couldn't ruin someone's life."

Hannah shook her head. Tears spilled from her swollen eyes. "Now what are we going to do, Luke? We're doomed. Now we don't stand a chance."

CHAPTER 22

I bounced the basketball hard against the driveway. Drove toward the backboard and sent up a hook shot. It bounced off the rim, back into my hands. I spun hard and sent up a two-handed shot that dropped through the net.

Overhead, clouds covered the moon. The garage lights sent white cones of light over the driveway. Behind me, the house was dark except for a square of orange light from my bedroom window upstairs.

I glanced at the roof. Men had worked all day to repair the broken and missing shingles. The fallen tree had been hauled away. One window—broken in the storm—was still covered with cardboard.

All my fault, I realized. All the damage to the house was my fault.

My dad was walking with a cane. He had a badly sprained knee from his fall down the stairs. But he was okay . . . for now.

That was all my fault too, I knew.

All my bad luck.

I heaved the ball angrily at the backboard. It thudded high, bounced back to the driveway. I picked it up and shot it through the hoop.

Luck . . . luck . . . luck . . .

The word ran through my mind like an ugly chant.

And then I heard Stretch's words again. Stretch actually saying something nice to me: "Luck had nothing to do with it, Luke. It was hard work and skill."

Hard work and skill.

Not luck.

"You cannot break the pattern," the Fate Master had said. "First you have the good luck—then you pay for it."

The pattern. You cannot break the pattern.

Not luck. Hard work and skill.

I shot the ball again. Dribbled, then shot again. Even though it was a cold, frosty night, sweat poured down my forehead. I wanted to work harder. Harder.

And as I practiced, those words repeated and repeated in my mind. And I knew what I had to do. I knew the only way I could end the bad luck for Hannah and for me.

The only way I could defeat the Fate Master.

I shot again. Again. I moved to the foul line and put up several foul shots.

I didn't stop when I saw the kitchen light flash on. The back door swung open. Dad stepped into the yard, wearing his bathrobe, leaning on his cane.

"Luke—what are you doing?" he called. "It's after eleven o'clock!"

"Practicing," I said, sending up another jump shot.

Walking unsteadily, he came up to the edge of the driveway. "But—it's so late. Why are you doing this?"

"I'm going to win *without* luck!" I replied. I sent up another shot and watched it drop through the hoop. "I'm going to win with skill! I shouted. "I can break the pattern! I can win without luck."

And then, without realizing it, I was screaming at the top of my lungs: "I DON'T NEED LUCK! I DON'T NEED LUCK!"

CHAPTER 23

My plan was simple. Maybe too simple.

But I had to give it a try.

I didn't tell it to Hannah. She was pretty much destroyed. I didn't want to give her any more to worry about.

I knew I didn't have much time—maybe a day or two at the most.

As soon as the Fate Master discovered that I still had the skull, that I hadn't passed it on to Stretch, he would come after me full force.

My plan?

It was to break the pattern.

To win. To win big. To have a major success. Without luck. Without needing any good luck.

If I could win with my own hard work, with my own skill, my own talent—it would be a defeat for the Fate Master. I would break his rule. I would break the pattern.

And maybe . . . just maybe that would free Hannah and me.

And that's why I practiced on my driveway. Practiced in the dark, in the cold until after midnight. Hard work and skill.

Hard work and skill.

Shawnee Valley played Forest Grove this afternoon. The last game of the season.

My last chance to win without luck.

As I changed into my team uniform, I knew I had to be great. I had to be a winner today. I had to win the game for my team.

And if I did?

If I did, maybe the nightmare would be over.

I was so nervous, I had to lace up my sneakers three times. I kept knotting them up. My fingers just wouldn't work.

"Go, Squires! Go, Squires!"

Guys were pounding their fists on the lockers, shouting, jumping up and down, getting pumped, getting ready.

Stretch gave me a playful slap as he jogged past. "Try not to bump heads today, Champ! We gonna beat these clowns?"

I flashed him a thumbs-up. "They're dead meat!" I shouted.

I tucked in my jersey, slammed the gym locker shut, and trotted out into the gym. I blinked under the bright lights. A big crowd nearly filled the bleachers. They were stamping their feet in time to some marching music over the loudspeaker.

I searched for Hannah but didn't see her.

The last game of the year, I thought as I picked up a basketball from the rack. My last chance . . .

I swallowed hard, trying to force down my fear.

Was the Fate Master here? Did he know that I lied to him? That I didn't give the skull to Stretch?

I don't care about that, I told myself. I'm going to be a winner today without his good luck.

I'm going to break the pattern.

I'm going to break the Fate Master!

I dribbled up to Coach Bendix. He slapped me on the shoulder as I passed. "Have a great game, Luke!" he called. "Keep it slow and steady. Remember—just focus. Focus."

"Okay, Coach," I called. "I'm ready. I feel good. Real strong. I think I'm going to—"

I felt a strong blast of cold air. It swept through the gym, like an invisible ocean wave.

And then I saw Coach's expression change very suddenly. He was grinning at me, flashing me a thumbs-up. And then his hand came down. His face went slack. His eyes appeared to fade, to glaze over as if a curtain had been drawn over them.

As if he'd been hypnotized or something.

"Hey, Luke," he said, motioning me back to him. He frowned, narrowing his eyes at me.

"What is it?" I asked, keeping up my dribble.

"Take the bench," he ordered, pointing to the team bench with his whistle.

"Huh?" I gaped at him.

"The bench," he repeated, his face a blank now, his eyes vacant, dull. "You can't play today."

"Hey—no way!" I protested. "What do you *mean*? I've *got* to play!"

He shook his head. "You can't play today, Luke. Your concussion—remember? I need a doctor's note. Have you been examined? You can't play until you're examined."

My mouth hung open. "Coach . . . I've been practicing so hard. Please. You've got to let me in the game today," I pleaded. My heart pounded so hard, I felt dizzy. My head throbbed. "Coach . . . I *have* to play. It's the last game."

He shook his head. "Sorry." He motioned to the bench. "We have to follow the rules."

Whose rules? I thought bitterly. The Fate Master's rules?

Coach Bendix gazed at me with those glazed, blank eyes. "Sorry. You've already played your last game, Luke."

"But—but—" I sputtered.

"You'll get 'em next year!" he said. He blew his whistle. "Stretch—you're in! You're playing the whole game!"

I stood there. I didn't move. I stood in the middle of the floor with my hands on my waist. Waiting for my heart to stop racing. Waiting for my legs to stop trembling.

Then I turned and slowly trudged to the bench.

I'd lost today. Score one round for the Fate Master.

No way I could break the pattern today. I was a loser today.

But I wasn't finished. I could still win.

If I had time . . .

CHAPTER 24

"Give the skull to Stretch," Hannah pleaded. "Maybe the Fate Master will go easy on us."

It was the next day. We were huddled at the back of the lunchroom. I could see Stretch laughing and kidding around with his friends at a table near the front. The Squires had won the game by two points, and Stretch had been a hero.

"I can't do it," I said, shaking my head. "Besides, you heard what the Fate Master said. He doesn't make deals. It won't help to pass it to Stretch."

Hannah let out a sigh. She had her head buried in her hands. "Then what are we going to do?"

"I'll find a way to defeat him," I said. I bit into my ham sandwich. "Hey—!" I felt something hard.

"Oh no," I moaned. I spit out a tooth.

In a panic I moved my tongue around the inside of my mouth. "My teeth," I groaned. "They're all loose. I'm going to lose all my teeth."

Hannah didn't lift her head. She whispered something, too low for me to hear.

"I've got to go," I said, jumping up. "I have some ideas, Hannah. Don't give up hope. I have some ideas."

I ran past Stretch's table, where the guys were laughing and blowing straw wrappers at each other. Stretch called out to me, but I didn't stop.

I made my way to the computer lab. The door was closed. I pulled it open and burst breathlessly into the brightly lit room.

"Mrs. Coffey? Mrs. Coffey? It's me—Luke!"

I felt another tooth swing loose in my mouth. I gritted my teeth, trying to press it down into place.

A chubby young man I'd never seen before came out of the supply room. He had short black hair on top of a round, pudgy face, and bright red cheeks. He looked like an apple with eyes! He wore a red plaid shirt over black denims.

"Is Mrs. Coffey here?" I demanded. "I need to talk to her."

He set down the disk drive he was carrying. "She's gone," he said.

"You mean she went to lunch?" I asked.

He shook his round head. "No. She left school. She got another job."

"I—I know," I stammered. "But I thought—"

"I'm Ron Handleman," he said. "I'm taking over the computer lab. Do you have a class with me?"

"Uh . . . no," I said. "But I have a project I was supposed to show Mrs. Coffey. She was going to send it to someone who might put it in a show. It's computer animation, you see. I've been working on it for two years and . . . and . . ." In my panic the words poured out of me. I had to stop to take a breath.

"Slow down," Mr. Handleman said. "She probably left me a note about it. She left me a stack of notes." He glanced around the cluttered worktable. "I put them somewhere."

How could Mrs. Coffey leave without seeing my project? I asked myself. How could she do that to me?

Didn't she realize how important it was? This could be my big triumph. If my computer animation is accepted for a show—because of my hard work, *only* because of my skill and hard work—it would break the pattern. It might defeat the Fate Master.

Didn't she *realize*?

"Uh . . . can you look at my computer animation?" I asked.

Mr. Handleman's cheeks grew redder. "When?"

"Tonight?" I asked, my heart pounding.

"Well . . . I don't think so," he replied. "Not tonight. I mean, this is my first day. I have so much to do here. Maybe next week . . ."

"No!" I screamed. "You have to look at it! Please! It's very important!"

"I'd love to see it," he said, picking up the disk drive, starting across the room with it. "But I have to get organized. Maybe . . ."

"Please!" I cried. "Find Mrs. Coffey's note. We've got to get it to the man who's putting together the computer art show. Please!"

He narrowed his eyes at me. He probably thought I was crazy.

But I didn't care. I needed a victory. I knew there wasn't much time.

"Okay," Mr. Handleman said finally. "Bring it in first thing tomorrow morning. I'll try to look at it during lunch."

Not good enough. Tomorrow might be too late, I realized.

"How late will you be here this afternoon?" I asked breathlessly.

"Pretty late," he replied. "Since it's my first day, I—"

"I'll run home after school and get it," I said. "I'll bring it to you before you leave tonight. Could you . . . I mean, would you look at it this afternoon? Please?"

"Okay, I guess. I'll be here till at least five," he said.

"Yesss!" I cried, pumping my fist in the air. I turned and raced out of the computer lab.

I can win! I told myself. I can defeat the Fate Master. My animation project is good. I know it is. I've worked for two years on it. I've put so much hard work into it.

I don't need luck. I don't need good luck at all.

After school I ran all the way home. I burst into the kitchen, tossed down my backpack, and started to my room. I stopped halfway to the stairs when I heard voices from the living room.

"Luke—is that you?" Mom called.

Mom and Dad were both there, sitting in the dark. Dad leaned heavily on his cane. Mom had her hands clasped tightly in her lap.

I stopped in the living room doorway. "Why are you both home so early?" I asked.

"I had to come home. I couldn't work," Dad said softly. "That fall I took. It was worse than we thought. Looks like I'm going to need surgery."

"Oh, no," I muttered. My fault. It was all my fault.

But I didn't really have time to talk to them. I had to get to my computer. I wanted to check out the animation one more time before I made a copy for Mr. Handleman. Then I had to rush back to school.

"But why are you sitting in the dark?" I asked. "Why don't you turn on some lights?"

"We can't," Mom said, shaking her head. "There's some kind of trouble with the power lines to our block. The electricity is off. We have no power. No power at all."

CHAPTER 25

I let out a horrified scream. "Nooooo! My computer!"

"You'll have to wait till the power comes back on," Dad said.

"But—but—" I sputtered.

"We're having so much bad luck all of a sudden," Dad murmured.

"We may have to leave the house tonight," Mom said, sighing unhappily. "Without electricity we have no heat. We may have to check into a hotel or something."

"Oh, no." I tugged at my hair. A big clump of it came out in my hand.

I was losing my hair. Losing my teeth. How could I fight back? How?

"He can't do this to me!" I screamed. "He can't! He can't!" I turned and grabbed the banister and pulled myself up the stairs.

"Luke? What are you saying?"

"Where are you going?"

I didn't answer. I dived into my room and slammed the door shut behind me.

Breathing hard, I stared at my computer. Stared at the dark monitor screen.

Useless. Totally useless.

Frustrated, I kicked the side of my desk. "Owww!" I didn't mean to kick it that hard. Sharp pain throbbed up my leg, up my side.

"Oh, wait." I suddenly remembered. I already made a copy!

Yes! I made a backup copy of my project. On my Zip drive. Yes!

I fumbled frantically through the pile of disks on my desk. And grabbed the Zip disk.

I still have a chance, I told myself. The Fate Master thought he shut me down. But I still have a chance.

I stuffed the disk into my jacket pocket. I hurled myself down the stairs two at a time. "Bye! I have to go back to school!" I shouted to my parents.

"Why?"

"What's going on, Luke? We need you here."

"Hey—come back and explain!"

I heard their cries, but I burst out the front door and kept running.

"I'll stop the bad luck," I said out loud. "I'll stop it. I'll stop the Fate Master—now!"

I found Mr. Handleman in the computer lab, leaning over a keyboard, typing an e-mail message.

He spun around when I shouted hi to him.

I held up the disk. "Here it is! Please! You've got to check it out!"

He motioned for me to sit down next to him. "I spoke to the producer of the computer show," he said. "He called me this afternoon. He said that if I liked your animation, I should send it over to him right away."

"Excellent!" I cried. "That's great news!"

"Aren't you going to take your coat off?"

"No," I answered breathlessly. I shoved the disk into the Zip drive. "No time. You have to see this. Right away."

He laughed. "Slow down. Take a deep breath."

"I'll breathe *after* you see it!" I said.

He leaned back in his chair and used his hands as a headrest. "You've been working on this for two years?"

I nodded.

I found the file in the disk directory and double-clicked it. "Here goes," I said. I was so nervous, the mouse trembled in my hand. My chest was so tight, it felt about to burst.

Is it possible to *explode* from excitement? I leaned forward to watch.

The screen was solid black. "It's starting now," I whispered.

I stared at the black screen, waiting for the bright burst of color at the beginning.

Waiting . . .

Finally a dim glow spread over the screen.

Two circles of light. Two red circles glowed in the center of the darkness.

Two red, glowing eyes.

The eyes stared out, unblinking, unmoving. Blank, round circles of shimmering red.

Mr. Handleman cleared his throat. His eyes remained locked on the monitor screen. "Are those eyes?" he asked. "Do they move or anything?"

I opened my mouth to answer, but no sound came out.

I stared frozen in horror at the glowing eyes. The evil eyes.

And knew I had been defeated again.

Mr. Handleman's cheeks were bright red now. "Is this all there is?" he asked.

"Yes," I whispered. "That's all."

My project was gone. My two years of work were lost.

The fiery eyes stared out at me in triumph.

I climbed to my feet and slumped out of the room.

I trudged down the empty hall, head down, hands shoved deep in my pockets. I've lost, I realized. I'm a loser forever now. Hannah and me both. Bad luck for the rest of our lives.

I turned a corner—and almost bumped into Coach Swanson. "Hey, Luke—how's it going?" he asked.

I muttered a reply under my breath.

"I was going to call you tonight," he said. "Andy Mason is sick. You have to swim in his place tomorrow."

I raised my head. "Huh? Swim?" I had nearly forgotten that I was on the swim team.

"See you after school at the pool," the coach said. "Good luck."

I'll need it, I thought glumly.

But then I realized I was being given one more chance.

One more chance to win *without* luck. One more chance to defeat Fate.

One *last* chance . . .

The next morning I wore a baseball cap to school so no one could see the bald patches on my head. When I brushed my teeth that morning, another tooth came sliding out between my lips.

My tongue was covered with hard, white bumps. My arms and legs itched. I was starting to get the same red blotches on my skin as Hannah.

Somehow I made it through the school day. All I could think about was the swim team race. Was there any way that I might win? That I might break the pattern and win the race and defeat the Fate Master?

I didn't have much hope. But I knew I had to try. I knew I had to give it everything I had left.

A few seconds after I lowered myself into the pool to warm up, Coach Swanson's whistle rang out, echoing off the tile walls. "Practice laps, everyone!" the coach shouted. "Do them half-speed. Let's see some warm-up laps."

At the other end of the pool I saw Stretch kick off and begin swimming with steady, strong strokes. I did a surface dive and started to follow him. The warm water felt good on my itchy skin.

I kicked hard. Picked up speed.

As I raised my head to suck in a deep breath, the water suddenly churned hard.

I swallowed a big mouthful. Started to choke.

I sputtered, struggling to clear my throat, struggling to breathe.

And then, to my horror, my stomach heaved hard. "Guuurrrrrrp." My lunch came hurling up.

I couldn't hold it back. I vomited a thick, dark puddle into the clear water.

"Ooh, gross!"

"Sick!"

"Yuck! Oh, wow—he's puking his guts up!"

A sick, sour smell rose up from the water. I heard kids shouting and groaning in disgust.

And then I heard Coach Swanson's whistle. And the coach shouting at me: "You're outta there, Luke! Get out. You're sick. You're not going to swim today!"

CHAPTER 26

No, I thought. This can't happen again. This is my last chance.

"Coach, I'm okay!" I shouted. "I just . . . swallowed some water. I can swim—really!"

Coach Swanson glanced around the pool. Andy Mason was in street clothes. Joe Bork, the other alternate, didn't show up.

"You've got to let me swim!" I pleaded.

The coach shrugged his shoulders. "There's no one else. I guess I've got no choice."

I'm going to do this, I thought. I'm going to win today. I'm going to do whatever it takes to win.

The race got off to a good start. I did a speed dive at the whistle and found myself gliding, stroking easily, in the lead.

Swimming steadily, keeping up a smooth rhythm, I stayed in the lead until the waves began.

Waves? They tossed up in front of me, rolled rapidly toward me, splashed over me. Wave after wave. Pushing me back. Slowing my pace.

Stroking harder to keep my rhythm, I turned to the side and glanced at the other swimmers. The pool was smooth, the water flat for them.

The waves were just for me! A strong current pushed at me, slowing me, shoving me back.

I ducked under the waves. Let them splash and roll over me. And swam harder.

Harder.

"Oh!" Something brushed my leg.

I felt something curl around an ankle. Something bumped my waist. I felt something slide around my knee.

With another gasp I turned—and saw the gray-green creatures. Eels? Were they *eels*?

Wrapping around my legs. Twining over my waist.

Long, fat eels. The water churned with them!

I cried out.

I saw the other swimmers, gliding swiftly through clear water. They didn't even notice my dark, churning water. They didn't even see the gleaming, wet creatures slithering between my legs. Tightening around my ankles, my legs.

Slapping me . . . slapping me hard . . . slapping me back.

"No!" I burst free. I kept swimming.

Into thick pink clusters of jellyfish. The jellyfish ballooned around me. Stung my arms. Stung my legs. Prickled the skin of my back.

I cried out in pain. The sticky creatures swarmed over me, stinging, stinging me again and again.

I could see the other swimmers moving smoothly, ahead of me now. Gliding in smooth, clear waters as I felt jolt after jolt of pain from the billowing jellyfish that clustered over me.

I slapped the water. Slapped and kicked.

And let out another cry of pain as the water sizzled and boiled. Scalding hot now. It steamed and bubbled. And my skin burned. My skin is going to burn right off me, I thought, struggling to breathe. Struggling to keep my arms moving through the scalding steam. Kicking . . . kicking hard . . .

The other swimmers ahead of me now. Moving so speedily, so steadily . . .

I shut my eyes and swam. You're not going to beat me! I thought. I'm going to win . . . going to win.

And the thought gave me a final surge of energy.

I shot forward to the wall. Plunged like a speeding torpedo to the finish.

My hand hit the wall. I slapped the wall.

Gasping . . . gasping . . . my chest heaving in agony . . . And knew that I had lost.

Too slow. Too slow.

I knew that I had lost again.

CHAPTER 27

Water poured down my face. I shut my eyes and struggled to catch my breath.

I heard a loud whistle. Then I felt a hand on my shoulder. A slap. "Way to go, Luke!"

I opened my eyes to see the coach. He grabbed my hand and pumped it hard. Then he slapped me a high five. "You won! You came from behind! What a race, Luke! Check out the time! You set a school record!"

"Huh? I did? I won?"

He helped me out of the pool. Guys were cheering and yelling congratulations.

But the cheering was cut short by a deafening cry from the middle of the pool. A shrill wail that rose like an ambulance siren. Higher . . . higher . . . until I was forced to cover my ears.

And then a mountain of water rose up from the pool. Red and steaming like a volcano. The water rose up—higher, higher—like a bubbling, boiling red tidal wave. And all the while the deafening wail rang out with it.

Everyone was screaming. We all were screaming.

And then, as suddenly as it rose up, the molten, red mountain collapsed back into the pool. Collapsed with a soft splash. The pool was flat and smooth again. And silent. Silent except for our stunned gasps and cries.

I turned to see Hannah running along the side of the pool. Hannah out of her wheelchair. Running. Running wildly, waving her arms excitedly, laughing, her red hair flying behind her.

"Luke—you did it! We're free! You defeated Fate! Luke—you defeated Fate!"

But it wasn't enough. Not enough for me.

I changed into my street clothes in seconds. Then I dragged Hannah down the hall to my locker. Locker 13.

I stopped at the janitor's closet. And I grabbed a huge sledgehammer.

Hannah cheered as I raised the sledgehammer to the locker, and smashed it . . . smashed it . . . smashed it.

Working feverishly, I pried the battered locker from the wall. Kicked it onto its side. Raised the sledgehammer again. Smashed it . . . crushed it . . . smashed it.

The battered locker door swung open. I heard a low groan from deep inside.

Hannah and I both leaped back as a skull rolled out onto the floor.

Not a tiny skull. A human-sized skull with glowing red eyes.

The eyes glowed for only a few seconds. Then the skull uttered a final groan, a groan of agony, of defeat. And the eyes faded to darkness. Empty darkness.

I took a deep breath. Ran up to it—and kicked the skull down the hall.

"Goal!" Hannah yelled.

We walked out of the school building arm in arm. Into the bright afternoon sunlight.

I took a long, deep breath. The air smelled so fresh, so sweet.

The houses, the trees, the sky—they all looked so beautiful.

I stopped at the bottom of the sidewalk. And bent down to pick something up.

"Hey, check it out!" I showed it to Hannah. "Is this my lucky day?" I cried. "I found a penny!"

THE NIGHTMARE ROOM
MY NAME IS EVIL

CHAPTER I

"Maggie, you're so evil!" Jackie Mullen said, laughing.

My mouth dropped open. "Huh? Me? Evil?"

Jackie pointed across the table to the cupcakes on my plate. "You took three cupcakes and only ate the icing."

Her sister Judy frowned at me. "What's wrong with them? I baked them myself—for your birthday."

I licked chocolate icing off my fingers. "There's nothing wrong with them," I told her. "They're wicked cool cupcakes. I just like icing."

Jackie laughed again. "Are you getting weird? You never say wicked cool."

I sneered at her. "I'm thirteen now. I can say whatever I want. Besides, I need a new image."

"Like a makeover," Judy said.

"Like a personality makeover," Jilly, the third sister said. "Maggie wants to be sophisticated now."

Jilly was right about that. I've always been the youngest in my class because I skipped second grade. But now I was turning thirteen. Now I was old enough to transform myself into a mature, confident person. And no one would treat me like "the baby" anymore.

"I am sophisticated," I said. "I'm thirteen now, and there's no turning back!"

"Well, you're off to a bad start," Jackie said. She pointed. "You have icing in your hair."

I groaned and reached up and felt sticky stuff up there. For some reason, the three sisters all thought it was a riot. Jilly laughed so hard, she choked on her cupcake.

Jackie, Judy, and Jilly Mullen are triplets, which means that I have three best friends. Everyone at our school—Cedar Bay Middle School—calls them the Three J's. And they're very close, although they try really hard to be different from each other.

Jackie and Judy look alike. They both have straight black hair and big, round brown eyes. They both always look as if they're suntanned.

But they're so eager for people to tell them apart, they have totally different styles. Jackie's hair is long, halfway down her back. She wears funky, old clothes, baggy jeans, old bell-bottoms from the seventies, oversized, bright-colored tops she finds at garage sales. She loves clanky jewelry, heavy beads, and dangling, plastic earrings.

Judy is much more preppy. She has her hair cut very short. She wears short skirts over black tights and neat little vests. Judy always looks as if she just washed her face.

Jilly was born last, and she doesn't look as if she belongs in the same family. She has long, golden blond hair, creamy, pale skin, and big green eyes. She looks very angelic, and she talks in a soft, whispery voice.

Jackie is funny, and kind of loud, and a real joker. She doesn't take things too seriously. I really want to be like that.

I have coppery hair and a slender, serious face. I've been quiet and pretty shy and serious my whole life. And I keep thinking if I hang out with Jackie a lot, maybe I'll be more like her.

Judy is the brain in the group. She is the perfect student. It's all I can do just to keep up in school. But Judy is always busy writing essays and doing projects for extra credit.

Judy likes to organize things. She's always joining clubs and committees at school. These days, she is organizing a huge Pet Fair to raise money for animal rights.

And Jilly? Well . . . as my mother would say, Jilly is in her own world. In other words, she's kind of a flake. She's really into boys, and music, and I-don't-know-what-else. She's kind of a dreamy person. You know. Like she's floating a few feet off the ground.

The only thing I've ever seen Jilly be serious about is her dancing. She takes ballet lessons five times a week after school, and she's really talented.

I'm into dance, too. But I've always been too shy to try out for anything. Not anymore, though. In a few days, the "new" me and Jilly are both trying out for a community ballet company. My whole life I've dreamed of dancing with a real company, but I'm not looking forward to the audition—because I have to compete against Jilly!

Anyway, those are my best friends, the Three J's. And of course I wanted to spend my thirteenth birthday at their house with them.

When we finished the birthday cupcakes and I wiped the chocolate icing from my hair, Jackie jumped up, clapped her hands once, and said, "Let's go!"

"Go where?" I asked.

"You'll see," Judy said. She started to pull me from the table. "Just follow us."

"To the carnival," Jilly added, tying her blond hair back with a blue, ribbony scrunchie.

I held back. "Huh? The carnival on the pier?"

All three girls nodded. All three were grinning. They had planned this.

So I didn't argue. I followed them to the carnival.

And that's when all the horror began.

CHAPTER 2

A short while later the four of us staggered off the roller coaster, laughing, holding on to each other to keep from falling over. I blinked, trying to stop the ground from tilting and swaying. The carnival lights flashed in my eyes.

"That was awesome!" Jilly declared, brushing back her blond curls with both hands.

I held my stomach. "Wow. I'm so glad I ate all those cupcakes!"

"Why do they call it the Blue Beast?" Judy asked. "The cars are bright yellow!"

Good question. Judy always wanted things to make sense.

"Who would want to ride on the Yellow Beast?" Jackie asked.

We all thought that was a riot, and we laughed our heads off as we made our way across the pier.

It was a warm, cloudy night. The air felt heavy and damp, more like summer than fall. I glanced up, looking for the moon. But the low clouds blocked it out.

"Wasn't this a great idea?" Jackie asked, taking my arm. Judy hurried up ahead to buy more ride tickets. "Isn't this the perfect way to celebrate?"

"Wicked cool," I replied, grinning.

Jackie shook her fist at me. "Go ahead, Maggie. Say it again. I dare you."

"I think there are some boys from school here," Jilly said. She has the most amazing Boy Radar! "Maybe I'll catch you guys later."

She started to wander off, but Judy pulled her back. "Let's stick together for a while, Jilly. It's a party, remember?"

The carnival opens on the pier every summer. It's kind of tacky, but we hang out there sometimes on weekend nights. There isn't much else to do in Cedar Bay.

Fall had arrived. In a week or two they'd be shutting the carnival down and packing up. Some of the rides were already closed. And the big Fun House sign lay on its side on the ground, the paint chipped and fading.

We wandered through a long row of game booths. "Try your luck, girls!" a man shouted, holding up three baseballs. "You can't lose! Really!"

I stopped across from a brightly lit booth. A young woman stood in front of a wall of balloons. "Hey—darts. Want to throw some darts? I'm pretty good at that."

Jackie shook her head. "No way. Let's do something wild."

I squinted at her. "Something wild?"

"Yeah. Something really crazy," Jilly chimed in, her green eyes flashing. "Something we normally wouldn't do. For your birthday."

"But darts is fun," Judy argued. "If Maggie wants to throw darts . . ."

That's why I like Judy. She's always on my side.

"Forget darts," Jackie said, pulling me across the row of booths. "I see the perfect thing. Awesome!"

She dragged me to the door of a low, square building. I gasped when I read the red-and-black hand-lettered sign next to the door: TATTOOS WHILE-U-WAIT.

"Whoa! No way!" I cried. I tried to pull back. But Jackie was too strong. She tugged me through the doorway.

The little room was dark and hot, and smelled of incense and tobacco. Red and blue tattoo samples on jagged pieces of paper were tacked up and down the walls.

Jackie hadn't let go of my arm. "Check them out. I'll buy you one for your birthday!" she said.

I stared at her. "You're kidding—right?"

"Ooh, look at this one!" Jilly gushed. She pointed to a blue half-moon circled by red stars. "That's the prettiest one. Or how about this red flower?"

"Doesn't it hurt to get tattooed?" Judy asked Jackie.

Jackie picked up a long needle from a workbench

against the wall. She pressed the tip against the back of my hand. "Zip zip zip, and it's done," she said. "Can you imagine the look on your mother's face when you come home with a tattoo?"

"No way!" I cried. "Come on—I don't want any tattoo!"

I tried to pull free of Jackie's grasp. And as I did, a large tattoo tacked up beside the door caught my eye.

It was so ugly. A dragon's head. A snarling green dragon with its jaws open, red flames bursting from its gaping nostrils. And beneath it, red words with blue shadows behind them. Bold, bloodred words:

My Name Is EVIL!

As I stared at the ugly tattoo, I felt a chill run down my back. It seemed to hypnotize me or something. I couldn't turn away from it. Couldn't take my eyes off it.

Finally Jackie's voice cut through the spell. "Pick one. Hurry."

"N-no," I whispered. "Let's get out of here!"

I headed for the door, but Jackie gripped my arm from behind. "Grab her," she ordered the others. "Don't let her get away!"

CHAPTER 3

They held on to me tightly, staring at me in cold silence.

Jackie broke up first. "Wow! I think you really believed us!"

Jilly laughed too. "You did! You thought we were serious."

Judy frowned. "Maggie, I told them it was a mean joke. But they wouldn't listen to me."

I stared angrily at Jackie. "You—you creep! You really scared me," I confessed. "How could you do that?"

Jackie laughed. "Easy!"

"Jackie has a sick sense of humor," Judy said, still frowning.

"Ha ha," I said, rolling my eyes.

Jackie shrugged. She put her arm around my shoulders. "I'm sorry, Maggie. I really didn't think you'd believe us."

I sighed. "I always fall for dumb jokes. Not too sophisticated, huh?"

"Forget about it," Jilly said. "Now you're thirteen, remember? Makeover time?"

I sighed again. I felt really dumb.

Why did I think that my best friends in the world would force me to do something I didn't want to do? Why did I panic like that?

The four of us stumbled out into the warm night. Across the path a tall girl was heaving baseballs at a target, trying to dunk a young man in a swim tank.

A mother hurried past, pulling two little boys. Both boys carried huge cones of pink cotton candy. They had the stuff stuck all over their cheeks and noses.

"Let's have some fun!" Jackie declared. She still had her arm around my shoulder. The four of us walked side by side in a solid row.

Jackie pulled back when she saw Glen Martin. I saw him, too. He was with two other guys from school. They were all singing some kind of song, snapping their fingers as they walked, bopping along.

"Oh, wow," Jackie muttered.

I glanced at her. What did she mean by that?

Everyone in school knows that I have a crush on Glen. Everyone except Glen, that is.

I watched him come nearer. He is tall and lanky, and he's so cute with his wild, curly brown hair, which he never brushes, and serious dark eyes.

Glen is always goofing, always cracking jokes. He's always in trouble in school for breaking up the class. He has the greatest laugh. And when he smiles, two cute dimples appear on his cheeks.

Glen doesn't live in my neighborhood. He lives in a tiny house in the old part of town. And the guys he hangs out with are kind of tough.

Sometimes I think about inviting Glen over or something. But I always lose my nerve.

That's going to change, too. It's makeover time, I reminded myself. And I'm going to invite Glen over real soon.

"Hey—it's the Three J's!" one of Glen's friends called.

"Yeah. Jokey, Jumpy, and Jerk-Face," Glen said.

Jackie tossed back her hair and sneered at him. "That's a compliment, coming from you—Tarzan!"

That's so mean, I thought. I can't believe Jackie is still calling him Tarzan! The name made Glen blush.

"Hey, guys. What's up?" Jilly walked over to Glen's two friends and started flirting with them.

Judy sighed impatiently. "Are we just going to stand here? Aren't we going to do any rides?"

Glen grinned at Jackie. "You'd better hurry. The Ugly Dog Contest is starting over there." He pointed to a tent at the end of the pier. "You could win a dog bone!"

Jackie scowled at him. "Shut up, Glen."

His dark eyes flashed. "You shut up." He grabbed the beaded necklace Jackie always wears and gave it a tug.

"Let go!" she screamed.

I stepped between them. "Come on—be nice," I said. "It's my birthday."

Glen turned to me and his eyes flashed, as if seeing me for the first time. "Maggie—hey. Is it really your birthday?"

I nodded. "Yeah. We all came here to celebrate, and—"

"Wow! It was my birthday yesterday!" he declared.

Before I could utter a reply, he grabbed my hand and shook it. "Happy birthday to us!" he cried.

And then, believe it or not, he raised my hand to his mouth—and planted a wet, noisy, slobbery kiss on the back of it.

His friends laughed. Judy and Jilly laughed, too.

I stood there stunned.

Glen started to back away.

Then Jackie shoved me from behind—shoved me into Glen. "Go ahead—kiss your boyfriend!" she cried.

Glen and I stumbled over each other and nearly tumbled to the ground. Everyone laughed. They thought it was a riot.

"Jackie—give me a break!" I shouted angrily. How could she embarrass me like that?

Glen backed away, blushing again. "Happy birthday. Catch you later." He flashed me a thumbs-up and started off with his friends.

A few seconds later the Three J's and I were hurrying away, heading past the Tilt-A-Whirl and FreeFall Mountain. Shrill screams rose up all around us.

Judy and Jilly were giggling about something. Jackie twined her arm around mine and pulled me along. "He is such a geek!" she exclaimed. "How can you like him?"

"He totally hates us!" Jilly declared.

"Especially Jackie," Judy added.

"And I don't blame him," I said. "Jackie depantsed him in front of the whole school!"

Jackie laughed. "What an awesome moment!"

"It almost caused a riot!" Jilly said. "Poor Glen was embarrassed for life!"

Judy sighed. "Another one of Jackie's great jokes."

"I can't believe you're still calling him Tarzan," I said. "That was a whole year ago."

Last year Jackie was in charge of costumes for the talent show at school. And Glen decided to do a crazy comedy act wearing a Tarzan costume. Well, Jackie had this insane idea. Somehow she rigged Glen's costume. She secretly removed most of the elastic.

And there was poor Glen, onstage in front of the entire school. And Jackie's trick worked. His pants dropped to his ankles in front of everyone!

"I'll never forget those black bikini briefs he was wearing!" Jackie exclaimed. All three sisters exploded with laughter.

"He looked like such a geek!" Jilly cried. "Standing there onstage in the stupid black under-pants, trying to cover himself up."

"He just stood there. He froze," Jackie remem-bered. "And the whole auditorium went wild. Everyone just freaked."

"We've called him Tarzan ever since," Jilly said. "It makes him blush every time."

"It was a year ago. You should let it drop. Give him a break," I said.

"Why? Because he's your boyfriend?" Jackie teased.

"It was so mean! Why did you do it in the first place?" I asked.

She fiddled with the tiny glass beads on her neck-lace and grinned. "I don't know. I just thought it would be funny."

"Hey, check it out. A fortune-teller!" Jilly said. She pointed to a small black tent that stood beside an ice-cream cart. "Can we do it? I love fortune-tellers!"

"No way," I said. "They make me nervous. I don't even like watching them in movies."

"Come on, Maggie. It's your birthday," Jackie said, pulling me to the tent. "You have to have your fortune told on your birthday."

"Let's see what the fortune-teller says about you and Glen!" Jilly teased.

"I don't think so," I said.

But as usual, they didn't give me a choice. A few seconds later we were standing at the doorway to the dark tent.

"We'll all have our fortunes told," Jackie said. "My treat."

"This is so cool!" Jilly whispered. "Do you think it's a real psychic? Do you think she can really tell the future?"

The three sisters started into the tent. I held back, staring at the red-and-black hand-lettered sign: MISS ELIZABETH. FORTUNE-TELLER. ONE DOLLAR.

I suddenly realized that my heart was racing.

Why do I feel so weird? I wondered. Why do I have such a bad feeling about this?

CHAPTER 4

I followed my friends into the tent. The air inside felt hot and steamy. Two electric lanterns on the back tent wall splashed gray light over the fortune-teller's small table.

Miss Elizabeth sat hunched with her elbows on the table, head in her hands, staring into a red glass ball. She didn't look up as we stepped inside. I couldn't tell if she was concentrating on the red ball, or if she was asleep.

The tent was completely bare, except for her table and two wooden chairs, and a large black-and-white poster of a human hand. The hand was divided into sections. There was a lot of writing all over the poster, too small for me to read in the smoky, gray light.

As she stared into the red glass ball, the fortune-teller muttered to herself. She was a middle-aged woman, slender, with bony arms poking out from the sleeves of her red dress, and very large, pale white hands. Squinting into the light, I saw that the polish on her long fingernails matched the red of her dress.

"Hel-lo?" Jackie called, breaking the silence.

Miss Elizabeth finally looked up. She was kind of pretty. She had big, round black eyes and dramatic red-lipsticked lips. Her hair was long and wavy, solid black except for a wide white streak down the middle.

Her eyes moved from one of us to the other. She didn't smile. "Walter, we have visitors," she announced in a hoarse, scratchy voice.

I glanced around, searching for Walter.

"Walter is my late husband," the fortune-teller announced. "He helps me channel information from the spirits."

Jackie and I exchanged glances.

"We'd like you to tell our fortunes," Jilly said.

Miss Elizabeth nodded solemnly. "One dollar each." She held out her long, pale hand. "Four dollars please."

Jackie fumbled in her bag and pulled out four crumpled dollar bills. She handed them to the fortune-teller, who shoved them into a pocket of her red dress.

"Who wants to go first?" Again, her eyes moved slowly over our faces.

"I'll go," Jilly volunteered. She dropped into the chair across the table from Miss Elizabeth.

The fortune-teller lowered her head again to gaze into the red ball. "Walter, bring me the words of the spirit world about this young woman."

I suddenly felt a chill at the back of my neck. I knew I shouldn't be frightened. The woman had to be a fake—right? Otherwise, she wouldn't be working in a tacky carnival like this one.

But she was so serious. So solemn. She didn't seem to be putting on an act.

Now she took Jilly's hand. She pulled it up close to her face and began to study Jilly's palm. Muttering to herself, she moved her long finger back and forth, following the lines of the palm, tracing them with her bright red fingernail.

Jackie leaned close to me. "This is cool," she whispered.

Judy sighed. "This is going to take forever."

Jackie raised a finger to her lips and motioned for Judy to shush.

The woman studied Jilly's palm for a long time, squeezing the hand as she gazed at it, murmuring to Walter in the red glass ball. Finally she raised her eyes to Jilly. "You are artistic," she said in her scratchy voice.

"Yes!" Jilly declared.

"You are a . . . dancer," Miss Elizabeth continued. "You study the dance. You are a hard worker."

"Whoa. I don't believe this!" Jilly gushed. "How do you know—?"

"You have much talent," the fortune-teller murmured, ignoring Jilly's question. "Much talent. But sometimes . . . I see . . . your artistic side gets in the way of your practical side. You are . . . you are . . ."

She shut her eyes. "Help me, Walter," she whispered. Then she opened her eyes again and raised them to Jilly's palm. "You are a very social person. Your friends mean a lot to you. Especially . . . boy friends."

Jackie and Judy laughed. Jilly flashed them an angry scowl. "I—I don't believe this," she told the fortune-teller. "You have everything right!"

"It is my gift," Miss Elizabeth replied softly.

"Will I make the new dance company?" Jilly asked her. "Tryouts are next week. Will I be accepted?"

Miss Elizabeth stared into the glass ball. "Walter?" she whispered.

I held my breath, waiting for the answer. Jilly and I were both trying out for the dance company. And I knew there was only room for one of us.

"Walter can find no answer," the fortune-teller told Jilly. "He only groans." She let go of Jilly's hand.

"He—groaned?" Jilly asked. "Why?"

"Your time is up," Miss Elizabeth said. She motioned to us. "Who is next?"

Jackie shoved Judy forward. Judy dropped into the chair and held her hand out to Miss Elizabeth.

Jilly came running over to join Jackie and me at the edge of the tent. "Isn't she amazing?" she whispered.

"Yes, she is," I had to admit. How did she know

so many true things about Jilly? I was beginning to believe Miss Elizabeth really had powers.

And now I didn't feel afraid or nervous. I was eager to see what the fortune-teller would say about me.

She squeezed Judy's hand and gazed deep into Judy's dark eyes. "You have great love in you," she announced. "Great love for . . . animals."

Judy gasped. "Y-yes!"

"You care for them. You work . . ."

"Yes," Judy said. "I work in an animal shelter after school. That's amazing!"

Miss Elizabeth ran a red fingernail down Judy's palm. "You also have an animal that you care about very much. A dog . . . No. A cat."

"Yes. My cat. Plumper."

Judy turned to us, her face filled with astonishment. "Do you believe this? She's right about everything!"

"I know! It's so cool!" Jilly exclaimed. She swept back her blond hair with a toss of her head. She kept bouncing up and down. She seemed too excited to stand still.

The fortune-teller spent a few more minutes with Judy. She told Judy that she would have a long, successful life. She said Judy would have a big family someday.

"Of kids? Of animals?" Judy asked.

Miss Elizabeth didn't answer.

Next came Jackie's turn. Once again Miss Elizabeth

was right on-target with everything she said. "Wow," Jackie kept muttering. "Wow."

Finally I found myself in the chair across from the fortune-teller. Suddenly I felt nervous again. My mouth was dry. My legs were shaking.

Miss Elizabeth looked older from close up. When she smiled at me, the thick makeup on her face cracked. Tiny drops of sweat glistened at her hairline.

"What is your name?" she asked in a whisper.

"Maggie," I told her.

She nodded solemnly and took my hand. She raised my palm close to her face and squinted down at it in the gray light.

I held my breath. And waited. What would she see?

She squeezed my hand. Brought it closer to her face.

And then . . . then . . . her eyes bulged wide. She let out a loud gasp.

With a violent jerk she tossed my hand away.

And jumped to her feet. Her chair fell behind her, clattering to the tent floor.

She stared at me—stared in open-mouthed horror.

And then she screamed:

"Get OUT! Get AWAY from here!!"

"Huh? Wait—" I choked out.

"Get OUT! You bring EVIL! You bring EVIL with you! Get OUT of here!"

CHAPTER 5

I stumbled out of the tent, my heart pounding.

The air felt cool on my face. I sucked in several deep breaths.

My three friends tumbled out after me. Jackie was the only one laughing. Judy and Jilly were shaking their heads.

I started to jog along the path between the rides. I wanted to get as far away from that crazy woman as I could!

Screams from the roller coaster rang in my ears. And over that shrill sound, the fortune-teller's frantic shrieks repeated in my mind.

"Get OUT! You bring EVIL! You bring EVIL with you! Get OUT of here!"

I stopped running and pressed my back against a tall wooden fence at the edge of the pier. The Three J's hurried up to me. "Wh-why did she say that?" I gasped.

Judy and Jilly both shrugged.

"It was . . . crazy!" Judy whispered.

"But why did she say that about me?" I repeated breathlessly.

Jackie laughed and gave me a playful shove. "Because you're a witch!" she cried.

"But—but—" I stammered.

Jackie imitated the fortune-teller's scratchy voice: "You're evil, Maggie. Get out of here! You're so evil, you're scaring Walter!"

Jackie sounded so much like Miss Elizabeth, I had to laugh.

"Let me see your hand." Jackie grabbed my hand and pulled my palm up to her face. "Yuck! You are evil!" she cried. "That's the most evil hand I ever saw!"

They started laughing all over again. But this time I didn't join in.

"She seemed so serious," I said, picturing the whole scene again. "And then when she looked at my hand, she really did look terrified. As if—"

"It was all an act," Jackie said. "I'm sure she does that all the time. To give people something to talk about and tell their friends."

"Maybe she wanted more money," Judy suggested. "You know. To tell us what the evil was."

"But why did she pick me?" I cried. "Why didn't she tell Jilly she was evil? Or Judy?"

"Because it's your birthday!" Jackie teased.

And then I had a thought. "You set this up—didn't you!" I cried. "You went to the fortune-teller earlier

303

and told her to say that to me!"

"No—" Jackie started. "Really—"

"Yes! You know I always fall for these things!" I insisted. "It's another one of your tricks. But I'm the new Maggie. I'm not going to fall for your little joke."

"We didn't set it up! Honest!" Jilly said, raising her right hand as if swearing an oath.

"I've never seen that woman before!" Jackie declared.

"Come on. Let's forget about it. Let's go on the Ferris wheel," Judy said.

"When we're up at the top, we can lean over and spit on Miss Elizabeth's tent!" Jackie said.

"No. I really want to get away from here." I shuddered. "Really. Let's go. I don't know what to think about that crazy woman. I just want to go."

Jackie put her hands on my shoulders. "You're shaking!" she said. "You didn't take that woman seriously—did you, Maggie? She's crazy!"

"I know. I know," I muttered.

But as we walked back to the Mullens' house, I kept examining my palm. I couldn't get that woman and her frightened face and her terrified cries out of my mind.

As soon as we got inside, we ordered pizza. Then I pulled out the magic kit my mom bought me for my birthday. And I started doing some of the tricks.

"Watch carefully. Which hand is the coin in?" I

asked, holding my closed fists in front of them.

Jackie rolled her eyes. "Your mother bought you this?"

I nodded. "Come on. Which hand?"

"Your mother must think you're five years old!" Jackie said.

"I had that same kit when I was seven," Judy chimed in.

"But you know I'm really into this stuff!" I protested. "You know I love magic. Check this out." I shoved the box in front of them. "The disappearing dollar-bill trick. And remember this one with the cups and the three red balls?"

"You're definitely weird," Jilly said.

"No, I'm not," I replied sharply. The fortune-teller flashed into my mind again. "I just like the idea of making things appear and disappear. I think it's so cool."

"Make the pizza appear," Jilly said. "I'm starving!"

"Okay," I agreed. I waved my hand three times toward the front door. "Pizza—appear!" I commanded in a deep voice.

And the doorbell buzzed.

Everyone laughed in surprise. "Yaay! You did it!" Jilly cried. She ran to the front door to get it.

"What did your father send you for your birthday?" Jackie asked.

I sighed. "He forgot again, I guess. He didn't call."

My parents have been divorced since I was four. My dad lives in Seattle, and he doesn't call that much.

I took out a silvery box from the magic kit. "Here. Let me show you a great trick before we eat. Jackie, lend me your necklace."

Jackie's smile faded. "My necklace?" She reached a hand up to the tiny, brightly colored glass beads.

"Yeah. Just lend it to me for a minute," I said, holding my hand out for it. "This is a really cool trick. You'll be amazed. Really."

She frowned. "Be careful, okay, Maggie?" She bent her head and started to slide the necklace off. "You know how much this necklace means to me. My great-grandmother gave it to me. I never take it off."

"She didn't give me anything," Judy griped.

"She didn't like you," Jackie snapped. The beads caught in her long, black hair. She carefully tugged them free and handed the necklace to me.

"Wow. It's so light and delicate," I said. "Now, watch carefully."

I slid open the silver box and carefully tucked the necklace inside. Then I turned the box over and over between my hands. "You watching?" I asked.

"Yeah. Sure," Jackie replied. Judy stared at the box without blinking. Jilly set the pizza down on the coffee table and watched the box twirl in my hands.

"This box leads to the fourth dimension," I

306

announced. "When I open it up, your necklace will not be inside. It will be in the fourth dimension."

"Jilly lives in the fourth dimension!" Jackie said. Judy laughed. Jilly stuck her tongue out at Jackie.

"The necklace is gone!" I declared. I slid open the box and showed them it was empty.

"Cool!" Jilly said.

"Good trick," Jackie said. "Very good."

I slid the box shut again. Then I turned it over. "Necklace—return from the fourth dimension!" I ordered.

I pulled open the box and peered inside. "Hey—!"

"It's not there," Jackie said.

"Whoa. Wait a minute," I said. I turned the box again and slid open the lid. "No. Not there. Hold on."

I raised my eyes to Jackie. She was glaring at me impatiently. "Maggie—?"

My chin trembled. "It's in here. I know it is!"

I turned the box and opened it again. No. I opened both sides. I slid open the secret compartment. No.

"Oh, wow!" I cried. "Oh, wow. Jackie—I—I'm so sorry! I don't know where it went!"

CHAPTER 6

With an angry cry Jackie jumped up from the couch. She grabbed the box from my hands and examined it. "Maggie, is this some kind of a joke?"

I couldn't keep up the act any longer. I laughed. "Of course it is!" I exclaimed. "It's a magic trick—right? Look in your pocket."

Jackie squinted at me suspiciously. "Huh?"

I pointed. "Look in your pocket."

She reached into her T-shirt pocket and pulled out the necklace.

"Wow!" Judy clapped her hands.

"That's so totally wild!" Jilly declared. "You're good, Maggie. You're really good!"

I took a quick bow.

But then I saw Jackie still glaring at me. "I think it was mean," she said through her teeth. She carefully returned the necklace to her neck.

"It was just a trick!" I protested. "Besides, it's not as mean as making someone's pants fall down!"

"But you know how much this necklace means to

me," Jackie said. "It's the most beautiful thing I own."

"Yes, it's beautiful," I agreed. I sighed. "I wish I had one like it. I'd never take mine off, either."

Jackie eyed me suspiciously. Finally a smile crossed her lips. "Well, if it ever really disappears, I'll know who swiped it!"

I laughed at that, along with Judy and Jilly.

I had no way of knowing that Jackie's necklace would disappear for real just a few days later.

Jilly brought paper plates and cans of Diet Coke from the kitchen. We each took pizza slices and carried them back to the living room to chow down.

"Maggie, do another trick," Jilly urged.

"No. Turn on the TV," Judy said. "See if there are any good movies on."

Jackie glanced at the clock on the mantel. "It's pretty late," she said to me. "Think you should call your mom or something? Tell her you're still here?"

"No. She had to work tonight," I replied. My mom is a nurse at Cedar Bay General. She has a different work schedule every week.

I started to lift my pizza slice to my mouth—when I felt a hard bump—like a heavy brick landing on my lap. "Plumper!" I cried. The pizza slice started to fall. I made a wild grab for it.

Judy's enormous orange-and-white cat pushed its fat body against my side.

"Plumper—get down!" Judy ordered. "Get off Maggie!"

Of course the cat ignored her.

The cat burrowed its fat head into my lap. "I don't believe this!" I cried to Judy. "Why does he always pick on me?"

"Plumper knows you don't like him," Judy replied.

"He's just so big and heavy, and he always jumps on me, and—and—" I sneezed hard. Once. And then sneezed again.

"You don't have to sneeze like that. We know you're allergic to cats!" Jackie said.

"Oh, yuck!" I cried. I held up my pizza slice. It had clumps of orange fur stuck all over it.

The cat stretched its paws over my lap.

"Plumper—what did you do?" Judy scolded. "Just shove him away, Maggie. You've got to be firm. Just push him."

I hesitated. I felt about to sneeze again. The cat was so heavy on my lap. Finally I gave him a soft shove. "Go away, Plumper. Go."

To my surprise, he tossed back his head, bared his teeth, and let out a long, frightening hiss.

Before I could move, the big cat swiped its claws over my arm.

"Owww!" I let out a scream. The pizza slice fell to the floor.

The cat hissed again, louder. It lowered its head—

and tried to sink its teeth into my arm.

With a cry, I leaped up.

I tried to back away, but stumbled over the coffee table.

Hissing furiously, the cat dived for me. Swiped both front paws over my jeans legs, clawing, snapping its jaws.

I fell hard onto my back. And before I could roll or spin away, the cat was on top of me. Hissing so loudly, so furiously. Hissing like an angry snake. And clawing, clawing at my face. Climbing over me. Clawing. Biting.

"Help me!" I shrieked. "Help! He's trying to kill me!"

"Plumper!" I could hear Judy scream. She sounded so far away. "Plumper—what's wrong with you!"

I raised both arms to protect my face.

The cat furiously clawed at my sleeves. Snapping. Crying. Hissing with such anger.

Judy grabbed the cat. Tossed him over her shoulder. And hurried out of the room, holding him like a big bag of laundry.

"Ohhhh." I let out a groan.

I struggled slowly to my feet. My whole body trembled.

"I never saw Plumper do that before!" Jilly declared, taking my arm.

Jackie hurried over to me. "Are you okay? Maggie? Are you cut?"

I checked myself out. My clothes were covered in orange fur. "I—I guess I'm all right," I said shakily.

"You have a small scratch on your hand," Jackie reported, checking me out. "But he didn't break the skin."

"Stupid, crazy cat," Jilly muttered. She started to pull clumps of fur off me.

Judy returned, shaking her head, pulling cat fur off her sweater. "I had to lock him in the back. That was so weird!"

"He's never done anything like that before," Jilly said. "He's always just fat, lazy, and contented."

"So why did he go berserk and attack Maggie like that?" Judy asked, her voice trembling.

Jackie's dark eyes lit up. "Because Maggie is evil!" she declared. "EVIL!"

CHAPTER 7

Her two sisters laughed.

But I didn't think it was funny.

"I'm not evil!" I protested shrilly. "That cat is evil!"

"I'll keep him away from you from now on," Judy promised, biting her bottom lip. "I—I don't know what made him do that. He just went . . . nuts. It's so weird. So weird . . ."

I turned and saw Jackie staring at me, studying me intently. "What are you thinking?" I demanded.

She blinked. "Nothing," she said. "Nothing at all."

I left their house a few minutes later. I didn't feel like eating pizza anymore. I kept picturing the slice with the orange fur stuck in the sauce.

The night air had cooled off a bit, but it still felt heavy and damp. Yellow-gray clouds covered the sky, hiding the moon and stars.

I still felt shaky as I turned toward my house. My

shoes scraped the sidewalk as I walked, the only sound except for the soft whisper of the trees.

That was so horrifying! I thought. The cat always sat in my lap before. Why did it decide to attack me tonight?

"Because you're EVIL!" Jackie had said.

It wasn't funny. It was so totally insane.

I'm not evil. I've never done anything evil. In fact, I'm the least evil person I know!

Jackie is more evil than I am, I told myself. She is. She definitely has a mean sense of humor.

Rigging Glen's Tarzan costume like that. Embarrassing him in front of the whole school. Pretending she was going to force me to get a tattoo tonight.

That's really evil.

Well . . . no.

I changed my mind. It's not evil. It's . . . mischievous, that's all.

Was tonight another one of Jackie's "mischievous" jokes? I wondered. Did she pay Miss Elizabeth to say those things about me? Jackie swore she didn't.

I thought about the fortune-teller. Pictured her solemn face again, leaning into the red glow of her crystal ball.

Why did she say I was evil? Why did she say that about me?

Why did she pick me?

Ask her, I thought. Just ask her, Maggie.

Make her explain. Then you'll never have to think about it again.

I stopped at the corner. A car rolled past, music blaring from the open window. I waited for it to pass, then took a few more steps—and stopped in the middle of the street.

My house was one block away. The carnival at the pier was four blocks in the other direction.

Go ahead, I urged myself. Go to the carnival. Get it out of your mind for good.

"Okay, I'm going," I whispered. I turned and started toward the pier.

I'm going to tell Miss Elizabeth how cruel that was, I decided. I'm going to tell her that she ruined my birthday with that lame act.

Another car rolled past, this one filled with teenagers. A boy yelled something out the window. I ignored him and kept walking.

I stopped under a streetlamp to check my watch. A little before midnight. My mom would probably kill me if she knew I was walking around by myself this late.

"Hey, I'm thirteen now," I said out loud. "I'm not a kid."

The carnival was probably closing down. I hoped Miss Elizabeth was still there. I began to feel angrier and angrier. People go to a carnival for fun—not to be frightened or insulted.

A strong wind came up, blowing against me, pushing me back. I leaned into it and kept going.

I reached the pier. It was nearly deserted. A few couples were leaving the carnival, carrying armloads of stuffed-animal prizes. The ticket booth stood empty. The entrance gate was open.

As I stepped through it, all of the lights dimmed. I blinked in the sudden darkness.

An empty Pepsi can rattled over the ground in a gust of wind. It rolled at my feet and I jumped over it.

The carnival music had been turned off, but the loudspeakers crackled with static. And over the sound of the static, I could hear the steady slap of water against the pier.

Workers closed up the game booths. Most of the booths were already dark and deserted. A young man was pulling a wooden gate over the front of his booth. He looked up when he saw me walk past. "Hey—we're closed," he called.

"I know," I called back. "I'm . . . uh . . . looking for somebody."

The crackling static in the loudspeakers grew louder as I made my way to the end of the pier. From nearby I heard a low howl.

An animal howl?

The wind through the pier planks?

More lights flickered out. Darkness washed over me. Someone in the distance laughed, a high, cold laugh.

I shivered. Maybe this was a mistake.

I heard scraping footsteps behind me.

I spun around. Just dead brown leaves, scuttling on the pier in a swirl of wind.

The empty cars on the roller-coaster track gleamed dully in the dim light. I heard a squeaking sound. The tracks rattled as if being shaken.

Finally the fortune-teller's tent came into view at the end of the pier.

I swallowed hard. My heart began to race.

I stopped outside the entrance. The tent flap had been pulled shut. Was she in there?

I had been rehearsing what I'd say to Miss Elizabeth. But now it all flew out of my mind.

I'll just ask her why she said that about me, I decided. That's all. I'll just ask her why.

I took a deep breath. Then I grabbed the tent flap with both hands and pulled it open.

"Hello?" I called in. My voice sounded tiny. "Anyone in here? Miss Elizabeth? Are you here?"

No answer.

I stepped inside—and let out a shocked gasp.

One of the two lanterns remained on the tent wall, casting the only light. I spotted the other lantern, the glass cracked, on its side on the ground.

The wooden table was overturned. A leg broken off.

Next to it, one of the fortune-teller's long, silky scarves lay torn and crumpled into a ball.

The chairs—the two wooden chairs were splintered

317

and broken. The poster of the human hand had been ripped in half.

And the red glass ball—shattered—shards of broken glass over the tent floor. The ball—the crystal ball—smashed into a thousand pieces.

CHAPTER 8

The next day in school I tried to shut the fortune-teller out of my mind. After school there was no time to think about her. I had a dance class.

Jilly was there, too. I watched her in awe. She is such a graceful dancer. She seems to float over the floor.

Dancing beside her, I felt like a circus elephant.

I can't compete with Jilly. But I'm going to the dance tryouts anyway, I decided. It's my dream to make that company. I'm not going to give up without trying.

I hurried home after the class. I had piles of homework.

It was a cool autumn day. The air smelled sweet and fresh as I jogged onto my block. I waved to some kids raking leaves on their driveway.

I stopped short when I reached my front yard. The backpack bounced heavily on my back.

Was I seeing things?

Or was that really Glen pushing the power lawn

mower over our front lawn?

"Hey—!" I called to him and waved.

He spun around. The mower roared. He cut the engine. "Maggie—what's up?" he called.

I ran over to him. "What are you doing?" I called. Dumb question. I felt my face grow hot and knew I was blushing.

He wiped sweat off his forehead with the sleeve of his gray jacket. "I mow all the lawns on this block," he said. "Didn't you ever see me?"

I shook my head.

"Your mom asked me to cut yours before winter comes." He wiped his hands on his jeans legs. "The mower keeps conking out. I don't know what its problem is." He kicked it with his sneaker.

It was chilly out, but he was sweating a lot. His curly hair—wild and unbrushed as always—glistened with sweat. I reached out and pulled a blade of grass off his cheek.

"Nice house." He pointed. "You could fit my house in there about ten times!"

"You want to come in?" I blurted out. "I mean—if you're thirsty or something. Come in and have a Coke or some Gatorade. When you finish mowing?"

He nodded. "Yeah. Maybe. Thanks. I have another lawn to do before dark." He bent to start the mower up. "Catch you later."

I hurried into the house. "He's definitely cool," I murmured. I stepped inside and called out,

"Mom—are you home?"

Silence.

I never can keep her work schedule straight.

I grabbed a can of iced tea from the fridge and made my way up to my room to start my homework. Chirpy, my canary, started chirping away as soon as I entered the room. I walked over to her cage in front of the window and rubbed her yellow feathered back with one finger.

And peeked out at Glen down below. He was leaning over the mower handlebars, moving quickly, making stripes across the grass. "So cute," I muttered to Chirpy. "Don't you think he's cute?"

The canary tilted her head to one side, trying to understand.

I trotted to the mirror and brushed my hair. Then I put on some lip gloss and a little eye makeup.

I decided to change. I pulled on a fresh pair of straight-leg jeans and my new white sweater.

I could hear the hum and roar of the mower outside. Wish Glen would hurry up and finish, I thought.

I knew I should start my homework. But I couldn't concentrate.

I went back to the window and watched him for a while. Then I picked up a deck of cards and started to practice a few new tricks. But I couldn't concentrate on those, either.

I heard voices outside. Girls' voices.

"Hey, Tarzan!" someone yelled.

I dived back to the window and saw Jackie and Judy coming up the driveway. They had stopped to tease Glen.

He just kept mowing. I could see that his face was bright red, and he was pretending to ignore them.

"Give him a break!" I said out loud. I hurried downstairs to let them in.

"Whoa. Way to go, Maggie. You got your boyfriend to mow the lawn!" Jackie teased.

"Mom hired him," I replied. "I didn't even know—"

"Were you in chem lab when Kenny Fields dropped the glass beaker?" Judy interrupted.

"No. I don't have lab on Monday," I said.

"It was a disaster!" she exclaimed. "It was some kind of ammonia or smelly acid—something really gross. It smelled so horrible, kids started to puke all over the place."

"First, one kid hurled, and then everyone was hurling," Jackie said. "It was awesome! Like an epidemic!"

"They had to evacuate half the school," Judy said. "How come you didn't know?"

"I wasn't there. We had a dumb field trip," I said, rolling my eyes. "To the art museum."

"Why don't you invite your boyfriend in?" Jackie asked.

"I already did," I told them. I could hear the

mower's roar, fainter now. Glen was nearly down to the curb.

Jackie pushed past me and started to the stairs. "I want to try all those new cosmetics you bought at the mall."

Judy and I followed her. "Where's Jilly?" I asked.

"More dance practice," Judy said. "She took an extra class today. She really wants to be perfect at that audition."

I sighed. "She already is perfect."

Jackie went right to my dresser. "It's like a make-up store in here!" she declared. She started picking up jars and tubes and examining them. "This is totally cool."

"If you're going to try all my makeup, you have to give me something in return," I said.

Jackie laughed. "Okay. I'll give you Jilly!"

"Ha ha," I said. I reached out my hand. "Let me try on your necklace."

Jackie hesitated.

"Just for a minute," I said. "You've never let me try it on. I just want to see how it looks on me."

Jackie shrugged and carefully pulled off the necklace of tiny glass beads. "No magic tricks?"

"No magic tricks," I promised.

She handed it to me and went back to pawing over all my new makeup.

"It's so beautiful," I said, gazing into the mirror, adjusting the delicate, sparkling beads around my throat. "I'd do anything to have one just like it."

I caught Jackie's smile in the mirror. "Anything?"

"Well . . . "

"Maybe I'll leave it to you in my will," Jackie said.

"Do you have a lot of homework?" Judy asked.

"Tons," I said, sighing. "I tried getting started on it when I got home. But my mind kept spinning. I couldn't concentrate."

Judy stood at the birdcage, petting Chirpy. She narrowed her eyes at me. "You're not still upset about that fortune-teller, are you?"

I laughed. "Thanks a bunch, Judy. Thanks for reminding me. I haven't thought about that all day!"

"You're evil," Jackie muttered, brushing thick, black mascara on her lashes. "You're so evil, Maggie."

"Shut up," I snapped. "That was totally dumb, and you know it. I don't know why I let it upset me."

Judy opened the cage and gently lifted Chirpy out. She let the canary perch on her finger. "Plumper would love you," Judy told the bird. "For lunch!"

"Don't mention that cat to me!" I cried. "That was so horrible! Your cat is a psycho!"

Judy frowned. "I'm really sorry about that. You know, I came over to ask if you'd help me with the Pet Fair."

"Not if I have to go near that cat!" I said.

"I'll keep Plumper away," Judy promised. "Will you help out?"

"I guess," I replied.

I glanced out the window. What's taking Glen so long? I wondered. Why doesn't he get finished?

Watching him moving back and forth, back and forth, I silently wished there was a way to speed up his mower.

"Hey—!" Judy's startled cry interrupted my thoughts. I spun around to see Chirpy fluttering in the air.

Judy grabbed at the canary with both hands. "Come back! Come back here, birdy!"

Chirping loudly, the canary flew up to the ceiling, hit the ceiling light, bounced off, and flew to the closet.

Judy and I both chased after him. "Come back!" I cried. "What's wrong with you?"

All three of us tried to grab the flittering, fluttering bird. Each time we nearly had her, Chirpy darted out of our reach.

At first it was kind of funny. But after ten minutes of chasing after the bird, it wasn't funny anymore. It was just frustrating.

"I don't believe this!" I cried breathlessly. I made another grab for the bird—and just missed! "Chirpy—stop it! You've never done this before! Come back! I could kill you for this!"

"Whoa. Don't say that!" Jackie declared. "Wouldn't you feel terrible if you said that and then Chirpy died?"

"I didn't mean it. It's just a stupid expression," I said. I stopped to catch my breath.

And Chirpy flew into her cage.

Judy slammed the cage door shut. "Gotcha!"

I was still breathing hard. I suddenly realized I still had Jackie's necklace around my neck. I took it off and handed it to her.

"Why don't we go down to the kitchen—" I started to say. But that's as far as I got. Because we all heard a scream of alarm from outside.

I dived to the window with Judy and Jackie right behind me. Peering out, I saw Glen chasing after his lawn mower. The mower was zigzagging wildly, roaring away from him. He was running after it full speed, shouting his head off.

My heart pounding, I shoved open the window. "Glen—!" I called. "What's happening?"

I don't think he could hear me over the roar of the mower.

He lunged forward and grabbed the handle. But the mower jerked away from him.

"Hey—helllp!" he shouted.

Jackie and Judy both giggled beside me. But I could see that Glen was really struggling, and very upset.

He grabbed the mower handle again and held on for dear life. But the mower roared forward, digging deep holes in the lawn.

Glen tried frantically to pull it to a stop. But the

mower zigzagged crazily, out of control, pulling Glen with it.

I slapped my hands to my ears as the mower shot into a tree with a deafening crash. It hit so hard, the whole tree shook.

I saw Glen hit the ground. He landed on his back.

And then over the roaring whine of the mower, I heard Glen's horrified shriek:

"My foot! IT CUT OFF MY FOOT!"

CHAPTER 9

"Nooooo!" I let out a scream and pushed away from the window.

All three of us went flying down the stairs—and out to the front yard.

"Glen—are you okay?" I screamed.

He was sitting on the grass, hunched over. He had his shoe off and was rubbing his left foot with both hands. As we ran down to him, the mower rocked against the tree, sputtered, and died.

"Your foot—?" I gasped.

"Sorry. I panicked a little," he said softly. "It's just a small cut. It hurt so much, I thought—"

"False alarm," Jackie said. "You scared us to death!"

"But what happened?" Judy asked.

"Beats me," Glen replied. "I don't understand it at all."

"Did you turn up the speed or something?" Judy asked.

He shook his head. "It just took off. It was so . . .

328

freaky! It . . . it's impossible! Lawn mowers aren't built to go that fast!"

He carefully slipped his shoe on and climbed to his feet. He took a few steps, testing his foot. "It's okay," he said.

He wiped sweat off his forehead, then raised his eyes to the mower. It had shot into the tree so hard, it left a deep gash in the tree trunk.

"Wow," Glen muttered. "Weird."

He made his way to the mower and wrapped his hands around the handles. He pulled it slowly off the tree. Then he turned to me. "Tell your mom I'm sorry, okay? The mower made a real mess here."

"Okay, I'll tell her," I said. "But—"

"Tell her I'll get the mower fixed and come back." He started to push it to the driveway.

"Don't you want to come in for a minute?" I asked. "Get something to drink?"

He pushed back his bushy hair. "No. I'd better get this thing home so my dad can look at it. Maybe he can figure out why it went berserk. See you."

I watched Glen push the mower down the driveway to the sidewalk. Then I turned and followed Jackie and Judy back into the house.

As we stepped inside, Jackie snickered.

"That was so scary!" I said. "What's so funny?"

Jackie's eyes flashed. "I thought you liked Glen, Maggie. Did you use your evil powers on his lawn mower?" She laughed.

"Stop it!" I cried angrily. "I mean it, Jackie. Stop saying that! You know I don't have evil powers! So stop it! It isn't funny!"

Her eyes went wide. I could see she was surprised by how angry I got.

"Sorry," she whispered. "I didn't mean it. I was only joking. Really. I was just trying to lighten up—"

"Well, don't!" I interrupted.

She put a hand on my shoulder. "I'll never mention it again. Promise."

We made our way back upstairs. The window was still open, and a cold wind filled my bedroom. The curtains fluttered and flapped.

I moved to close the window, but stopped halfway across the room.

A tiny yellow feather floated in the air in front of me.

I turned. And stared at the birdcage.

Stared at Chirpy. Stared at my canary, lying so still . . . so still.

Dead on her side on the floor of the cage.

CHAPTER 10

When I got over the shock, Judy helped me wrap the poor little bird in tissue paper. I carried him out behind the garage. Jackie dug a shallow hole in the soft dirt back there. And we buried Chirpy.

We stood silently, staring down at the little grave. All three of us felt weird. Especially Judy, who loves animals so much.

Jackie kept her promise and didn't say anything about evil powers. I think we were all thinking the same thing. When I was chasing Chirpy around the room, I shouted, "I could kill you for this."

And a few minutes later the little canary lay stiff and dead.

But no one believed that I was really responsible. And for once, Jackie didn't joke about it.

The afternoon sun began to set behind the trees. I shivered as the air grew colder. Fat brown leaves fell from the trees, scattering over the freshly cut lawn.

My friends and I were returning to the house when I saw Mom's brown Taurus pull up the driveway.

Jackie and Judy lingered behind, but I went running to meet the car.

"What are you three doing out here without jackets?" Mom asked. She climbed out of the car and straightened the skirt of her white nurse's uniform. "And what happened to the front lawn? Why is it so torn up?"

"It's a long story," I said, sighing.

As we walked into the house, I told her about Chirpy and about Glen and his runaway lawn mower.

Mom tsk-tsked. She dropped her pocketbook onto the kitchen counter and gazed at me. "That's so strange about Chirpy," she said. "The bird was only a year old."

Jackie hoisted her backpack off the floor. "Judy and I should be going. It's getting late."

"I have tons of homework, too," Judy said to me. "It's like they all piled it on today."

"I guess the bird got overexcited, flying around your room like that," Mom said. She tossed her coat on a kitchen stool. "Probably had a heart attack."

She carried the teakettle to the sink and filled it with water. "Sure you girls don't want to stay and have something hot to drink?"

"No. Thanks. We really have to go," Jackie said.

I followed them to the front.

We were passing the bookshelves in the front hallway when Jackie suddenly stopped. She stooped down and examined the bottom shelf of books. "Whoa. Maggie—what's this?"

"Huh?" I knelt down beside her to see what had caught her eye. The shelf was filled with old books, the covers frayed and faded. "What about them—?" I started to ask.

But then I read some of the titles. And I saw what the old books were about. Witchcraft . . . the Dark Arts . . . Magic . . . and the Occult.

"I—I've never noticed these down here before," I said.

Jackie stared hard at me.

"Big deal," I said sharply. "So, it's a bunch of old books. Why are you looking at me like that?"

Jackie shrugged. Then she climbed quickly to her feet and gave Judy a shove toward the front door. "Call you after dinner," she said.

"Bye," Judy said. "Sorry about your canary. She was sweet."

I closed the front door after them and turned to find Mom in the hallway.

"Mom, can I ask you something?" I said. I knew it was crazy and stupid. I knew it was totally ridiculous. But the question just popped out of my mouth.

"Mom, am I weird? Do I have some kind of evil powers?"

She narrowed her eyes at me. She took a breath. "Well . . . yes," she said finally. "Yes, you do."

CHAPTER II

"Huh?" I gasped. I could feel my heart skip a beat.

"Yes," Mom said. "And every night after you go to sleep, I take out my broomstick and fly to Cleveland!"

She laughed.

I just stared at her with my mouth hanging open.

She wrapped her hand tenderly around the back of my neck, the way she used to do when I was little. "Maggie, why on earth would you ask such a crazy question?"

I swallowed hard. "Well . . ." I hesitated. Then I figured I might as well go ahead and explain.

So I told her about the fortune-teller at the carnival and about how Jackie had been teasing me ever since. And how Judy's cat suddenly attacked me for no reason.

"You know you're perfectly normal, Maggie," Mom said. "You know you're not a witch or anything."

"I know, Mom, but—"

"Besides, if you have these evil powers, why didn't you use them before?" Mom asked. "Why did you start two nights ago? You went thirteen years, and now all of a sudden you're evil?"

"You're right," I said. "I don't know why that woman at the carnival got me so upset."

"She was just having her little joke," Mom said. "What happened to your sense of humor, Maggie? You've gotten very serious lately. You've got to lighten up."

I started to agree again. But then the bottom shelf of books caught my eye. "Mom—" I pointed. "Those books . . ."

Mom sighed. She squeezed my neck again. "I wrote my senior paper on strange beliefs. I told you that. Remember? I've had those old books since college."

"Oh. Right."

Now I really felt stupid. "Sorry, Mom. I'll never mention the whole thing again. I knew it was dumb. But—"

My phone rang upstairs in my room. "I'd better get that. Call me for dinner," I said, and I hurtled up the stairs two at a time.

I grabbed the phone after the third ring, and panted, "Hello?"

It was Jackie on the other end of the line, and she sounded frantic. "My necklace—" she choked out. "You forgot to give it back."

"Huh? No," I protested. "I handed it to you. Don't you remember?"

"You couldn't have returned it!" she screeched. "I don't have it!"

"Calm down, Jackie," I said softly. "I know I gave it to you. Let's try to think—"

"I don't have it!" Jackie repeated shrilly. "It's not in my coat or in my backpack. It's got to be somewhere in your room, Maggie. Look for it—okay? Look for it."

"Yeah. Sure." I turned and glanced quickly around my room. No necklace on the dresser . . . the bed . . . the desk . . .

I tried to picture Jackie as she left the house. She was wearing the necklace. I was sure she had it around her neck.

"I—I don't see it," I told her. "You were wearing it. I know you were."

"Find it!" Jackie shrieked. "You've got to find it! Find it, Maggie—please!"

The next morning at school between classes, I ran into Glen. "Where are you going?" I asked.

"Gym," he said. "How about you?"

"Spanish." I yawned. "How's your foot?"

"It's okay." He grinned. "I was lucky. I still have all six toes!"

We bumped through the crowd. Cedar Bay Middle School is too small. Between classes the halls look like cattle stampedes.

I yawned again. "Sorry. I stayed up past midnight doing homework." I shook my head. "I'm in great shape for the dance tryouts tonight. I'll probably yawn in the judges' faces."

Glen shifted his backpack on his shoulders. "Are you nervous?"

"Yes," I admitted. "Even though I know I don't stand much of a chance. Jilly is so much better than me. She's an awesome dancer."

Glen nodded thoughtfully. Then he reached out and solemnly shook my hand. "Good luck," he said. "Break a leg."

I laughed. "I think you say that to actors. I don't think that's the right thing to say to a dancer."

He turned the corner and gave me a little wave. "Catch you later."

I followed the crowd, thinking about the dance tryout. Why am I even bothering? I asked myself.

I answered my own question: Because it's the new, bold me.

I vowed on my birthday that I would change. That I wouldn't be so shy, so timid. That I would go after what I really wanted.

And that's why I had no choice. I had to go to that dance audition after dinner.

I turned a corner and headed to the stairs. I was on the second floor. My Spanish class was in the language lab on the first floor.

I grabbed the railing and started down the steep, tile stairs. I had only taken a step or two when I spotted Jilly halfway down the stairs.

Suddenly I had the strangest feeling. My arms started to tingle. My hands felt all prickly, as if they'd fallen asleep. And then my hands started to burn. They were burning hot.

I tried to ignore it. "Hey, Jilly—!" I called. But she didn't hear me. I elbowed my way through the students.

"Jilly." I tapped her lightly on the shoulder—and I saw her hands fly up like two birds taking flight.

Then I saw her shoes slide off the step.

And I saw her eyes go wide and her mouth pull open. Her shrill scream rang through the stairwell.

And she fell. Fell forward. Her hair flying behind her.

Jilly swooped straight down. Down . . . down . . . bumping the hard tile stairs.

Thud . . . thud . . . thud . . . thud . . .

Screaming all the way down.

She landed hard. I saw her head bounce against the floor.

She uttered one last groan.

And then she didn't move.

CHAPTER 12

My knees started to crumple. I gripped the railing to hold myself up.

"Nooooo!" I wailed. "Jilly? Jilly—?"

She lay sprawled on her stomach at the bottom of the stairs, one arm tucked under her body, the other straight out. Her hair had come loose and spread over her head, hiding her face like a furry yellow blanket.

"Jilly—? Jilly—?" I shouted her name as I ran down the stairs.

She raised her head off the floor. "Why . . . why did you push me?" she choked out.

"Huh? I didn't push you!" I cried. "I just tapped you!"

Jilly pulled herself to a sitting position. She had a cut on her shoulder. It was bleeding through her white top.

Her eyes remained locked on me. "Yes, you did. You pushed me, Maggie."

"No—!" I cried. Some kids had stopped to help

Jilly. Now they were all staring at me. "No. I didn't touch you. You know I wouldn't push you. I—I called out, and then—"

She rubbed her sweater, feeling the dampness of the blood. "You—you're lying. I felt your hand on my back. You shoved me. I felt you shove me, Maggie."

"N-no," I protested. "I swear. I didn't touch you. You just fell."

Everyone stared hard at me now. I could feel their accusing eyes.

Why didn't they just go away? Why didn't they all go to class?

I turned and saw that Jilly's leg was cut too.

"Hey—!" I cried. "Your shoelace. Jilly—look. Your shoelace is untied."

She groaned and rubbed her side. "Huh?" She squinted at her shoe.

"See?" I said. "That must be it. That must be what happened. You tripped over your shoelace."

"You shoved me," she insisted. "I felt you push me. You could have killed me, Maggie. Does the dance tryout mean that much to you? You could have killed me!"

"No," I repeated, shaking my head. "No, no, no."

We were such good friends. Why was she accusing me?

I didn't push her. I know I didn't.

• • •

After school I hurried over to the Mullens' house to see if Jilly was okay.

Judy answered the door. "Oh. It's you!" She seemed surprised to see me.

"Is Jilly here?" I asked, following her into the den. "Is she okay?"

The TV was on—some talk show with all the guests screaming at each other. Judy clicked it off.

"Jilly is still at the doctor," Judy said, plopping down on the green leather couch. "She's getting her ankle taped."

"She—she didn't break it—did she?" I asked.

Judy shook her head. "Just a sprain. She'll probably be able to try out tonight."

I let out a long, relieved sigh and dropped into the armchair across from Judy. "I'm so glad she's okay," I said. And then my voice shook: "She—she accused me of pushing her down the stairs. But that's crazy!"

Judy brushed back her short hair. Her eyes were locked on me, studying me intently.

"I didn't push her," I said. "I didn't bump into her, or anything."

I held my breath, waiting for Judy to reply.

Finally she said, "Even if you did bump her, it had to be an accident." She tucked her slender legs beneath her on the couch. "I know you'd never deliberately try to hurt her."

"Of course not," I said. "I'm so glad you believe me. If only—"

I stopped when I heard the front door slam. Jackie came running into the room. Her mouth dropped open when she saw me. "You're here!"

I turned in the chair. "Yes, I—"

"Did you find it?" Jackie demanded breathlessly. "I've been looking for you all day. Did you find my necklace?"

"No," I said. "I searched everywhere. I turned the whole house upside down."

"But—but—" Jackie sputtered. Her long hair was wild and unbrushed. One side stood straight up. Her expression was frantic.

"Then where is it?" she cried. She rubbed a hand over her throat as if she hoped to find it there.

"I even searched behind the garage," I told her. "Where we buried the canary. No sign of it."

"I'm desperate without it," she said. "I'm totally desperate."

"I'm really so sorry," I said, lowering my eyes. "I'll keep looking. I promise."

She shut her eyes and sighed. "It's just so weird."

Then she startled me. She ran across the den, wrapped her arms around me, and hugged me. "I wasn't accusing you, Maggie," she whispered. Her cheek was burning hot against mine. "You know that—right? You're my friend. My best friend."

Without waiting for an answer, she spun away and hurried from the room.

Judy must have seen how stunned I felt. "Jackie

has been a little emotional," she said. "Ever since her necklace disappeared."

I settled back in the armchair. But I didn't have time to relax.

I heard the rapid thud of soft footsteps over the carpet.

And then I let out a frightened cry as Judy's huge cat Plumper leaped onto my lap.

"Get him off!" I shrieked. "Get him off me!"

Judy jumped up. "Plumper—come here!" she called.

But to my surprise, the big orange cat burrowed his face into my chest and purred.

"Judy—" I gasped. "He—he—"

Plumper settled into my lap, purring softly.

"I don't get this," I murmured, still trembling. "One night he tries to claw me to pieces—"

Judy smiled. "He's trying to make up," she said. Her smile grew wider. "Isn't that adorable?"

Purring louder, the cat rubbed its head against my T-shirt.

"Go ahead. Pet him," Judy instructed. "See? He wants you to be nice to him."

I swallowed hard. The cat was so unpredictable. What if I tried to pet him and he started slashing at me again?

"Pet him," Judy urged. "He's waiting for you to pet his fur."

"I—I don't really want to," I said, staring down at

the fat, orange creature.

"He wants you to," Judy replied. "He wants you to make up."

"Well . . ." I took a deep breath. I raised my hand slowly, carefully. And . . .

CHAPTER 13

My hand started to tingle again. Both of my arms were tingling. It felt like a million pinpricks. Once again my hands started to burn.

Why is this happening again? I wondered.

The cat purred.

I lowered my hand and smoothed it gently over Plumper's furry back.

Would he attack? Would he go nuts again?

No. He purred louder.

I rubbed his back. He burrowed his head against me.

"Now you two are friends again," Judy said, beaming happily.

I glanced at the grandfather clock against the wall. "I'd better go," I said. "That dance audition tonight." I gave the cat one more rub. "I hope Jilly and I can be friends again," I said with a sigh.

But Jilly cut me dead at the audition that night.

She glimpsed me standing there in the auditorium aisle. She turned her head and kept walking.

And when I followed after her, begging her to let me talk to her, she pretended I wasn't there.

I felt so bad. I had to fight back the tears.

It was so unfair.

One of my best friends hated me now. And it wasn't my fault in any way.

I could see that she had a slight limp as she climbed onto the bare stage and began to limber up. Her right toe shoe bulged, and I could see that her foot was bandaged beneath her tights.

Ms. Masters, the dance adviser, waved to me to come up to the stage. Then she moved to a CD player on the floor against the curtain and put on some warm-up music.

I sat down on the edge of the stage to tie my ballet slippers. I felt so awkward. I kept glancing at Jilly. She deliberately turned away every time I looked in her direction.

There were only four girls trying out for the one opening in the dance company. Not a big crowd. Just Ms. Masters and four girls onstage. So it would be pretty hard for Jilly and me to ignore each other completely.

My hands fumbled with the laces. I'm too upset to audition, I thought. I'll just leave.

I glanced at Jilly again. She was twirling on her bad foot, testing it.

"Hey, Jilly—looking good!" I called.

She stuck her nose in the air and ignored me.

346

This is ridiculous! I decided. She has no right to treat me like this.

I'm going to audition. I'm not going to let Jilly drive me away. And I'm going to dance the best I've ever danced!

I finished lacing my toe shoes and hurried onstage to warm up.

Well . . . I didn't exactly dance the best I've ever danced. But I didn't embarrass myself, either.

I was glad when Ms. Masters asked me to try out first. It meant I wouldn't have to stand around and get more and more nervous watching the others.

Jilly and the other two girls—Marci and Deena—had to watch me. And as I danced a short section from Swan Lake, I knew they were standing there at the side of the stage, arms crossed in front of them, watching my every move.

But I concentrated on the steps and the music and shut them from my mind.

Afterwards Ms. Masters clapped her hands and smiled. "That was very nice, Maggie," she said. "I'm impressed."

Struggling to catch my breath, I thanked her and padded off, feeling light as a feather, trying to make my exit graceful.

Yes, I knew I had slipped once or twice. And I got behind the music a few times. I guess I was concentrating too hard on the steps, on not messing up.

But over all, I felt pretty good about it. The truth is, it's not easy to get a compliment from Ms. Masters.

Now I leaned against the stage wall and watched as Jilly stepped out, toe shoes tapping the floor so lightly, like little bird feet.

Normally we would have wished each other luck. Normally she would have congratulated me on doing such a good job.

But that was before today. Before . . .

Ms. Masters started the music, and Jilly raised her arms, pasted a smile on her face, and started to dance.

She's a wonderful, graceful dancer. Moving so lightly, so effortlessly, her blond hair tied back, her arms so slow and lovely, she really looks like an angel onstage.

My heart was still pounding from my dance. I wiped perspiration from above my upper lip and watched Jilly.

Such perfect jumps. Such quick feet.

I felt jealous. I couldn't help it. I really, really wanted to be in this dance company. Jilly was into all kinds of activities and clubs and sports at school. But this was the only thing I wanted.

My hands started to tingle and burn. I clasped them tightly together. Why did this keep happening?

Marci, one of the other dancers, leaned close to me. "Wow," she whispered, her eyes on Jilly. "Wow."

I nodded, clasping and unclasping my burning hands.

"We might as well go home," Deena whispered.

Jilly looks so comfortable onstage, I thought. So natural . . . So happy.

But then I saw her expression suddenly change. Her smile faded. She looked surprised. Confused.

All three of us gasped as Jilly started to twirl.

She was near the end of the dance. She had her hands high above her head. As she started to lower them, she raised up on her right foot—and started to spin.

"That's not part of the dance," Marci whispered.

"Is she showing off?" Deena asked.

My arms prickled. I tightened them around myself as I watched Jilly in amazement.

Round and round she twirled. Kicking her left leg out with each spin.

Faster . . . faster . . .

"Unbelievable," Deena said, shaking her head. "What a show-off."

"Wow," Marci repeated.

Jilly twirled even faster now, her arms flying wildly. Her right leg remained stiff and straight as she spun. Her left leg kicked out. Faster . . . harder . . . Her blond ponytail whipped around behind her.

I let out a cry when I caught her expression. Her eyes were wide with fright. Her mouth open in a silent scream, as she spun . . . harder . . . faster . . .

My whole body shuddered in dread. Jilly wasn't showing off.

"She—she can't stop!" I shrieked. "She's out of control!"

My hands burned as if on fire. They throbbed with heat. I clenched my fists tightly, as if trying to keep my hands from exploding! Wave after wave of pain shot up and down my arms.

I gaped in horror as Jilly twirled.

Kick, spin. Kick, spin.

Ms. Masters cut off the music.

But Jilly didn't stop.

Kick, spin. Kick, spin. She hurled herself around and around, her hands flailing.

Silence now. A heavy silence as we all watched in horror.

"Help me—!" Jilly's shrill cry rang out. "Ohhhh, help—!"

And still she spun. Hurling herself harder . . . Hair flying wild now . . . Hands frantically thrashing the air.

"Help me! Pleeeeease!"

And then, still screaming, still moaning in pain, still heaving herself around, Jilly sailed across the stage. Sailed into the wall.

Her body made a sick thud as she hit it.

And then, twirling, still twirling . . . she crumpled to the floor.

CHAPTER 14

"What happened?"

"Why did she do that?"

"Why couldn't she stop?"

"Did she break something? She hit the wall so hard!"

Our frightened voices rang out in the auditorium. We hurried over to Jilly.

Sprawled awkwardly on the stage floor, her eyes shut, her mouth hanging open, legs bent at odd angles, she looked like a broken doll.

"Stand back, everyone," Ms. Masters ordered shrilly. "Stay back. Let me examine her."

"Why was she screaming like that? Why couldn't she stop?" Marci cried. Tears glistened in her eyes.

"Did she lose her balance?" Deena asked, shaking her head. "Did she just spin out of control?"

Holding one hand over my mouth, I stared down at my friend in silence. A heavy feeling of dread rolled over me. My stomach lurched.

"Is—is she breathing?" The question escaped my

lips without my realizing it.

Ms. Masters was down on the floor, bending over Jilly. "Yes, she's breathing," she answered. "Open your eyes, Jilly. Can you open your eyes?"

My eyes moved to Jilly's feet. Her right foot was swelling like a balloon.

My stomach lurched again. I felt really sick.

I swallowed hard several times, forcing my dinner back down.

"Somebody call for an ambulance," Ms. Masters instructed.

"I have a cell phone," Marci said. She ran to get her bag.

"Jilly? Can you hear me?" Ms. Masters asked softly. "Can you open your eyes?"

Jilly finally stirred.

A dry, hacking sound burst from her lips. A gob of saliva ran out of her open mouth, down her cheek.

"Jilly?" Ms. Masters called. "Jilly? Can you hear me?"

Jilly groaned. She blinked several times. "It . . . hurts," she whispered. She moved a hand to her rib cage—then quickly jerked it away. "Ohhhh."

"Lie still," Ms. Masters said. "You might have broken a rib when you crashed into the wall."

Jilly sighed. "Wall?"

"You were spinning so hard," Ms. Masters said. "You lost control and—"

Jilly groaned again. "My foot. I . . . I can't move it."

"Don't try to move anything," the teacher said. "We'll get you to the hospital. You're going to be okay."

"What . . . happened?" Jilly asked groggily. And then suddenly her expression changed. She uttered a sharp gasp as she saw me. Saw me standing there so tensely, my hand still clapped over my mouth.

"Maggie!" she cried hoarsely.

I started toward her, but her cold, angry eyes made me stop.

"Maggie." As she repeated my name, her face twisted in disgust. "You did this!"

"N-no—!" I stammered.

Jilly pointed an accusing finger at me. "I don't know how, but you did this."

Marci and Deena were staring at me.

"Jilly, lie still." Ms. Masters patted Jilly's hand. "I think you've had a concussion. You're confused. No one did anything to you, dear."

"Just like Glen and the lawn mower," Jilly whispered, her finger trembling in the air. "Jackie told me what happened with Glen's lawn mower. The fortune-teller was right. You're evil! You're EVIL!"

"Don't say that!" I screamed. "Jilly—don't! It's not true! You know it's not true! It can't be true! Don't say that!"

Jilly shut her eyes and uttered a moan of pain. "You did this to me! You did it, Maggie!" she whispered.

Her words made everyone turn to me. They were staring at me.

Staring at me as if Jilly had told the truth. As if I really had caused horrible things to happen.

As if I really was evil.

And then, I couldn't hold back. I couldn't hold my hurt, my anger in.

I began screaming at the top of my lungs. Shrieking like an insane person. Screaming at them all:

"I'm not evil! I'm not! I'm not! I'm not!"

CHAPTER 15

A few minutes later the paramedics arrived to take Jilly to the hospital. Ms. Masters hurried out to the hall to phone the Mullens.

Marci and Deena got changed quickly, whispering to themselves. They would have to audition some other time. They kept glancing over at me, but they didn't talk to me.

I changed into my shoes and pulled a jacket over my leotard and tights. I just wanted to get out of there. To get away from their whispers and suspicious looks.

How could Jilly say such a thing about me? How could she blame me like that?

We've been friends since fourth grade. She knows me so well.

She knows I wouldn't hurt her.

I stared at my hands. They didn't burn anymore. Why did that happen again? I wondered.

Every time my hands start to burn, something terrible happens. Every time. But that doesn't mean I'm causing these things to happen—does it?

I shoved my hands into my pockets. I didn't want to think about that. I jumped down from the stage and ran up the auditorium aisle to the exit. I couldn't wait to get home, to the safety of my room.

But Ms. Masters stopped me in the hall. She put a hand on my shoulder. "Jilly was just upset," she said softly. "She didn't mean the crazy things she said."

"I . . . I know," I whispered.

"She must have been in shock," Ms. Masters said. "That's the only explanation."

I nodded.

"Try to put it out of your mind, Maggie. Jilly probably won't even remember she said those things later."

"Probably," I repeated. I grabbed her arm. "But what did happen out there, Ms. Masters? Why did Jilly spin out of control like that?"

My voice shook. "It . . . it was so horrible . . . so frightening. It really looked as if . . . as if some force was controlling her!"

Ms. Masters shook her head. "I'm not sure what happened, Maggie. I think I'm still in shock, too."

She patted my shoulder. "I guess this means you'll be in the dance company. Deena and Marci will have their auditions. But they're not at your level. I'd say congratulations. But I know you're upset about your friend."

"Yes." I nodded again.

A thin smile crossed the teacher's face. "Well, congratulations anyway. We'll celebrate some other time, okay?"

"Thanks, Ms. Masters." I turned and jogged away.

"Try not to think about what Jilly said," she called after me. "She was in shock. I'm sure she'll apologize when she's better."

"Sure," I muttered.

And then I was out of the building. Into the cold, fresh night air. Pale silver moonlight washed over the school grounds. Dead leaves danced across the grass.

I felt like tossing back my head and screaming. I felt like crying.

Instead, I lowered my head into the wind and started running. I didn't go far. I was almost to the corner when I ran right into someone.

"Hey—!" He uttered a startled cry and leaped to the side. "Slow down."

"Glen!" I cried. "What are you doing here?"

He pushed back his wild mop of hair and smiled at me. "Wow. You should try out for track, Maggie."

"Sorry. I didn't see you. I—I wasn't watching. I mean . . . What are you doing here?" I repeated breathlessly.

"Following you," he said.

I gaped at him. "Huh?"

He laughed. "No. I'm kidding. I was down the block, collecting money from people. For mowing their lawns. And I remembered you had that dance thing tonight. So I thought—"

"Don't ask me about it," I said, shuddering. "It was horrible." I started to walk, heading toward home.

He hurried to keep up with me. "You didn't get in?"

"I did get in," I replied. "But—but—" And then I blurted it out. "Jilly got hurt, and she blamed me."

He jumped in front of me to block my path. "Whoa. What happened? You tripped her or something?"

"No. I didn't push her," I said. My voice trembled. I felt about to cry again. "I didn't push her. But she broke her ankle, and she blamed me. Just like this morning at school. She fell down the stairs and blamed me for that. I didn't push her. Really!"

Glen knotted up his face, trying to sort out what I was saying. "Twice in one day?" he said. "She got hurt twice today? Twice before the dance tryout? And you were there both times?"

"Y-yes," I said. "But I never touched her. That's the truth."

He stared hard at me.

"You believe me—don't you?" I demanded. "Don't you?"

He lowered his eyes. "Of course," he said. "I believe you."

But something in his voice had changed. He wasn't looking at me. He suddenly seemed nervous.

He doesn't believe me, I realized.

He thinks that Jilly getting hurt twice in one day is too big a coincidence.

But it was a coincidence. I know it was.

A cold blast of wind made the trees shift and creak. Leaves showered down all around us. I shivered, suddenly feeling cold, so cold all over.

"Jilly is my good friend," I said. "I would never hurt her. No way."

"Of course not," Glen said. But he still avoided my eyes.

"I—I've got to get home," I said. I took off, running hard. "Later."

"Later," he called after me.

I ran about half a block and stopped at the corner. When I turned around, I saw that Glen hadn't moved. He was still standing there in front of the school, hands shoved in his pockets, watching me, staring hard at me.

And even from so far away, I could see the unhappy, troubled look on his face.

I didn't go home. I went to Jilly's house instead.

I knew that Jilly's parents were probably on their way to the hospital. But I wanted to tell Jackie and Judy what had happened.

Judy opened the door. Her eyes were red-rimmed.

She looked as if she'd been crying. "What a horrible night. Mom, Dad, and Jackie are on their way to Cedar Bay General," she said in a rush. "Maggie—what happened? Is Jilly going to be okay?"

"Yes," I said, stepping past her into the house. The house smelled of fried onions. I heard the dishwasher chugging away in the kitchen. Judy had her homework spread out all over the living room floor. "Her ankle was really swollen. It's probably broken. But she should be okay."

Judy started pacing the living room tensely. "But what happened? Did she slip or something?"

I sighed. I still felt so cold. I decided to keep my coat on. "It's hard to explain. It was totally weird, Judy. She just started spinning. It wasn't part of the dance or anything. She was spinning and . . . I guess she lost control."

Judy shook her head. "Poor Jilly. She worked so hard for this."

I dropped down heavily into an armchair. "She might have cracked some ribs, too," I added softly.

Judy grabbed her side, as if feeling Jilly's pain. "Wow. I—I should have gone to the hospital. I didn't know it was so bad."

I nodded. I didn't know what else to say.

Should I tell Judy that her sister blamed me for the whole thing? That she accused me of using my evil powers on her?

No, I decided.

Ms. Masters was right. Jilly was in shock. She didn't know what she was saying.

Judy suddenly stopped pacing. Her expression changed. She crossed the room and sat down on the arm of my chair. "Can I ask you something?"

"Yeah. Sure," I said.

Judy's dark eyes locked on mine. "Remember when you were over here yesterday and you were petting Plumper?"

"Of course," I replied. "How could I forget it? I was so shocked. First the cat goes psycho. Then he decides he likes me."

Judy swallowed. She continued to stare at me. "Well, were you wearing any weird kind of lotion or cream or anything on your hands?"

I blinked. "Excuse me?"

"You know. You're always trying new cosmetics, right? So did you have anything on your hands yesterday? Some kind of hand cream?"

"No. No way," I said. I gazed up at Judy, bewildered. "Why?"

Judy frowned. "I'll show you," she said. She slid off the chair arm and disappeared from the room.

A few seconds later she returned carrying Plumper in both arms like a baby. The big cat lay limply in her arms.

I climbed to my feet. I could tell instantly that something was weird. He never let Judy carry him around.

"Did you wash your hands in some new kind of soap?" Judy asked. "Think hard. Did you touch anything strange in chemistry lab yesterday?"

I shook my head. "No way. What is the problem?"

"Look at him," Judy replied, setting Plumper down on the floor.

I let out a gasp when I saw the cat's back. It took me a while to realize that the wide stripe I stared at was yellow-pink-splotched skin. Bare cat skin. Skin where the thick, orange fur had been.

"Look at that," Judy said sadly. "All the fur on his back. It all fell out after you left, Maggie. In big clumps. It just all fell out. Only where you touched him . . ."

CHAPTER 16

I hurried home. The house was dark except for the front hall light.

I found a note from Mom stuck to the fridge. It said that she was called for emergency room duty. She'd be at the hospital all night. The note ended: "Hope you danced up a storm! Love, Mom."

Well . . . there was a storm, all right! I thought bitterly.

Then I realized: If Mom is on emergency room duty, she'll probably see Jilly come in. And she'll get the whole horrible story from Jilly.

Will Jilly blame me in front of my own mother?

With a weary groan I tossed the bag with my ballet slippers onto the kitchen counter. I suddenly realized I was still in my tights and leotard. I pulled open the fridge, grabbed a diet soda, and hurried up to my room to get changed.

I pulled on a long, woolly nightshirt and a pair of heavy, warm white socks. I was standing in front of my dresser mirror, absently running a brush through my hair, thinking . . .

What is going on?

So many strange, horrible things had happened in the past few days. Since my birthday . . . since the fortune-teller read my hand.

Glen's lawn mower out of control. Poor Chirpy. Judy's cat attacking me. Then losing all his fur. And Jilly . . . falling down the stairs at school . . . twirling out of control onstage . . . and accusing me . . . accusing me!

Such an ugly jumble of pictures in my mind.

Was it possible that I was causing these things to happen? Was it possible the fortune-teller had seen the truth about me?

No . . . no . . . no . . .

There's no such thing as evil powers.

I was still gazing into the mirror when the phone rang.

It must be Jackie or Judy to tell me how Jilly is doing, I decided.

My heart started to pound. I had a sudden, heavy feeling of dread in my stomach.

What if she isn't okay?

What if her injuries were worse than everyone thought?

I grabbed the phone, pressed it to my ear, and uttered a tense, "Hello?"

"Hello, Sugar?"

Not the voice I expected to hear. Through heavy static, I recognized the voice of my dad.

"Sugar? It's me."

I absolutely hate the fact that he always calls me Sugar or some other cutesy name. He never calls me by my name. Sometimes I think it's because he doesn't remember it!

"Hi, Dad."

"Am I calling too late?"

"No. It's only eleven," I said, glancing at my bed table clock. "Where are you?"

"I'm in the car," he replied, shouting over the static. "On the freeway. Not a very good connection." He said something else, but a loud buzz covered it up.

"How's your mother?" he asked when the buzzing stopped.

"Okay," I said. "She's at work."

"Sorry I missed your birthday, Punkin," he said.

It's only the tenth birthday in a row that you've missed! I thought.

But I said, "That's okay."

"Did you—" More static drowned out his question.

"What did you say, Daddy?" I shouted, pressing the phone tighter against my ear. "This horrible connection—"

"Did you get my present?" he repeated.

"No," I said. "Not yet."

I knew he hadn't sent a present. No way. He

didn't even remember to call!

"Keep watching for it," he said, followed by more static. "What's new at school, Sugar? Tell me some news."

I hunched down on the edge of my bed. "Well . . . I had a tryout tonight, and it looks as if I'll be in the new town dance company."

A long pause. "Dance company? Really?" he asked. "I didn't know you were into dance."

Only my whole life!

"Yeah. I'm really into it," I said.

"I'm sorry. This is such a bad connection, Punkin. I'd better say good night."

"I—I'm glad you called," I shouted over the static.

And then—I had to ask.

I don't know why. I knew it was totally crazy. I knew Dad would only think I was weird.

But I had to. I had to ask while I had him on the phone.

I stood up. "Can I ask you a question, and you promise not to laugh at me?" I shouted.

"What?" he replied. "Oh, yeah. Okay. Go ahead."

"Dad . . . Is there something strange about me? Do I have some kind of weird powers?"

A burst of static on the other end. I pressed the phone tighter to my ear.

What did he say? What was his answer?

"I can't talk about it."

Is that what he said?

That couldn't be it—could it?

No. I didn't hear him right.

"Dad? Dad?" I cried. "Are you still there? What did you say?"

Silence.

"Dad? Dad?"

Silence.

The connection was lost.

I stared at the phone. I knew I hadn't heard correctly. I knew I got it wrong.

"I can't talk about it."

No. No way.

What kind of an answer was that?

CHAPTER 17

Before school the next morning I ran into Glen at his locker. "How's it going?" I asked.

"Okay." He slammed the locker door shut.

I shifted my backpack on my shoulder. "Where are you headed? What's your first class?"

He glanced nervously from side to side, as if searching for someone else to talk to. "Music Appreciation," he said. "Hey, I gotta go." He hoisted his backpack up by the straps with one hand and hurried away.

He was so unfriendly.

He seemed afraid of me, I realized.

Across the hall I saw Deena and Marci staring at me. They looked away when I waved to them. But I made my way over to them.

"Hey—hi!"

I was still thinking about how unfriendly Glen had been. But I tried to sound cheerful. "I like your vest," I told Marci. "Cool color."

Marci didn't reply. She glanced at Deena.

"Did you hear anything about Jilly?" Deena asked.

"Not yet," I said. I gazed down the hall. "I'll ask one of her sisters when they get here."

They both nodded coldly. Then they turned and started to walk away.

"That was so horrible last night," I called after them.

Marci spun around to face me. Her pale cheeks reddened. Her eyes burned into mine. "Why did Jilly say that stuff about you last night, Maggie?"

I swallowed. "Excuse me?"

"Why did Jilly blame you for what happened? Why did she say you were evil?"

"I don't know!" I cried shrilly. "I don't know why she said that! I really don't! You've got to believe me!"

They both just stared at me. As if I were some kind of lab specimen or strange creature from another planet.

They didn't say another word. They turned and hurried away.

I stood there in the middle of the hall, breathing hard, my heart racing. I felt so bad. I could feel hot tears on my cheeks.

Did Marci and Deena believe what Jilly said?

Did Glen think I did something to Jilly so that I'd make the dance company?

How could they think such a crazy, horrible thing?

When I spotted Jackie striding down the hall, I was so happy to see a friendly face. I wanted to grab her and hug her.

Wiping the tears away with both hands, I ran toward her. "Jackie—hi! How is Jilly?" I called.

She shrugged. "I guess she's okay," she said. "I mean, it could have been a lot worse."

"What did the doctors say?" I asked breathlessly.

Jackie sighed. "Well . . . she has a badly sprained ankle. And two bruised ribs."

"Oh, wow. Is she . . . is she home?" I asked.

Jackie shook her head, her long, black hair tumbling out from beneath her purple down coat. "Not yet. The doctors want to keep an eye on her a little while longer. They said maybe this afternoon."

She unzipped the coat and crossed the hall to her locker. "It's just so weird," she said. "How could she spin out of control like that? It's crazy!"

"I—I want to see her," I stammered.

Jackie had opened the locker. She was kneeling to pull some books from the bottom. But she turned and gazed up at me. "Not a good idea," she said, frowning.

I opened my mouth to say something, but the words caught in my throat.

"She blames you," Jackie said, standing up. "She thinks you cast a spell on her or something. To make her spin out of control."

"But that's totally insane!" I screamed.

A group of kids turned to stare at me.

"Of course it is," Jackie said. She sighed again. "But Jilly keeps talking about that fortune-teller at the carnival. She keeps saying the fortune-teller wasn't joking. The fortune-teller told the truth. Jilly says what happened to her last night proves it."

"But—but—" I sputtered.

"The doctors tried to explain to Jilly," Jackie continued. "They tried to tell her she probably got carried away last night by the excitement of the dance tryout. She wanted to show everyone what a great dancer she is, and she just lost control."

"Yes. That explains it," I said in a whisper. My throat suddenly felt so tight and dry.

"But Jilly isn't buying it," Jackie said. "Jilly says she could feel a force—a really strong force—making her spin. She says she tried desperately to stop. But she couldn't. She couldn't stop no matter what she did! Something was forcing her to spin!"

I grabbed Jackie's shoulder. "You don't believe that—do you?"

Jackie shook her head. "I don't know what to believe," she muttered. She raised her eyes sadly to me. "I guess I should tell you. There's more."

"Huh? More?" I realized I was holding my breath.

"Judy isn't in school," she said softly. "She and Mom had to take Plumper to the animal hospital this morning."

"Oh, no," I whispered.

"The cat lost his fur. On his back. Where Judy says you petted him. And now he's getting big red and purple sores all over his back."

"No . . ." I repeated. I grabbed Jackie's arm. "You don't believe that's my fault, too—do you? I mean, Judy doesn't blame me for that. She can't. She can't!"

Jackie started to reply. But the bell rang. It was right above our heads, and the jarring electronic buzz made me jump a mile.

Jackie closed her locker and clicked the lock. "Gotta run," she said. "I'm sorry about all this, Maggie. But—"

"Can I come over after school?" I asked desperately. "You and I could study together. Or just talk. Or—"

"Not a good idea right now," she replied. "Maybe I should come to your house instead."

So after school Jackie and I walked to my house together.

We talked about our classes. And our teachers. And a movie Jackie had seen. And about guys in our class.

We talked about everything except Judy and Jilly. I think we both wanted to pretend that none of the bad, frightening stuff from the last week had happened.

In the kitchen I grabbed a bag of pretzels, a couple of apples, and some cans of Sprite. And Jackie and I made our way up to my room.

"I need to see your government notes," I told her. "I know we're supposed to write down everything Mr. McCally says. But I can't listen to him. He puts me right to sleep."

"I think I have the notes with me," Jackie said. "But—first things first." Her eyes lit up as she crossed the room to my dresser and began going through my cosmetics collection. "You're so lucky, Maggie," she said. "Mom won't let us have any of this stuff."

I tore open the pretzel bag and pulled out a handful. "The new stuff is in the top drawer," I told her.

"Yesss!" Jackie cried happily.

She pulled open the top dresser drawer. Began to paw inside. And then I saw her expression change.

Her smile faded. Her eyes bulged.

She gripped the sides of the drawer with both hands.

And opened her mouth in a horrified scream.

"Jackie—! What is it? What is it?" I shrieked.

CHAPTER 18

Jackie let out another high scream.

Her face distorted—in horror, in shock—she reached into the drawer.

"Jackie—?" I cried.

I heard a clattering sound.

She lifted something from the drawer and spun around to show it to me. Raising it in front of her, shaking it, her face wild with fury.

Her beaded necklace!

"You did take it!" she shrieked. "You're a liar, Maggie! You are evil!"

I stared at the shiny beads, glittering, trembling in her raised hand. A wave of nausea rolled over me.

I felt sick. So sick.

"Jackie—listen to me!" I shrieked. "I don't know how that got there. You've got to listen to me!"

I dived across the room.

But she dodged to the side, angrily scooting away from me.

Gripping the necklace tightly in one hand, she

raised her other hand and pointed at me. "Evil," she muttered. "Evil."

My hands burned again. And my arms tingled.

I stared in horror at Jackie's finger, jerking in the air, pointing, accusing me.

And as I stared, Jackie's finger suddenly tilted up. Up—and then back.

"Hey—!" Jackie let out a startled cry as the finger bent back . . . back . . . back . . .

"Stop it, Maggie!" she pleaded. "It hurts! Stop it!"

Back . . . back . . .

And then the finger snapped.

The finger made a sick snapping sound. The sound of cracking bone.

Jackie was screaming now, her eyes bulging, her mouth gaping in howls of pain.

I screamed too, pressing my burning hands against the sides of my face.

The crack of her finger repeated in my ears, again and again.

And then, holding her hand high, Jackie lurched out into the hall. She went flying down the stairs, hurtling them two at a time.

"Please! Listen to me!" I pleaded.

She jerked open the front door. She didn't turn around. She leaped off the front stoop and ran full speed down our gravel driveway. Gravel flew under her shoes.

"Jackie—stop!" I screamed.

She let out a cry as she fell. Stumbled on the stones of the driveway and sprawled face forward. She landed hard on her knees and elbows. Her backpack thudded away from her.

"Jackie—" I ran after her.

But she was on her feet. Hair flying wildly around her flaming red face.

"Jackie—come back!" I begged.

But she scooped up her backpack with her good hand. Then, trembling, she turned furiously to me. "Leave us alone, Maggie!" she shrieked. "Leave my family alone! You've done enough! Just leave us alone!"

I slumped to the ground. I buried my face in my hands. My whole body was shaking.

I took a deep breath and struggled to stop the powerful shudders. When I uncovered my face, Jackie was gone.

For a moment I thought it had all been a bad dream. Some kind of frightening nightmare.

I'm going to wake up in bed, I thought. And none of this will have happened.

But no. Here I was on the front stoop. The front door wide open behind me. Awake. Wide awake.

I climbed to my feet and made my way back up to my room. The top dresser drawer stood open. I slammed it shut with an angry cry. Then I threw myself down on my bed and buried my head in the pillow.

How did that necklace get in there? I asked myself. How?

Why did Jackie's finger snap back like that?

Why are these things happening?

Jilly was back in school on Friday. She walked on crutches. She had a cast on her foot.

She wouldn't talk to me.

Jackie wouldn't talk to me, either. She and Jilly turned their backs whenever I came near.

I felt so upset, I could barely speak.

"Give them time," Judy told me. "They're totally upset now. But they'll come around, Maggie. They'll realize there's no such thing as evil powers." She squeezed my arm. "I'm still your friend. And I know you would never do anything to hurt us."

Judy cheered me up a little. But word about my so-called evil got around school quickly.

In the lunchroom at noon kids were staring at me. I passed a table of laughing girls—and they all stopped laughing when I came near.

Carrying my lunch tray, I searched for an empty seat. The whole lunchroom grew quiet. An unnatural hush.

Everyone stared at me. Everyone hoped I wouldn't sit next to them.

I tried to talk to some guys I always kid around with. But they ignored me and leaned across the table to talk to each other.

They're all shutting me out, I realized to my horror.

They're all afraid of me. They all believe the rumors. That I'm weird. That I have powers. That I'm evil.

Overnight I've become an outcast. A freak.

I sat down by myself in the far corner and set down my food tray. Kids kept glancing at me, then quickly looked away.

Near the front I saw the Three J's at a table with a couple of guys. Jilly's crutches were propped against the side of the table. She sat at the end so that she could stretch out the leg in a cast.

Jackie said something, and everyone else at the table laughed. Then Jackie and Judy started arguing about something, a playful argument. More laughter.

None of them looked my way.

I couldn't touch my food. My stomach felt hard and tight, like a solid rock. It took all my strength to keep from breaking down and crying my eyes out.

I can't just sit here by myself for the rest of the school year, I told myself.

I can't let everyone in school think I'm some kind of evil freak.

I know I'm not evil. I know I have no strange powers of any kind. No powers at all.

Now I have to prove it to my friends. I have to prove to my friends that I'm just me, just the same normal me they've always known.

But how? How can I prove it to them?

I stared at the three sisters across the room, laughing and enjoying their lunch. I stared hard at them, thinking . . . thinking . . .

And suddenly I had an idea.

CHAPTER 19

I left my food behind, took a deep breath, and crossing my arms tightly in front of me, I walked over to the three sisters' table. "I want to talk to you," I said. My voice came out tight and tense, almost like a growl.

Jackie swallowed a bite of her sandwich, then stared down at the cast on her hand. "Maggie, please go away," she said softly.

"No," I insisted. "I want to show you something."

Jilly stared at her food. Jackie scowled at me. "I asked you nicely," she said. "Please don't bother us."

"I—I'm going to prove that you're wrong about me," I said, wrapping my arms around myself tighter to stop my trembling. "We've been friends for a long time. You owe it to me. Just give me two minutes to prove to you that you're wrong."

Jackie kept scowling, her face growing redder and redder. But I stared her down.

"Two minutes?" she said finally.

I nodded. "Yes. Two minutes. I'm going to prove

to all of you that I have no powers. That fortune-teller was crazy. I'm totally normal. I'm not a witch, and I'm going to prove it."

"Give her a chance," Judy said. "Come on. Give her a chance."

"Can I sit down?" I asked.

Jackie nodded. "Go ahead. Two minutes. We'll give you two minutes. Then do you promise you won't do any more horrible things to me and my sisters?"

I pulled out the chair and slid into it. "I haven't done anything to you," I said.

"How are you going to prove it?" Judy asked.

I turned to watch the lunch line. I saw Marci pick up her food tray and carry it to the cash register to pay.

"See Marci over there?" I asked, pointing.

The three sisters turned their heads to look at her.

"I'm going to concentrate on her as hard as I can," I told them. "I'll try to make her stumble and drop her lunch tray. I'll concentrate all my powers. And you'll see. Nothing will happen."

Jilly laughed. "That's so stupid!" she sneered.

Jackie shook her head. "We're not idiots, Maggie. We know what you'll do. You'll only pretend to concentrate. You can make Marci trip if you want to—but you won't do it. You'll pretend. You'll fake the whole thing."

"Anyone can say they're concentrating when

they're not," Jilly added. "It's no kind of test at all."

"But I promise!" I said. I placed my hand over my heart. "I swear it! I swear I'll concentrate as hard as I can to make Marci trip. Believe me. Please— believe me. There she goes. Watch. She won't trip. She won't—because I have no powers."

Balancing the tray in both hands, Marci moved away from the cash register. She gazed around the crowded room, looking for a friend to sit with.

I narrowed my eyes on her. Concentrated . . . concentrated all my energy. And my hands started to burn. I felt tingling up and down my arms. And my hands . . . my hands felt as if they were on fire.

It's happening again, I realized. Is it some kind of power? Some kind of force flowing through me—a force so powerful it burns?

My hands smoldered as if I were holding them on a stove burner. The pain throbbed up my arms.

I turned away from Marci. Don't look at her, I thought. If you don't look at her, nothing bad will happen.

I grabbed a cold can of soda from the table. I gripped it tightly, wrapped my burning hands around it, trying to cool them off.

But my hands grew hotter.

I stared hard at the soda, willing my hands to cool down.

I stared at the soda so I wouldn't look at Marci.

But my eyes lifted. They bored into Marci. No!

No! I thought. Don't look at her!

I tried to turn away, but I couldn't.

I tried to shut my eyes, but they wouldn't close.

Marci took three steps toward the tables—and stumbled over her own feet.

She let out a startled cry—and her tray went flying.

She fell and landed hard on her stomach. The tray clattered to the floor beside her, plates bouncing, food spilling, her apple juice overturned, puddling over the floor.

I uttered a horrified cry. Turned to see Jilly and Jackie glaring at me, their faces twisted in shock, in fear.

Before I could say anything, I heard another loud cry from the back of the lunchroom. I turned in time to see a boy crossing the room with a tray. His hands flew up, and he tumbled to the floor. His tray fell, bounced once on the edge of a table, and crashed to the floor.

Some kids laughed and cheered. But the room was mostly silent now.

Am I doing this? I wondered, staring at my burning hot hands.

If I am, I've got to stop it. I've got to concentrate on stopping it.

Stop! I thought. Stop! I concentrated hard, repeating the word over and over in my mind. Stop! Stop!

In front of the cash register, Cindy, a girl from one

of my classes, stumbled and fell—and her food tray flew out of her hands, sailed high, and came down on her head.

Two girls fell off their chairs. The chairs toppled over on top of them.

More laughter. But I heard startled gasps, and a few kids were screaming.

Stop! I thought, concentrating hard. Stop this—now!

I let the soda drop to the floor.

I pressed my hands against my ears as another tray crashed. A girl in the food line fell into a plate of spaghetti.

I heard a loud groan. A boy jumped up from his chair, leaned over the table—and let out another hoarse groan, opened his mouth, and vomited his lunch onto the table.

Screams and cries now.

I turned and saw Jilly screaming: "Maggie—stop it! Stop it!"

"Please—stop it!" Jackie was shrieking, too.

Trays crashed. Food splattered over the tables, over the floor. A girl waved her hands wildly above her head. Then she jumped up and began to puke, groaning and heaving.

Two more kids jumped up and started to vomit. Another lunch tray went sliding over the floor. Large platters of food sailed off the counter, soared into the air, and crashed against the wall, sending their contents splashing over the lunchroom.

I saw a girl covered in tomato sauce. Kids were falling, screaming, running for the door. A boy leaned on our table. His eyes rolled back in his head, and he puked his lunch into Jilly's lap.

"Nooooo," I moaned. "This isn't happening. It isn't . . ."

"Maggie did this!" Jackie screamed.

She jumped onto the table. She cupped her hands around her mouth and bellowed at the top of her lungs, "Maggie did this! Maggie did it!"

Kids stampeded to the doors. Others turned to stare at me.

"She's evil!" Jackie screamed, standing on the table, frantically pointing down at me. "Maggie is evil! Maggie did it!"

CHAPTER 20

I covered my ears, trying to force out the shrieks and groans and cries of horror. And I ran, ran out of the lunchroom, and tore through the deserted hall.

"Maggie! Stop!" a voice called.

I spun around. "Glen—!" I cried.

His eyes locked on mine. "Let's get out of here," he said softly. "Some kids and teachers are coming after you."

I gasped. "You—you're helping me?"

He didn't answer. He pushed the door open and guided me outside. "Come on. Run," he whispered.

I heard the thud of rapid footsteps behind us in the hall. I didn't turn around to see who was coming.

I lowered my head and started to run, following Glen across the playground. It was a gray, windy afternoon. Heavy, low clouds made it seem nearly as dark as night. Our shoes crunched over dead leaves as we ran.

I heard shouts from the school behind us. Glen and I crossed the street and kept running.

We didn't stop until we were two blocks away and the school building was no longer in sight. I dropped onto the grass of someone's front lawn, gasping for air, waiting for the pain in my side to fade.

Glen lowered himself beside me. His face was bright red. His hair was so wild about his head, he looked as if he'd been in a hurricane!

"I was in the lunchroom," he said, swallowing. "It . . . was so weird."

I nodded, still struggling to catch my breath.

"Kids said it was your fault," Glen continued, his eyes searching mine. "They said you have evil powers or something."

I snickered bitterly. "Do you believe them? Aren't you afraid of me?"

He swallowed again and brushed back his hair with one hand. "Yeah. I guess I am. A little." He lowered his eyes. "But I saw you needed help. So . . ."

I reached out and squeezed his hand. "Thanks for sticking with me," I whispered.

He looked embarrassed. He pulled his hand away quickly. "What happened back there, Maggie?"

I shook my head unhappily. "I—I don't really know. I don't know if it was my fault or not. I wanted to show Jilly and Jackie that they were wrong about me. But then . . ." My voice trailed off.

My brain was doing flip-flops. I felt dizzy. And so confused.

Glen was still studying me intently. "Do you really have powers?"

"I—I don't know!" I screamed. I didn't mean to scream. It just burst out of me. I jumped to my feet. "I don't know! Stop asking me questions!"

My head felt about to explode. I spun away from Glen and took off.

I saw the startled expression on his face. But I didn't care. I couldn't explain to him what had just happened in the lunchroom. I couldn't explain it to myself!

I had to get away from him, too. I had to go somewhere and think.

I couldn't go back to school. At least, not until things calmed down. And I couldn't go home. Mom would probably be there—and how could I explain?

So I kept running . . . running in a daze. Ignoring the ache in my side from running so hard. Ignoring the pictures of horror from the lunchroom that played over and over in my mind.

A loud wail of a car horn snapped me from a daze. I heard the squeal of brakes and saw the red car swerve—and realized I had run into the street without even looking.

"Are you crazy?" The young man in the driver's seat swung a fist out the window at me. "Want to get killed?"

"Sorry," I called as he roared away.

I shut my eyes. Close call, I thought.

But somehow the shock of the close call had calmed me down. I had stopped trembling. My heart no longer thudded against my chest.

Where am I? I wondered.

The heavy clouds seemed to lower over me. Squinting into the darkening light, I saw that I was only a block from the Cedar Bay Mall.

In the middle of the afternoon the mall would be a safe place to sit down and think, I told myself. Everyone I knew was in school. I didn't have to worry about running into anyone there.

I'll find a quiet place to sit down, and I'll try to figure this all out, I decided.

I'll try to figure out a way to talk to Mom about what happened. I'll force her to tell me the truth about myself.

Mom lied before. I know she did.

I can't kid myself anymore. I have to admit to myself that I do have powers. I've been denying it, denying it, denying it.

But after the scene in the lunchroom, I know better.

I caused those people to trip, those lunch trays to fly. I caused those kids to be sick. My evil thoughts caused it all. I can't deny it any longer.

What am I going to do? I wondered, feeling my panic start to return. I couldn't stop what was happening. I tried to stop it—but it was out of control.

How will I have a normal life? How will I ever have any friends?

I waited for the traffic to clear, then crossed the street and made my way through the parking lot to a mall entrance. Inside, I gazed down the long aisle. The mall was practically empty. A mother pushed her sleeping baby past me in a stroller. An elderly couple, both leaning on bright blue canes, peered into the window of a shoe store.

I passed by a Gap, an Urban Outfitters, a CD store, and a bookstore. Somehow, the blur of bright lights and colors and the bouncy, brassy music from the loudspeakers was comforting.

Normal life. Everything so clean and bright . . . and normal.

I suddenly pictured Glen, the startled look on his face when I took off and ran away from him.

I'll have to apologize later, I decided. That wasn't nice of me at all. He was only trying to help me. He was the only one who wanted to help me.

I took an escalator down one flight. My stomach growled. I remembered that I hadn't eaten any lunch.

I'll grab something to eat at the food court, I decided. Then I'll find a place in a corner where I can sit and think.

I rode down to the lower level. Turned down the aisle that led to the food court—and stopped.

"Oh." I stared hard at the woman in the brightly colored flowered dress coming toward me. I recognized her instantly—and to my shock, she recognized me.

Miss Elizabeth. The fortune-teller.

Her dark eyes bulged. She dropped her shopping bags. Then she scooped them up quickly. Turned. And, long black hair bouncing behind her, started to hurry away.

"No, wait! Please!" I cried, running after her. "Please—wait!"

CHAPTER 21

Miss Elizabeth dropped a shopping bag again. She stopped to pick it up, and I caught up with her.

"Please—" I said.

"I remember you," the fortune-teller said, her eyes studying me coldly.

I stepped in front of her so she couldn't run away. "Tell me the truth," I pleaded. "That night . . . at the carnival . . ."

"I sensed the evil," she said. "I saw it."

"But how can that be?" I asked. "My whole life, I—"

"I can sense it now," Miss Elizabeth interrupted. "The evil you carry. It's so strong."

"I—I just don't understand!" I cried. "I never used to be evil. Up until my birthday I never had any powers!"

The woman stared at me coldly. I caught the fear in her eyes. Her bottom lip trembled. "Let me go now," she said.

"No, wait. Please." I blocked her path. I held up

my hand. "Look at it again. Just look at it. Maybe . . . maybe you made a mistake."

She shook her head. "No. I must go." She raised the shopping bags in her hands. "I have been shopping a long time. My family is waiting."

I shoved my hand into her face. "It will only take a second," I said. "Please—look at my hand. You were wrong the first time. I know you were."

Miss Elizabeth sighed and set down her bags. She reached for my hand and turned it so that the palm was up.

She raised my palm to her face and squinted at it for a second or two.

And then she opened her mouth in a shrill cry—and tossed my hand away as if it were burning hot!

"The evil!" she cried. "It's there on your hand! I made no mistake. It came with your birthday! Thirteen is a powerful number!"

She took a step back, her eyes wide and frightened.

"Wait," I pleaded. "Are you sure—?" I stuck out my hand again.

"Please—don't hurt me!" the woman begged. "Don't hurt me! I have a family. They are waiting."

"I . . . I won't hurt you," I whispered. "I'm . . . sorry." I lowered my hand—my evil hand—to my side. And turned away from the poor, trembling woman.

She grabbed up her bags and scurried away. I

watched her as she rode up the escalator, staring down at me, clutching her bags tightly in front of her as if shielding herself from my evil magic.

At home I shut myself up in my room and didn't even come out for dinner. Mom kept banging on my door, asking what was wrong. "Are you sick? I'm a nurse, remember? Let me look at you."

"No. I just want to be left alone," I called out.

I felt relieved when she left to work the night shift at the hospital. I sat down at my desk and grabbed the telephone.

I'd been thinking hard, thinking for hours.

At first my thoughts were filled with anger. Anger and despair.

My life is over, I thought. I'm doomed—doomed to a horrible, lonely life.

A life without friends. With everyone hating me, terrified of me.

But then I started thinking about my powers. I have powers, I knew. I definitely have powers. But do they have to be evil?

I thought about those old TV shows they run on Nickelodeon all the time at night. The one with the genie who is always popping in and out, doing cute magic. And the other show—Bewitched—with the cute, blond witch.

Everyone thinks they're funny, I told myself. No one hates them. Everyone thinks they're terrific!

I knew they were only TV sitcoms. There wasn't anything real about them. But they started me thinking in a whole new way.

They gave me a little bit of hope.

So I sat down at my desk and phoned Jackie.

At first she didn't want to talk to me. "Haven't you caused enough damage?" she asked angrily. "What more do you want, Maggie?"

"I want my friends," I said. "I want you and your sisters not to hate me. I don't want everyone in school to stare at me like I'm some kind of freak, and hide from me, and think I'm evil."

"But—but you are evil!" Jackie sputtered. "You proved it—in the lunchroom. Even Judy had to admit it."

"No—!" I protested. "Listen to me, Jackie. Please don't hang up. Give me a chance."

"I've got to study," she replied. "I can't spend time on the phone. I have that algebra test first thing tomorrow morning, and you know it's my worst subject."

"I have the test, too," I said. "Listen, I've been thinking . . ."

"I've got to go, Maggie. Really—"

"Maybe I do have powers," I continued. "In fact, yes. Okay—yes. I do have powers. I don't know how. I don't know why. But I seem to have them."

"Maggie, you've already hurt my family so much!" Jackie declared.

"Well—what if I use my powers for good?" I asked. "If I can do evil things, I can do good things, too—right?"

"I don't know," Jackie said impatiently. "The whole thing is too creepy, too yucky. Everyone is scared of you now, Maggie, and—and so am I."

"But what if I do something good tomorrow? What if I use my powers to get you an A on the algebra test?"

Jackie uttered a startled cry. "Excuse me?"

"I'll get you an A tomorrow," I repeated. "I'll concentrate all my powers. I promise. I'll—"

"Concentrate your powers? Like in the lunchroom?" she interrupted.

"I'll concentrate all my powers and get you an A on the test," I said.

"Well . . ."

"I want you to stay my friend," I told her. "I'll do it for you. Really. You'll see. And if I do it, you have to promise not to hate me."

Again, she hesitated. "Well . . . we'll see, Maggie. See you tomorrow." And she hung up.

I sat at the desk, gripping the phone, staring out the window at the black night sky.

I just made a big promise. Can I do it? I wondered.

Can I?

CHAPTER 22

The next morning I met Jackie outside the algebra classroom. I ignored the kids staring at me up and down the hall. I saw them whispering as I passed. And I saw several kids back away, as if I carried a disease or something they might catch.

"Ready?" I asked her.

She eyed me intently, as if she'd never seen me before. "I'm sorry," she said. "I—I don't know what to think. You've done so much harm. Poor Jilly had to stay home today. Her ribs hurt too bad. She could barely get out of bed."

I lowered my eyes. "I'm really sorry," I muttered. "I didn't mean to hurt Jilly or you. You've got to believe me. It was before I realized—"

"Let's just go in," Jackie said sharply. "Kids are looking at us." She started into the classroom.

"I'm going to do what I promised," I whispered as I followed her in. "I'm going to concentrate all my powers. You'll see. I can do good, too."

We took our seats. Jackie sat in the same row as me, two seats away.

When I sat down, Cory Hassell, the boy who sits next to me, scooted his desk as far from mine as he could. Then he leaned over to me and whispered, "Are you going to make everyone puke their guts out today?"

I rolled my eyes. "Give me a break, Cory. That was not my fault yesterday. I don't know how these dumb rumors start—do you?"

He didn't answer. He sat back up and pretended to study his algebra textbook.

The bell rang. Mrs. Rodgers got everyone quiet. Then she walked up and down the aisles, passing out the tests.

She stopped when she got to my desk, and peered down at me. "How are you feeling today, Maggie?" she asked.

"Fine," I replied. I took the test from her.

She stared at me for a few seconds more. She looked as if she wanted to ask me another question. But she didn't. She moved on down the row.

"Everyone begin," she instructed when she had returned to her desk. "It's a difficult exam. But you should have enough time to complete it."

A heavy silence fell over the room. I glanced around at all the heads bowed low over the test questions. Pencils scratched. One girl was already erasing violently.

Did she get her name wrong? I wondered.

I shut my eyes and started to concentrate.

I concentrated on Jackie. I pictured her in my mind, filling out the test, getting all the answers right.

Jackie will get a perfect score, I told myself.

I was catching on to how these powers worked. I just had to concentrate on something—and it came true.

So I lowered my head and shut my eyes, and wished for Jackie to get a perfect score on the algebra test. Wished . . . concentrated hard . . .

And yes. Once again, the skin on my arms started to prickle. My hands burned . . . burned so hot . . .

My eyes snapped open when I heard a sharp cry. I recognized the voice. Jackie!

I turned down the row—in time to see Jackie leap up from her seat. "Oh! Oh, nooo!" she wailed.

Bright red blood poured from her nose.

The blood splashed onto her test paper. It ran down the front of her yellow T-shirt.

Mrs. Rodgers looked up from her desk. "Oh, what a bad nosebleed!" she declared.

The blood flowed from both of Jackie's nostrils. Two rivers of gleaming, scarlet blood.

Jackie jammed her hand over her nose. But it didn't stop the nosebleed. In seconds the blood flowed over the side of her hand.

Mrs. Rodgers ran up beside Jackie and took her by the elbow. "Quick—go to the nurse! She'll know how to stop it. Hurry, Jackie! Oh, my. I've never seen so much blood!"

Jackie staggered to the door, cupping her hand over her nose, leaving a bright trail of blood on the floor.

"I'd better go with you," Mrs. Rodgers said. "Just keep doing your tests, everyone. And no talking." She hurried after Jackie.

Jackie stopped at the classroom door. She turned and pointed at me. "Evil!" she cried.

One word.

That's all.

Evil.

Then she and the teacher disappeared out the door.

"Whoa. That was so gross!" someone said.

"Poor Jackie."

Then the classroom returned to silence. I lowered my head and shut my eyes again. I was trembling so hard, I gripped the sides of my chair to steady myself.

My breath caught in my throat. My chest ached.

Evil. I can only do evil, I realized.

I wanted to help Jackie. I tried to help her. But my powers can be used only for evil.

And I can't control them. I do these horrible, evil things to my friends because I have no control over my powers!

Then, behind me, I thought I heard a boy begin to chant—softly at first, and then louder.

And then some girls joined in. Then more voices. More voices chanting.

And as I sat there trembling, sick, terrified, it sounded as if the entire class chanted, slowly, in a slow, steady rhythm, softly, so softly, like distant thunder.

All of them.

All of them, leaning over their test papers, chanting:

"EVIL . . . EVIL . . . EVIL . . . EVIL . . . EVIL . . . EVIL . . . EVIL . . ."

CHAPTER 23

After dinner that night I rode my bike over to Glen's house.

I didn't know where else to go. Who else could I talk to?

He seemed really surprised to see me. He led me into a tiny den beside the living room. It looked like some kind of hunting lodge from an old movie. The walls were covered with huge art posters of tigers and elephants. The chairs and couch were all beat up, cracked, dark brown leather. A long hunting rifle was mounted over the doorway.

"I don't know what to do," I said. "I thought maybe you—"

What did I think? Why was I there?

I suddenly felt very confused.

Glen motioned for me to sit down in one of the broken leather chairs. "I heard about Jackie," he said, dropping into the chair across from me.

"And did you hear . . ." I started. But it was hard to force the words out. "Did you hear that everyone blames me?"

He nodded. "It's crazy," he murmured, lowering his eyes to the floor. "I keep hearing rumors about you, Maggie. Kids are talking. You know. After that thing in the lunchroom . . ." His voice trailed off.

I sprang up from the chair. "What am I going to do now?" I wailed.

He shook his head. "I don't know what to say. It's so . . . scary." He narrowed his eyes at me. "You're not going to do something evil to me—are you?"

I let out a sigh. "Of course I'm not. But . . . that's the scariest part. Don't you see, Glen? I don't know why these evil things are happening. And I can't control them when they do happen!"

He continued to stare hard at me.

"I don't mean to hurt anyone!" I cried. "How can I prove that to everyone? How can I stop everyone at school from thinking I'm some kind of evil witch?"

Glen shrugged. "I don't know. Maybe . . . maybe if you showed kids you were normal . . . If you showed them that bad things don't always happen when you're there . . . After a while, kids would forget about the rumors."

I bit my bottom lip. "Yes, that's true. But—"

"I know!" He jumped to his feet. "How about the Pet Fair tomorrow morning?"

"Huh? What about it?"

"It's at the Community Center. Just about everyone from school will be there, Maggie. If you show up and help out—"

"I was supposed to help out," I interrupted. "Judy wanted me to help her, but—"

"Great!" Glen cried excitedly. "If you help out at the Pet Fair, and nothing bad happens, kids will start to see that you're not evil. That you're totally normal."

I hesitated. "Well . . ."

"Do it!" Glen urged. He grabbed my hand and squeezed it. "Do it, Maggie. It's worth a try! Do it! What can you lose?"

CHAPTER 24

The Community Center is a long, red brick building with a gym and an auditorium, built beside the Cedar Bay public swimming pool. It's used mainly for town suppers and parties. Kids don't hang out there, but sometimes my friends and I like to explore the thick woods that stretch behind the building for miles.

I woke up early Saturday morning. Pulled on a clean pair of khakis and a sweatshirt. Grabbed a glass of orange juice and an untoasted Pop-Tart for breakfast. And rode my bike through the chilly morning fog, across town to the Pet Fair.

My plan was to get there early so that I could help Judy set up. But as I parked my bike in the rack at the side of the building, I heard cat yowls and barking dogs from inside.

I stepped inside and saw that the big, brightly lit gym was already filled with kids and their pets. As I waited for my eyes to adjust to the bright light, I glimpsed cats in cages and boxes, hamsters, ferrets, and dogs of all sizes and colors. A boy from my class had a fat, green-and-yellow snake curled around his wrist.

Most of the animals didn't seem happy to be there. They were all yowling and howling. Kids were shouting and laughing and showing off their pets. At the front of the gym some blue-uniformed workers were setting up a podium and microphone.

I searched for Judy and finally found her at the far side of the room. She was scurrying around from one group of kids to the other. "All cats against this wall!" she shouted, motioning to the front wall. "Please—try to keep your pet with you!"

"When is the judging?" a girl shouted to Judy.

Judy's answer was drowned out by two dogs growling fiercely at each other.

"Please! Keep your pets calm!" Judy shouted. "All cats over here! Dogs against that wall!"

At the front a man started to test the microphone. It let out a deafening, shrill whistle. That made all the dogs go crazy—howling, barking, straining to pull free of their leashes.

Judy definitely needs my help! I told myself.

I started to make my way to her through the pets and pet cages. But I stopped when I saw a cat I recognized.

Plumper!

Somehow, Plumper must have escaped from his carrier. The cat was slinking low across the gym. His yellow eyes were locked on a cage on the floor, a cage filled with white mice!

I saw Plumper's back arch as he prepared to attack the mice.

"Plumper—no!" I cried. I swooped down on him and lifted him into my arms.

Plumper screeched his unhappiness. He swiped a paw at me, but I held him away from my body. He couldn't reach me.

"Judy—!" I called, running to her, the squirming cat in my arms. "Plumper got free! He—"

Judy spun around at the sound of my voice.

"Here. Here's your cat," I said breathlessly. I reached Plumper out to her. "I—I came to help out."

To my surprise, Judy let out an angry shriek. She grabbed Plumper from me. "Give me that cat!" she screamed. "Don't touch my cat! Get out! Get out of here! We don't want you here!"

Trembling, I backed away.

I saw kids looking at me.

The gym grew quiet.

"Get out! Get out!" Judy screeched at the top of her lungs. "You're evil! Get out!"

"N-no—!" I cried. "Please—don't do this!"

Everyone was staring at me in silence now. Even the animals were quiet.

"You're evil, Maggie!" Judy shrieked. She raised Plumper out toward me as if preparing the cat to attack me. "We don't want you here! Get out! Out!"

My legs were trembling so hard, I could barely move. Somehow I backed to the gym door. My breath came in loud sobs.

So many eyes staring at me. All the kids . . . all the kids I knew . . . staring at me so coldly . . . with so much fear . . . so afraid of me.

They all hate me! I realized. Everyone . . . everyone I know.

It was too much. Too much to bear.

I started to back out the door. And then I stopped. And I pointed to Judy.

"Judy—!" I screamed her name. "Judy—! You shouldn't have done that!"

My arms tingled. Heat soared through my hands. I gasped as a bright red flame shot out of a finger.

I heard an electric crackle. Sparks burst from my hands.

In shock I jerked up both hands—and long, angry flames shot out from all my fingertips.

Screams of fright rang out across the room.

And then the screams were drowned out . . . drowned out by the wails and howls of the animals.

Dogs howled and struggled to tear free of their leashes.

Cats began to hiss. So loud and shrill . . . hissing in rage . . . The most terrifying sound I ever heard . . . like rushing water . . . like air escaping . . . The hiss of evil, of true menace.

And then I stumbled back as the hissing cats

408

began to claw furiously through their cages and carrying cases.

Across from me a black cat's eyes glowed bright yellow. With an almost human cry it swiped a claw at its owner. Then sank its fangs into her leg.

Screaming in panic, she struggled furiously to kick the cat off.

I turned to see a Dalmatian puppy begin to froth at the mouth. Its eyes spun wildly in its head. It tossed back its head and let out a fierce roar.

"No," I whispered. "Nooooo."

A snake curled itself around a girl's waist, tightening, twisting. The girl screamed, tugging at it helplessly with both hands, red in the face, struggling to breathe.

White mice, squealing, snapping their fat pink tails behind them like whips, stampeded across the floor.

Two wild, snarling dogs attacked each other. Their snapping teeth ripped off huge chunks of fur and skin. Bright red blood puddled beneath them as they battled.

Cats clawed at their owners. Dogs frothed and howled.

Kids scrambled over the floor, wrestling, fighting, frantically struggling to escape their howling, raging pets.

My hand still burned. Flames crackled from my fingertips.

I saw Judy against the back wall. Her hands were raised high as if in surrender. Her mouth was open in an endless scream of horror.

I pointed to her and called. "Judy—! Judy—!"

And to my shock the animals all turned. Turned away from their noisy, angry battles. Broke away from their horrified owners.

The animals all turned. And moved forward as if following orders. They circled Judy. A tight circle of frothing, growling creatures. Chests heaving. Eyes glowing with menace.

They began closing in on her.

Lowering their heads. Arching their backs. Snapping frothy jaws. Drooling hungrily. Preparing to attack.

Closing in. The circle growing tighter . . . tighter.

Judy hunched helplessly in the middle. Trembling. Her entire body shuddering.

They're going to kill her, I realized.

They're moving in for the kill. And it's all my fault.

What can I do? What?

Suddenly I knew. I had to leave. If I left the hall, maybe . . . just maybe . . . the animals would return to normal. And Judy would be saved.

So I spun away. Stumbled shakily, dizzily out the door—and started to run.

Out of the building. Back into the cold morning, still foggy and gray.

Past the parking lot and the bike rack. Around the side of the building.

Into the woods. Into the clean, sharp-smelling woods. Into the darkness, the safe darkness under the autumn-bare trees. Twigs and leaves cracking and snapping beneath my shoes.

I followed a twisting, bramble-choked path that curved through the old trees and the low, tangled shrubs. I ran . . . ran blindly . . . ran till I couldn't hear the cries from the building any longer.

And then I stopped just beyond a line of evergreen shrubs. Stopped to catch my breath.

And heard the thud of rapid, approaching footsteps.

The kids in the gym—they're following me! I realized.

They're coming to get me!

CHAPTER 25

With a sharp gasp I ducked low behind the ever-green shrubs. Brambles clung to my sweatshirt sleeves. Wet leaves stuck to my shoes.

I couldn't stop my wheezing breaths.

I struggled to hear the footsteps. Had anyone seen me?

What were they going to do to me when they caught me?

My side ached. My chest felt about to burst.

I peered over the top of the shrub.

"Glen—!" My cry came out in a hoarse whisper. "Glen—it's only you!"

I was so glad to see him. I jumped to my feet, my heart pounding.

His denim jacket flapped around him as he ran. "Are you okay?" he asked, his eyes studying me. "I heard—"

"It was so horrible!" I cried. "I—I'm evil. I—I just did a terrible thing. I can't ever go back. I—I have no friends now. I have no life!"

He raised a finger to his lips. "Sshhhhh. Try to calm down, Maggie."

"How can I?" I shrieked. "I'll never calm down. Never! Don't you understand, Glen? I'm all alone now. A freak! A horrible, evil freak!"

He kept his finger to his lips. "Maggie, I'm still your friend."

"But—but—" I protested.

"It's you and me now," he said softly. "You and me against all of them."

"But my friends," I whispered. "My friends . . . Jackie and Judy and Jilly—"

Glen's expression changed. His eyes grew cold. His whole face tightened. "They deserved it," he rasped. "They deserved everything they got."

I swallowed hard, startled by the change in his voice, the icy expression on his face.

"But, Glen—"

"They're total phonies," he sneered. "Good riddance to them, Maggie. That's what you should be saying. Good riddance."

"No, you're wrong," I protested. "Those girls have been my friends for a long, long time. And—"

"All three of them are so cruel, so cold," Glen continued, ignoring my words. "And they're so totally jealous of you, Maggie. Didn't you see how jealous they were?"

"No," I replied sharply. "That isn't true. They—"

"They've always been jealous of you," Glen

insisted. "I can't believe you're so blind to them. They were never your friends. Never."

He shut his angry eyes for a moment. I saw that he was grinding his teeth, his jaw working back and forth tensely.

When he opened his eyes, he appeared even angrier.

"You should never have trusted those three," he said, shaking his head. "Never. Believe me, they can't be trusted. Know what, Maggie? I'll bet Jackie hid her necklace in your dresser drawer just to make you look bad."

"Huh?" I let out a gasp and staggered back, away from him. A wave of fear swept over me. My whole body trembled.

"Glen—!" I cried. "How—how did you know about Jackie's necklace? I never told you about that!"

CHAPTER 26

Glen stared at me without blinking. "What difference does it make?" he said finally. "It's you and me now. Us against them."

"But—how did you know about that?" I repeated.

Dizzying thoughts flashed through my brain. Glen knew about the necklace in my dresser drawer. And he was always there . . . always there right after something horrible happened.

I gasped. I couldn't hold the words back. "It was you all along—wasn't it!" I whispered. "You—you're evil!"

To my surprise, Glen tossed back his head and laughed, a cold, cruel laugh. "Of course it was me!" he said. "Did you really think you had powers?"

"Y-yes," I answered. "I—I had that strange feeling each time. My hands burned. Flames shot out. I did think I had powers."

"No way," Glen said, grinning a sick, ugly grin. "It was all me. I shared some of my powers with you.

You don't have any powers, Maggie."

And then, the grin fading, he added bitterly, "You're just a normal girl. A normal, average girl. You're not like me."

I stared hard at him, stared hard until he blurred into the dark shrubs and trees.

Suddenly I remembered. I remembered my birthday. The carnival. Before I went in to see the fortune-teller, Glen held my hand. He was goofing around, and he kissed my hand.

The hand the fortune-teller read.

Miss Elizabeth— she saw Glen's evil on my hand! She sensed his evil. Because he held my hand and spread his evil onto me.

And in the mall. When I ran into the fortune-teller in the mall . . . I had squeezed Glen's hand on the way to the mall, just before I saw her.

Miss Elizabeth never saw my evil on my hand. Because both times she was reading Glen's evil!

The sky darkened. The shadows of the trees lengthened over us.

Glen's eyes sparkled in the fading light. "You're figuring it out—aren't you!" he said softly. "You're figuring out how I did everything. And you understand—right? You understand why I had to pay those sisters back."

"Because of what Jackie did to you onstage in front of the whole school?" I asked. "Because of the Tarzan costume? Because none of them would stop teasing you about it?"

He nodded.

"But—but—what about your lawn mower?" I asked. "Your lawn mower went out of control and crashed. You almost cut off your foot."

Glen snickered. "Good one, huh? I faked that one. I wanted everyone to think you were responsible. I wanted everyone to think you were evil. Then I could get my revenge on those sisters—and everyone would blame you!"

He seemed so excited now, so pleased with himself. "You are so helpless, Maggie. You have no powers of any kind. But I can give you powers. I can share my powers with you. With just a touch."

He swiped his hand at me.

"No—!" I cried. "I don't want them! I don't want any powers, Glen. I just want—"

He didn't seem to hear my protests. "It's you and me now," he said, his eyes glowing in the shadowy light. "Just you and me against all of them."

He reached his hand out. "Come on. Share the power. Shake hands. Shake hands again, Maggie. It's you and me now. We'll show those sisters."

"No!" I cried again. "I—I won't!"

Eyes glowing wildly, he grabbed for my hand.

But I spun away from him. Stumbled over a fallen tree branch. Caught my balance and started to run.

"You can't run away from it!" he called after me.

And I gasped as I felt a force, a powerful force

holding me, pushing against me, holding me back.

"Nooooo!" I howled, and slammed my fists against the invisible wall in front of me. I dug my shoes into the dirt. I lowered my shoulder and pushed hard against the wall I couldn't see.

But he was holding me, using his strange power to hold me prisoner.

I ducked low. Tried to spin free.

But the invisible wall was all around.

"I warned you, Maggie!" he called. "You can't escape! You can't!"

And then dead leaves rushed up from the ground. Clumps of wet, dead leaves swooped up, swirled like a tornado— and swept over me. Weeds slapped at my face. Twigs and limbs snapped and swung at my waist, my legs.

"Stop!" I wailed. "Please—stop!"

The twigs, and weeds, and wet leaves stopped their wild whirl and sank around my shoes. And as they dropped back to the ground, I heard footsteps, hurrying toward us along the curving path.

Three grim-faced figures marching in a single row. The three Mullen sisters—swinging their fists as they walked. So angry. All three of them, so furious I could see it on their faces and in their stiff-legged, menacing steps.

I'm trapped, I realized.

Glen behind me, using his evil to hold me here in

place. And the sisters marching, advancing on me with such fury.

Trapped. Trapped . . .

What am I going to do?

CHAPTER 27

I stared in horror at the sisters as they made their way toward us through the woods.

Jackie with her long hair flying behind her, beaded necklace bobbing up and down at her throat.

Judy, her clothes ripped and stained—but alive, alive!—marching in the middle, her eyes narrowed in anger.

Jilly, leaning on a crutch, struggling to keep up, her blond hair bouncing against her back, shaking her head, a scowl on her pale face.

They were my best friends, I thought bitterly. And now . . .

They think I am ruining their lives. All three of them—they believe I am trying to destroy them.

And so they are coming after me.

And in a few seconds . . . they will get me.

I took a deep breath and turned to Glen. "Okay!" I called in a whisper. I glanced over my shoulder, watching the sisters come closer.

"Okay, Glen. It's you and me," I whispered.

I reached out my hand to him. "I'll share the power. Let me have some of the power."

I could feel the invisible wall fade away. I took a step toward Glen. Then another. I could move again.

His eyes burned into mine. "You're serious? You'll help me destroy them for good?"

"Yes," I whispered, holding out my hand. "Yes. Hurry. I want the power again. They're almost here! Hurry!"

He stepped forward. Reached out to me. Grabbed my hand.

And squeezed it hard.

"Thank you!" I cried. "Yes! Thank you!"

CHAPTER 28

"There they are!" Jackie cried, pointing.

"Maggie—" Jilly called, breathless from pulling herself through the woods with a crutch.

"Stay back!" I warned. I raised my hand, the hand Glen had just squeezed. "I'm warning you! Stay back!"

"This has to stop!" Judy shouted. "Those animals—they wanted to kill me!"

"Yes. This has to stop," Jackie repeated. "Now!"

I turned to Glen in time to see a cruel grin spread over his face. "The evil hasn't started yet!" he declared.

"It was Glen!" I cried, turning back to the sisters. "It was Glen the whole time! He has the powers! He—he was using me!"

"Yes!" Glen shouted, beaming with pride. "Yes, it was me all along! My power! My magic! But I made you believe your friend was evil. I made you believe!"

I saw the shock on the sisters' faces. But I didn't

wait for them to react. I knew I had to act quickly.

I spun around to face Glen. I raised my hand and waved it at him.

I concentrated all my thoughts . . . concentrated . . . concentrated . . . My arms tingled. Once again, my hands started to burn . . .

Glen opened his mouth in a cry of surprise. He was so stunned. He had no time to fight back.

And then he started to spin. Twirling like a top, he whirled around and around on one foot.

"Hey—!" He managed to call out. He tried to point at me. Tried to use his powers to stop me.

But I made him spin faster . . . faster. So fast he was sending up clouds of dirt and dead leaves.

"Thanks for sharing the power, Glen!" I shouted. "Thanks for sharing!"

And then I concentrated harder—and sent him flying off the ground. Higher . . . above the trees . . .

Spinning, his arms thrashing the air. Twirling faster and faster inside a cyclone of leaves, and twigs, and dirt.

And then I changed my thought. Concentrated . . .

I sent Glen crashing to the ground. He landed hard on his stomach. Let out a whoosh of air. Bounced once. Twice.

And before he could move, I changed my thought again. Pointed my finger down at him.

And watched his body shrink . . . shrink . . .

. . . Until he was a tiny, brown-and-white-striped chipmunk.

His tiny paws scrabbled over the dirt. He glanced up at me once with his round, black eyes. And then he scuttled around a fallen log and vanished under a blanket of dead leaves.

Finally I lowered my hand to my side. I started to breathe again.

Jackie rushed up to hug me. "You tricked him?"

I nodded.

"It's all over? The horror is over?" Judy asked. "It was Glen the whole time? Glen's evil powers?"

"Yes," I whispered. "He—he used me."

And then we were all hugging each other, all four of us at once. Hugging and laughing and crying all at the same time.

Finally, I let out a long sigh. "I can feel the power slipping away. I'm starting to feel normal."

"No—wait!" Jackie cried. "Before the power is gone for good—one favor!"

"Huh? What kind of favor?" I asked.

"Can you change our algebra grades?"

I laughed. Then I shut my eyes and concentrated . . . concentrated . . .

"Guess what?" I told them. "All four of us just made the Honor Roll!"